D1649384

Hattie Moore's OFFICIAL SECRETS

DO NOT READ THIS

SERIOUSLY

IT IS NOT A BLOG

HANDS OFF

I WILL KNOW IF YOU DO

YES, NATHAN – IT IS AN OLD-FASHIONED
DIARY THING BUT GRAN BOUGHT IT FOR
ME FOR CHRISTMAS AND I WANT PEOPLE
TO REALIZE JUST HOW CRAPTACULAR
YOU ACTUALLY ARE.

000002065441

* Rae Earl *

OMG!

is this

ACTUALLY

my Life?

HATTIE MOORE'S
Unbelievable Year!

**WALKER
BOOKS**

DUDLEY PUBLIC LIBRARIES	
000002065441	
£7.99	JF
28-Mar-2017	PETERS
JFTX	

This is a work of fiction. Names, characters, places and incidents are either the product of the author's imagination or, if real, used fictitiously. All statements, activities, stunts, descriptions, information and material of any other kind contained herein are included for entertainment purposes only and should not be relied on for accuracy or replicated as they may result in injury.

First published in Great Britain 2013 by Walker Books Ltd
87 Vauxhall Walk, London SE11 5HJ

6 8 10 9 7 5

Text © 2013 Rae Earl
Cover artwork © 2013 Sarah J Coleman
Cover photographs courtesy of Shutterstock.com: raw bacon by Richard Griffin, puppy beagle by Eric Isselee, old mobile phone by thumb, elderly people sign by Aquir, fresh mackerel fish by Evlakhov Valeriy, Canada goose by Miao Liao, blueberry muffin by Paul Turner, ripe melon by Viktar Malyshchyts, coffee cup by Valentyn Volkov, classic donut by Aaron Amat
Interior illustrations © 2013 Walker Books Ltd

The right of Rae Earl to be identified as author of this work has been asserted by her in accordance with the Copyright, Designs and Patents Act 1988

This book has been typeset in GFY Brutus
Printed and bound in Great Britain by Clays Ltd, St Ives plc

All rights reserved. No part of this book may be reproduced, transmitted or stored in an information retrieval system in any form or by any means, graphic, electronic or mechanical, including photocopying, taping and recording, without prior written permission from the publisher.

British Library Cataloguing in Publication Data:
a catalogue record for this book is available from the British Library

ISBN 978-1-4063-4001-3

www.walker.co.uk

For my Harry.
For making my day job
mainly just being silly.

Sunday 28th December

9.23 a.m.

OMG — I'M IN PRISON!

It's actually my bedroom but it might as well be a cell.
I've seen what prison is like in *EastEnders* and except
for the fact I'm in heart-print Primark pyjamas there's
no difference.

10.12 a.m.

Mum just came up — she is the hardest screw ever
(that's what you call prison officers when you're inside).
Apparently I've "disgraced myself" and I'm growing up "way
too fast".

OMG — THIS is from the woman who had her first
cigarette at 11. Gran remembers because she made Mum
eat it. And because it was one of hers and the last one
in the packet. She's still mental about it now!

10.32 a.m.

Gran just rang — she says she feels a bit guilty and it's
basically her fault. I agreed. She is going to talk to Mum.

10.41 a.m.

Mum says I cannot blame Gran as I am responsible for
my own actions and Gran is a delicate old woman with
crippling arthritis. A delicate old woman with crippling
arthritis who does Zumba on a Tuesday at the community
centre and who asks for a "Britain's Hottest Firemen"
calendar for Christmas EVERY year!

11.16 a.m.

Just spoke to Dimple. She was zero help. She agrees with Mum. Plus she said if she'd done what I did her dad would have called the police.

11.31 a.m.

Just spoke to Weirdo Jen. She said that she would burn some lavender as it encourages forgiveness in "her wider spiritual world" (?).

She thinks I should also eat 8 mistletoe berries as they are good for detoxifying mind and body.

I might as well eat mistletoe. I'm not going to get any action under it this Christmas. AGAIN.

11.39 a.m.

Weirdo Jen rang back in a panic. She said I should cancel the mistletoe berries as they are actually deadly poisonous. She meant blueberries.

Dying might be preferable now though.

11.54 a.m.

Rob has been up. He forgives me but he says he needs a new miniature china pagoda and he's had to flush 2 of his angelfish as they were on their last legs.

12.12 p.m.

Mum has been up again. She doesn't forgive me. When I said, "Why?" she said, "BECAUSE, HATTIE, BEING SICK IN YOUR STEPFATHER'S FISH TANK IS UNFORGIVABLE!"

So I was sick in a fish tank?! This is not the worst thing that has ever happened. And it IS Gran's fault. She was the one who said, "Let Hattie have a glass of sherry – it's Christmas!" Mum said, "No, don't be silly – she's under-age." But I helped myself to one. Then I felt really sick. And then I thought I am actually going to be sick. And the nearest thing to be sick in was Rob's fish tank.

I don't even think it was the sherry that caused it. It was more likely the half a massive tin of Quality Street that I'd eaten before that.

12.42 p.m.

It was the sherry.

2.14 p.m.

Rob has also now had to flush a Malawi Firefish Peacock and 5 guppies – he says it's probably the shock.

I am an alcoholic mass-murderer.

2.54 p.m.

Mum just came in and said if she hears that my Facebook status has been changed to

Hattie Moore has been sick in a fish tank

she will ground me for all next year.

3.01 p.m.

Mum has been back in to say, "That goes for chirping too." I said, "Mum, it's TWEETING and I am not going to tell anyone because it's TOTALLY EMBARRASSING.

Perhaps it was cool to drink sherry and throw up in a fish tank when you were 13 but not now!" Mum went mental and said she would have never been "like this in her day because people respected aquatic life".

3.26 p.m.

Just rang Gran. She said when Mum was 7 she went through 2 pet goldfish in a month. ANOTHER MUM LIE TOTALLY EXPOSED.

5.32 p.m.

The verdict is in. I'm grounded for a week BUT I still have to take Gran sales shopping on Tuesday. Gran the TOTAL mental who ALWAYS finds the most disgusting item of clothing in ANY shop she visits. No Gran — you cannot wear neon green — you are 67.

That really is the bum cherry on my crapcake of a day.

MONDAY 29TH DECEMBER

8.12 a.m.

Why do these diaries start a week before they are meant to anyway? It's like they want you to remember just how bad the year before was!

9.37 a.m.

My brother is threatening to spread it about the fish tank. He says if I iron his shirt on a Saturday for the next 3 weeks he will keep it quiet. I can't risk Miss Gorgeous Knickers at school knowing about this. She had a *Sex and the City* cocktail party 2 months ago and is well known for being able to drink loads and still look like Carrie Bradshaw.

10.12 a.m.

Carrie Bradshaw when she was 13. Not like she is now — someone's mum!

4.55 p.m.

I've decided because of yesterday I need to examine my life fully. Why am I turning to sherry and Quality Street? Especially the purple ones with the hazelnut. Why do I keep messing up?

6.01 p.m.

Asked Gran about why I keep messing up. Gran says I have to stop "bloody navel-gazing" and help her plan which bus we are getting tomorrow. She doesn't want to walk too far because she's wearing her FOUL white stilettos. It's so she can dig her high pointy heel into the feet of anyone who tries to buy anything she wants. She nearly put someone in hospital over a bag once!

TUESDAY 30TH DECEMBER

7.15 p.m.

That is the last time I EVER go shopping with my gran.

In the Debenhams changing room she told one woman trying on a Lipsy dress that she looked like a sausage about to burst. THEN she tried on a pair of FOUL skinny jeans (4 sizes too small!) and BROKE THE ZIP!!! Instead of saying sorry she told the assistant "when things say they

---

should stretch THEY SHOULD STRETCH" and that she "wasn't going to pay for them as they already inflated the prices to allow for retail wastage".

Yet she thinks all shoplifters and burglars should be sent to Siberia with just a pack of sandwiches and a winter coat.

8.23 p.m.

I have nicked my mum's Dr Phil book. He'll know exactly what's wrong with me. Bet even he can't help Gran though.

9.17 p.m.

Flicked through the book. Basically I need to fully examine everyone in my life and ask myself, WHERE AM I NOW? Only through doing this can I truly understand my "life strategy" – because if it's happening NOW we are going to deal with it NOW.

HATTIE NOW:

* 14 in 6 weeks. OFFICIAL YAY!
* I am a 32 AA. BOO. But I am POSITIVE-THINKING my breasts bigger.
* My mum is generally annoying and takes bad-mood tablets daily. I put this mainly down to the fact that she stares at bread for most of the day, has to make builders' fry-ups, never wears make-up and always smells of bacon. The woman needs a GLAM-INJECTION.

* My stepdad, Rob, is a geek from the planet Doofus who likes car boot sales and calls me "Bones" – but he's actually all right.
* My brother is the devil and must die.
* My gran is a mental but I LOVE her. And at 67 she still has her hair done 3 times a week.
* No boyfriend as have no breasts.
* BUT Dimple and Weirdo Jen, my best friends, are TOTES excellent.
* And Goose next door who I have known FOR EVER is a MASSIVE dork but sweet really. Plus he's pretty much lent me his iPod for good.
* School is DULLSTER VON DULLSTER.

Likes – my friends, getting gorgeoused-up, dancing my brain out of my head, LOUD music, BIG lattes.

Dislikes – eggs.

LIFE STRATEGY:

I need to read the rest of Dr Phil's book before I can truly say what it is.

WEDNESDAY 31st DECEMBER

11.35 a.m.

Weirdo Jen just invited me to her mum and dad's New Year party. No point even asking Mum if I can go. I'm still getting the semi-silent treatment. Mainly because the fish tank snails have now also died.

2.43 p.m.

Dr Phil's book is big on families and people being GOOD PARENTS (my mum definitely has NOT read this book!). The fact is, I don't even know who my actual real DAD is! No one will talk about him and all I ever get from Mum is: "Rob has been around since you were 6 months, Hattie. That's what a REAL father does." And then I have to stop asking because Mum starts welling up. BUT I NEED to know. What about family diseases and conditions that can be passed down, Mum?! And how big were my other grandma's breasts? And will mine ever get that big? VITAL QUESTIONS!

8.05 p.m.

Just asked Mum what my real dad's surname is. She said, "Hattie, honestly... I don't think it's the right time to be discussing this." When I said, "WHEN will be the RIGHT time?" she YELLED, "Well NEVER during *Casualty* for a start!"

9.27 p.m.

Casualty has finished and it's STILL not the right time apparently. I'm not stupid. I know why. It's because Mum thinks if she gives me his surname I can find him in a SECOND on Google. She'd never say that though. But it's true.

Bet it's a better name than "Moore". I have had to endure so many craptacular Moore jokes through my mum giving me HER surname. Jack Pearson and his posse of pukesters once sang Britney Spears' "Gimme More" at me for an entire lunch break. Only they sang "Gimme More – NOT!"

10.32 p.m.

It's 10.32 p.m. and everyone in this house is in bed. It's NEW YEAR'S EVE. This family is a miracle as it is both dysfunctional AND DULL.

11.12 p.m.

Gran just rang. She's at an over-60s party. She's on vodka jellies because they are "easy to handle at her age". I asked her who was bringing her home. She said she hadn't decided yet but "not to worry as she's put her name and address on her dentures if she gets lost".

All I want is someone who isn't mental who gets ME!

Dad, come and save me!!!

THURSDAY 1ST JANUARY

11.01 a.m.

NEW YEAR. NEW LIFE. NEW HATTIE MOORE.

HATTIE MOORE OFFICIAL ANNOUNCEMENT:

THIS YEAR I AM GOING TO FIND MY REAL DAD. I DESERVE THE TRUTH. I NEED TO FIND HIM. I know he will get me like no one else on Earth. I can just feel it. I WILL FIND HIM.

Also THIS YEAR...

1.   I will become a TOTAL HOTNESS GODDESS.

2.   I will.

3.   Actually I think that's it really.

4.   Except for: I will generally be lovely to everyone. Unless they are a known force of evil.

5.   Known forces of evil – my brother, Miss Gorgeous Knickers at school, the chav-mongous dog 3 doors away.

6.   I would probably even be nice to the dog as I'm sure he only barks because he's forced to wear a fake Burberry collar.

Might start by going to Pets 'R' Us and buying the dog a decent collar.

I'll get Goose to put it on him though.

2.56 p.m.

Just spoke to Goose next door. He thinks finding my real dad will be mahoosively hard. He also thinks I should probably wait as I need help from my family and currently none of them are talking to me as I am the "aquarium assassin".

He's right.

And as for putting anything on the dog 3 doors away, he said it would be a TOTAL suicide mission and no way is he doing it.

He's right about that too.

3.01 p.m.

I didn't ask him about how to become a Total Hotness Goddess as Goose is a boy and therefore clueless.

3.23 p.m.

Just thought – Gran is still speaking to me! I'll ask her about my dad.

3.40 p.m.

Just remembered Gran has been on the vodka jellies. She won't make any sense for about a month.

6.12 p.m.

Gran just called me. She got home safely. I was going to ask her about my dad but I didn't as I thought she'd clearly had a few too many drinks.

You can't have a chat about your family tree with an old lady who answers every question you ask by singing "Yellow Submarine".

FRIDAY 2ND JANUARY

7.20 p.m.

Nothing happened today except I grew more spots. My brother now calls me "Zit Farm" and says by the time I'm 20, face transplants (which they currently only give to people who have been attacked by a rogue Labrador) will be a normal everyday operation.

9.35 p.m.

Told my mum about my brother calling me "Zit Farm". She just said, "It's teasing Hattie, and you give as good as you get." In what way is calling someone a TOTAL no-hoper-craptacular-thon as bad as calling someone a zit farm?! My brother's rubbish life is his fault — I cannot help my actual face.

Yet another example of everyone ganging up on me in this house. EVERYONE is either Team Nathan or Team Mum. NO ONE is Team Hattie.

Can't wait to start the hunt for Dad once the fish are forgotten.

SATURDAY 3RD JANUARY

2.19 a.m.

18 minutes ago Gran called my mob. Conversation as follows...

Gran:	Hattie, it's your gran — can you help me?
Me:	Are you OK?!
Gran:	Yes. I've accidentally texted a … rude joke to my dentist.
Me:	What?
Gran:	I've texted a rude joke to my dentist and I need to un-send it. I meant it to go to my friend Denise but I got the wrong name on my address list

Thinking, oh my God, she might be having a heart attack or something.

```
          thing — the dentist was the
          next one down.
Me:       You can't do it, Gran. Once the
          message has gone it's gone.
Gran:     Well, what can I do?
Me:       Nothing, Gran. What was the joke
          about?
(PAUSE)
Gran:     Old ladies' boobs.
Me:       Why is your dentist's number in
          your phone anyway?
Gran:     When you've got gums like mine,
          Hattie, you need a hotline.
Me:       Sorry, Gran, there's nothing you
          can do... Got to go. Love you.
          Bye.
```

↖ I say that just in case
she dies in her sleep.

At that point Mum storms into my bedroom
(KNOCK FIRST PERHAPS?!), going mad. She blahhed at
TOP volume: "Hattie, who is calling you? I'm going to take
that phone off you." (Yeah, Mum, of course you are. Life
is actually not safe without a mobile.) "I've got to be in
the shop in 5 hours for a delivery."

I didn't get a chance to say, "Actually, WOMAN, I was
trying to stop YOUR MUM DISTRIBUTING ACTUAL
PORN." It's just so typically NOT ON. I know she works
hard and everything — but she never actually listens to
the REASONS why things happen.

7.36 a.m.
Why has my gran got a mobile anyway? She gets confused
by her hand-held blender, and that's only got one button!

7.45 a.m.

Thinking about it, Dimple's granny just sits there watching Indian soaps on telly and growing facial hair. WHY do I get lumped with the mental?

8.49 a.m.

AND lack of sleep gives you wrinkles.

7.15 p.m.

My STUPID brother is going out tonight so I have to iron his STUPID shirt so he doesn't spread the story about the fish tank. So tempted to pin a sign to the back saying,

> NATHAN MOORE CRIED AT
> THE END OF THE LION KING

but the information he has on me could actually end my life. Miss Gorgeous Knickers and her gang hunt for stuff like that. They had T-shirts printed once with a photo of Dibbo Hannah from school dressed as a squirrel. She was 5 at the time — but Miss Gorgeous Knickers doesn't care.

SUNDAY 4TH JANUARY

11.15 a.m.

Mum in such a major mood this morning. It only stopped when Golden Boy got up. I don't know what it is with my older brother but in my mum's eyes he can't do a thing wrong, despite being Mr AS Level dropout. My stepdad Rob thinks my brother is just someone who'll take more time in life to "find his way".

Rob forgets that my brother washed his face in puddles up to Year 8.

12.11 p.m.

Also, my stepdad puts Reggae Reggae Sauce on everything — including toast — so what does he know?!

I have decided I am going to keep on writing this probably for the rest of my life. It's good practice for when I have my own column in *Vogue* and it's nice to have something to BLAB to about the things that REALLY matter.

8.46 p.m.

Went round Gran's. She's not heard from her dentist but she says he has a holiday cottage in the Peak District and he can't get reception there. She said she hoped her text had got stuck in the satellite for ever.

How does my gran know where her dentist goes at weekends?

9.47 p.m.

OMG — is my gran snogging her dentist?! Her dentures wobble when she talks (probably because she put them out of shape when she wrote her address on them!). They couldn't handle a full-on tongue!

9.56 p.m.

Just googled <u>snogging with dentures</u> 🔍 — you can get special glue that keeps them in.

Why did I look that up?! I need to concentrate on MY love life not my gran's. At least I have some things going for me. I have my own teeth for a start.

MONDAY 5TH JANUARY

6.10 p.m.

Getting uniform ready to go back to school. I am the only 13-year-old in the history of time not to have any matching underwear at all. Some of my pants actually have days of the week written on them.

6.39 p.m.

Mum says my bras and knickers are fine and functional. Of course she does.

She thinks I am still 4 and never listens to a word I say. EVERYONE in this house thinks I am 4.

8.28 p.m.

Gran rang — her dentist loved the joke and to date has sent 6 more back. She also managed to get in next week with him as an "emergency". She says it pays to stick out from the crowd. I said, "Gran: a) I don't need to know about your teeth situation, and b) rude jokes on text are just always crap." Gran then accused me of being a prude. I'm not a prude. I have flirted in ways so subtle that she would never even know! Like with Ant Spicer. 6 months we waited at the same bus stop and not once did he realize I was giving him my psychic-connection-love-eye-stare that Weirdo Jen taught me.

8.32 p.m.

Actually that may be the problem. Am I too subtle? Do I need to hit boys with a MASSIVE love ATTACK?

TUESDAY 6TH JANUARY

5.48 p.m.

COOLEST first day back at school today EVER-EVER-EVER. First Dr Richards demonstrated the difference between a noun and a verb by the use of SNOG! SNOG is a noun. TO SNOG makes it a doing word — it's a verb. It's the first time I've actually understood it. Then Dibbo Hannah accidentally called Dr Richards "DAD". DURGGHHH times 2 million!

Goose next door grabbed me on the way to school and walked with me. He actually invited me to a car boot sale. I said, "Goose, why would I want to get up at stupid o'clock on a Sunday to go and look at my gran's ornaments in the pouring rain?" Goose reckons that you can make a fortune buying tat and then selling it on eBay. One woman he'd heard about bought a plant, and the bowl it was in was worth £30,000.

I don't know why Goose doesn't get the message that I'm older now and our interests are different. I am too mature to be playing *Sesame Street* in his garden. Yes, he did let me always be Cookie Monster, but so? Don't get me wrong — I love Goose — but only in a chronic way.

7.50 p.m.

Sorry that should have read "platonic way". That means when you love someone but you don't actually want to snog them.

8.12 p.m.

According to loads of people on the advice thread on Digital Spy, platonic relationships do not actually exist and if a man likes you then he fancies you — unless he is gay!

8.34 p.m.

Just texted Goose. He is not gay. So that proves MoleinaHole and BunkBed do not have a clue what they are actually talking about and should be banned from the Internet for ever.

WEDNESDAY 7TH JANUARY

1.15 p.m.

In Geography this morning, me and Dimple made the best code ever to rate how gorgeous a boy is:

- ♥ "He studies at the University of (Sick Noise)" — means we would actually be ill if we had to kiss him.
- ♥ "He was born in Muntershire" — he is very ugly.
- ♥ "He is Toky-OK" — he is just all right.
- ♥ "He holidays in Torreme-CUTE-tos" — he is cute (that one may be a bit obvious).
- ♥ "He's from the Hotswolds" — we may die if we NEVER get to snog him.

We also talked about the Dr Phil book. We agree with him when he says you have to love yourself before you can date. Dimple thinks she might love herself a bit but I don't think I love myself at all. We were going to go through the reasons for me not loving myself but Mrs Cripps went mad that we weren't concentrating on her stupid coastal erosion diagram. EXCUSE ME, MRS CRIPPS? WHAT'S MORE IMPORTANT? MY SELF-ESTEEM, OR YOUR PICTURE OF A CLIFF DISAPPEARING?!

9.36 p.m.

Weirdo Jen just texted me the best joke ever.

> How many men does it take to change the toilet roll? No one knows – it's never happened!

LOL!

10.03 p.m.

Weirdo Jen just texted to say she got that text from Gran. What else is she sending out and to who? I must tell Mum. She needs to be stopped.

THURSDAY 8TH JANUARY

8.02 p.m.

Today will go down in history. SERIOUSLY.

This is one of the most important days EVER. Today, 3 girls sick of life being so unfair, decided to make things better for all WOMEN. Because today was the day we HAD ENOUGH.

It all started when Dimple wanted a Kit Kat on the way home. Because of the STUPID, STUPID SIGN that Mr Patel has on his door that says:

> *NO MORE* THAN 4 UNACCOMPANIED SCHOOLCHILDREN IN THE SHOP AT THE SAME TIME.

we ALL had to wait out in the pouring rain because 4 boys from St Gilbert's were in there already, perving over *Nuts* magazine. We got soaked through, we were freezing cold, and WHY? Because we are young. AND HOW CAN WE HELP THAT?!

There are just so many things that just SUCK. Not being allowed in shops. Being banned from wearing mascara, lipstick AND eyeshadow in school because "school isn't about looking good" (?). And Dimple said, "Why do we just sit down and take it?" And I said, "That's such a good point, Dimps – we are empowered women of the 21st century – we CAN make a change." Then Weirdo Jen said her mum had actually been in a society at university called "Women RULE", where they all decided they didn't have to wear bras, and that "group action" was the only way to get things done.

Anyway, we went to Bertie's Coffee Shop and worked it all out. We are the "NOT FAIR PROTEST GROUP". We are the trio of justice. WE ask the questions. We are going to write down what isn't fair in our lives and then we are going to SORT IT OUT. We pledge to do this without slagging people off OR doing down our fellow women. From now on I, Hattie Moore, will record how just 3 normal girls made all the difference. We will do it together and we will do it in fine GORGEOUS style. First meeting is going to happen next Thursday. CANNOT WAIT.

And THEN just to prove that some days turn out to be packed AND stuffed FULL OF YUM after days of TOTAL dullster, I can now officially confirm to you — please tell *Heat* magazine IMMEDIATELY — that I am IN LOVE! TOTAL MASSIVE HUGE AWESOME LOVE, LOVE, LOVE!!!

It's been going on for a while, and I think that, like Dr Phil says, I have been in denial. But today I just couldn't fight it ANY LONGER. I LOVE THE BOY THAT WORKS AT BERTIE'S. HE FROTHS THE LATTES AND HE MAKES ME HOT, BABY! He is McFittie from Fitshire in the Hotswolds. HE is the chocolate sprinkle on my cappuccino. He is the CROWN KING OF FIT BUMS. I must snog him or die.

There is a MASSIVE problem though. Every time I see him I am in uniform. It's impossible to look good in brown. No wonder other schools call us the "Walking Turds". But I can't let the fact that I look like a giant poo stop me from FULL-ON LOVE.

9.55 p.m.
Keep thinking about Jen's mum and her society at university. Why wouldn't a woman want to wear a bra?

Especially Jen's mum. She has the world's biggest breasts and they are REAL.

11.12 p.m.

Actually, are we a bit geeky forming a protest group?

11.35 p.m.

No – it's the sort of thing celebrities do all the time and EVERYONE in the world EVER fancies them.

FRIDAY 9TH JANUARY

4.34 p.m.

Got home tonight to talk to Mum about Gran, and the conversation went like this...

```
Me:    Mum, can we have a talk?
Mum:   Hats, I haven't got time for
       this right now.
Me:    But, Mum, we need to talk!
Mum:   Why?
Me:    Because Gran is sending
       out porn!
```

Which isn't what I wanted to say at all but she just makes me SO mad ... and what's the point anyway? She never listens. Mum just said that Gran would never do that as she is so LAST CENTURY. (Gran's still furious with Mum for getting pregnant when she wasn't married.)

Sometimes I think Mum doesn't realize what a true mental Gran is.

SATURDAY 10TH JANUARY

6.07 p.m.

I'm sorry but I have totally given up on Dr Phil. I think it's actually written for people who are a bit older than me, as it asks what you have learned from previous relationships. I have had no previous relationships. I actually may be the most tragic person on the planet except for....

OMG, I can't actually think of anyone more tragic.

7.15 p.m.

Yes, I can – Danielle Lance at school. She went with her ACTUAL MUM to see *The Sound of Music* AND she wears socks with mini zebras on them.

I am officially still tragic though. I have never snogged a man or felt man-bum.

SUNDAY 11TH JANUARY

7.02 a.m.

Just got woken up by my stepdad. He's up at a stupid time to take Goose next door to a car boot sale. He says the first one after Christmas is full of gifts everyone's trying to get rid of and did I want to come? *No* – not unless someone got a brand-new pair of big breasts for Christmas that they don't want.

11.01 a.m.

Actually, I think Dr Phil may have made me feel slightly depressed. I am probably the only nearly-14-year-old in the history of the world that hasn't had a relationship.

Miss Gorgeous Knickers at school had her first boyfriend at 9! And she regularly has to wear polo necks to cover her love bites. I can wear low-cut tops as I have no bites and, in fact, no breasts.

2.34 p.m.

Stepdad just came home with a lampshade in the shape of an elephant.

I was so right not to go.

11.09 p.m.

Just done my weekly tit test in front of the mirror. When I jump up and down they STILL don't move.

Goodnight, breasts. Please grow a bit overnight so I can bounce to school.

MONDAY 12TH JANUARY

7.23 a.m.

Good morning, breasts. You are still tiny and I hate you.

5.29 p.m.

NON-TRAGIC MARVELLOUSNESS! Netboreball was cancelled because it was raining! Me, Dimple and Weirdo Jen spent indoor Core PE talking about what we want from LOVE. Dimple says she wants a good friend who's romantic. We thought Dimple got her husband chosen for her, but apparently her parents will only "suggest" people if she reaches 30 and still isn't married. Weirdo Jen wants something intense and "consuming". Between you and me. I think she's waiting for a vampire! LOL! I'll just settle for a rich guy who owns a farm but doesn't mind me travelling to London every week for a job in fashion. He can look after the animals on his own — it won't be a big place. In fact, just some chickens will do. I think that's all Stella McCartney has. And her dad is loaded.

7.35 p.m.

Keep thinking about my wedding now. Who will walk me up the aisle? Rob will want to but what if Mr REAL Biological Dad turns up?!

8.43 p.m.

By the way, Weirdo Jen likes being called Weirdo Jen. I'm not being a cow or anything. She says it adds to her "mystical aura of otherworldness"!

TUESDAY 13TH JANUARY

7.45 p.m.

After school just the best thing ever — McFittie from Fitshire in the Hotswolds was serving in Bertie's. AND LISTEN TO THIS — HE DID NOT ASK DIMPLE IF SHE WANTED A BISCOTTI BUT HE ASKED ME!!!

Even Dimple had to agree that it was special treatment, because we watched all the people that went after us and he didn't ask them if they wanted biscotti either. IT'S THE BISCUIT OF LOVE! THEN he seemed to come over and wipe our table first. Perhaps I am reading too much into it, but there seemed to be definite interest!

OMG — I think my tragic life may actually be about to end.

8.59 p.m.

I just want to say I love Dimple. We have so much in common — like the fact we are both named after film stars. Only she's named after a gorgeous Bollywood actress. I'm apparently named after a fat woman that used to play nurses. Still it's all TOTAL glamour.

Actually my auntie is a nurse and one time she had to shave an old tramp's arse, so scrap the glamour thing. I'll just tell future men in my life I'm named after ... hats or something. The point is, I WILL make McFittie mine.

WEDNESDAY 14TH JANUARY

9.57 p.m.

Dimple and me have just spent 2 hours on the phone going over fully what happened yesterday. She says that McFittie MUST like me. Thinking back, I've got a feeling she might be right. I just can't quite believe that someone that gorgeous actually likes me!

Come on, Hattie — you are not completely Ugly City. Gran says I am even classic supermodel material in my uber skinnyness. It's just I also have this voice telling me I am a hideous munter monster.

I think this voice might sound like Miss Gorgeous Knickers.

10.15 p.m.

I know why I have low self-confidence. It's a totally well-known actual fact (google it!) that girls who do not know their fathers think they are ugly and pick rubbish men. I may pick a craptacular boy and it won't even be my fault! It will TOTALLY be my mum's.

10.32 p.m.

Just been on drphil.com and he says one of the worst things you can do when you split up with your partner is "sabotage your child's relationship with the other parent". MUM – ARE YOU LISTENING?!

10.54 p.m.

I need to start looking for my REAL dad. The fish thing HAS to have been forgotten by now. Actual people murderers eventually get forgiven!

I need help though – I don't really know where to start.

11.36 p.m.

Just remembered that Citizens' Advice place that Gran went to when one of her neighbours started keeping a goat on his balcony. I'll try them tomorrow. They must have people in all the time who have mislaid a parent.

THURSDAY 15TH JANUARY

4.03 p.m.

We had our first official meeting of the Not Fair Protest Group at lunch today. The injustices were as follows:

! Mum HAS to realize just how UNFAIR she was
the other night when she told me off because
of Gran. She HAS to start actually listening
to what I say. She also has to STOP giving the
excuse that she hasn't got time to listen because
she has 70 ham and salad rolls to make up for
the shop tomorrow and she has to nip to the
cash and carry to get 3 boxes of Doritos.

! Mr Patel has to STOP discriminating against
people under 18 and allow unlimited young people
in his shop at any time.

! It's a complete injustice that ALL cosmetics
are banned at school. Limited make-up SHOULD
be allowed if it's an expression of someone's
religious faith or because of the music they like.
Jen says she is emo Goth and that is technically
a belief, so she should be able to express it.

! Many people are having their days (and nights!)
unfairly RUINED by old people who can't use
their mobiles properly. ALL over-40s to be
given compulsory mobile phone lessons. In fact,
there should be a mobile phone licence for the
over-40s with an exam they have to pass.

I am tackling my mum, Jen is making an appointment
to see the head Mrs Cob, and Dimple is talking to Mr
Patel. That's not racist — it's not because she is Indian
or anything. It's because her PMT makes her into a
chocolate mental and she is Mr Patel's best customer.

I wanted to add it's not fair that McFittie and me aren't snogging yet, but it seemed a bit selfish. The Not Fair Protest Group should be about helping our fellow women and solving injustice – not about me getting full-on love action. It's just McFittie is SO LUSH – black hair, green eyes and big chunky-monkey, hairy, FIT, BUFF arms. Dimple reckons he looks like an orang-utan, but I'm just relieved we don't fancy the same people. Dimple is UBER gorgeous. In fact I'm a bit annoyed her parents aren't arranging her marriage because it means she's shopping in the snog supermarket at the same time as me. "Love IS a battlefield" – so one of my mum's CDs says.

4.50 p.m.

Feel bad about the last bit. Dimple is my best friend. It's good she doesn't have to marry an ugly.

5.09 p.m.

The Citizens' Advice Bureau can't give me an appointment for 4 WEEKS!

4 WEEKS!!!

The woman there was really nice but she said it was due to "unprecedented demand" and the fact that "everyone is going bankrupt or getting divorced".

WHAT IS ACTUALLY WRONG WITH EVERYONE?!

I'm seeing the CAB on 13th February. On the last day that I am 13. All those 13s. It must mean something.

6.13 p.m

Jen says that 13 can actually be lucky for some people. She wasn't sure who though.

She also says that if you go bankrupt you don't have to pay ANY of your credit cards back and can basically shop like Paris Hilton. It all makes more sense now.

6.43 p.m.

Dimple says if you go bankrupt you can't buy a house though. Who cares if you've got a decent Gucci bag!

FRIDAY 16TH JANUARY

8.35 p.m.

Like an idiot I blabbed to Gran about the Not Fair Protest Group. This was a big mistake as she thinks it's a great idea and is going to draw up a list of unfair things that affect her. What does she expect me to do about them?!

I told Gran about talking to Mum. AND she says what she ALWAYS says: "Hattie, be gentle with your mum — she's had it hard. When your dad left you were only a baby. She had to start all again." I said, "I KNOW that, but that was nearly 14 years ago, Gran, and I've got over it so why shouldn't she?" Then Gran said, "But have you really got over it, Hattie?" with one of her laser looks.

So I went for it. I said, "Gran, OF COURSE I HAVEN'T. I wonder where he is and why he hasn't sent me a birthday card. It's SO hard. Dimple's dad adores her and even Weirdo Jen and her Weirdo dad bond over her frill-

necked lizard. But I HAVE TO PRETEND TO BE OVER
IT mostly because no one wants to listen. I want to know
who he is and where he is!"

Gran looked at me for about 10 minutes and said, "Hattie,
I know it's hard, duck (as soon as Gran uses DUCK you
know it's bad). But sometimes you just have to accept
that other people know best and they are protecting you
FOR A REASON. Now subject closed – can you help me
with my puzzle?"

THEN she had an angina attack and had to have a spray
of her mad medicine.

I WILL GET TO THE TRUTH. I WON'T BE STOPPED
BY SUDOKU.

I couldn't ask Gran any more then though. She was gasping
for breath! It would have been evil to carry on.

10.23 p.m.
OMG – do you think my gran might have been pretending
to have an angina attack just to shut me up?! No,
Hattie – that IS you being a cow.

SATURDAY 17TH JANUARY

6.09 p.m.
Tried to speak to Mum today – but she didn't have time.
When I said, "You NEVER have time for me – it's not
fair," she said, "Life isn't fair, Hattie."

I TOTALLY know that, Mum — I am the only 13-year-old I know without any decent lingerie AND without a dad. Even people at school who don't know their dads at least have decent knickers!

Then Goose from next door suggested I put toothpaste on my zit farm. I went MENTAL: "Yes, thanks, Goose — perhaps you would like to play dot-to-dot with them too. You are not meant to point them out." Goose looked really upset and said he was just trying to help. I said, "You can help, Goose — by not mentioning them."

I also asked Goose how he deals with not having a dad. It's different for boys but it's still worth asking. Goose said he did think about his real dad occasionally but he's decided, "The man must have bad taste as I am actually an OK kind of guy and well worth knowing." I said, "Goose, do you REALLY think that?" and Goose went, "Yeah — seriously."

9.56 p.m.
REASONS WHY MY DAD MAY HAVE LEFT:

* Something I did wrong. Perhaps I was one of these total nightmare babies that cried all the time and did chemical warfare poos.
* Something my brother did wrong. He has always been evil. He put his hamster — Hammy — in my stepdad's model plane to see if he "enjoyed air travel". He didn't. He died.
* Something my gran did wrong. She is a mental.

*   Something my mum did wrong. This is TOTALLY likely. But what?

10.47 p.m.

I bet they were just going to pretend that Rob was my dad but they couldn't because Rob is from Guyana and actually black.

SUNDAY 18TH JANUARY

5.34 p.m.

Gran has given me her *Not Fair List* – honestly I am frightened:

1. People at her pensioners' club who have asthma or breathing problems don't have time to say "bingo" before the caller has read out the next number. Gran's friend Denise missed out on the £1,000 jackpot last week because of her wheezing. Please can the caller slow down.

2. Just because Gran is of mature years does not mean that she has "given up". Therefore when she goes into Topshop she would like to be treated like a normal woman and not asked if she is shopping for her granddaughter. She particularly likes the jewellery.

3. Dating websites should not have ← VOM VOM VOM!!! an upper age limit.

After thinking about Number 3 I'm worried my gran may be after a toyboy. She may in fact be a COUGAR! I've never seen her with any men though. I thought she was happy with Inspector Barnaby from *Midsomer Murders,* but perhaps she is on the prowl for young meat? Like Madonna!

7.32 p.m.

I am officially stressed. I have to finish a project on the dairy industry (press the snooze button), sort out my gran's life, keep Mum off my back (yes, I *will* clean under my bed, Mum), AND get McFittie to actually like me.

I think finding my dad may have to wait for a bit. I'll look less tragic if I have a boyfriend when I meet him anyway.

MONDAY 19TH JANUARY

5.09 p.m.

Nightmare day. It was double Art. Scary Mrs Matfield – the only woman in the world who is capable of making Art NOT a laugh – decided we had to recreate old classic paintings, using ... STRING AND WOOL! She says it's about "experiments in textures". We say it's about her having even more reasons to shout at us when the impossible goes wrong. I am currently trying to make the *Mona Lisa* – this ancient munter woman. I'm using red wool that won't do as it's told, even when I use half a ton of glue. Apparently the *Mona Lisa* is meant to look enigmatic (had to google this – means "mysterious"). Mine doesn't. She looks like Grandad after his stroke.

Why can't I make McFittie from string? He is a masterpiece and should be framed for me to look at ALL DAY!

7.48 p.m.

Dimple just rang. She is going to see Mr Patel tomorrow in the evening, when it's quiet during *EastEnders* – to find out why he hates teenagers.

TUESDAY 20TH JANUARY

9.34 p.m.

Dimple went to see Mr Patel, who said that he HAD to put the sign on the door as he was losing hundreds of chocolate bars a week and several magazines. He said that most children and pensioners were natural thieves, and that they needed to be watched at all times.

So Dimps said, "Why don't you discriminate against pensioners too?" Mr Patel said that old people were "easier to watch".

I think he means because they all need hip replacements they don't move as fast. He DID then agree with Dimple that it was only fair that he put a sign up saying:

> ONLY 4 PENSIONERS WILL BE ALLOWED
> INTO THIS SHOP AT ANY ONE TIME.

He's putting it up tomorrow, so we are counting that as our first *Not Fair Protest Group* victory.

WEDNESDAY 21ST JANUARY

7.13 p.m.

OMG!!!

Gran has heard that Mr Patel is only allowing 4 old people in his shop at a time. I didn't tell her that it was our doing! She has mobilized a protest group and they are starting a blockade of his shop. Plus they are going to take it in turns to press the button on the pedestrian crossing outside his shop so it's constantly in use. They are doing it on Saturday.

What have I started?

McFittie – why aren't you in my life yet?

THURSDAY 22ND JANUARY

5.17 p.m.

My *Mona Lisa* string picture is a disaster. The red wool has left a mark all over the paper – the woman looks like she has been stabbed. Mrs Matfield said it was typically shoddy slapdash work and Leonardo da Vinci would be turning in his grave. All his paintings would have been crap too if he had had Matfield for a teacher. She is basically Hitler with a stupid big wooden orange necklace.

7.16 p.m.
I LOVE DIMPLE RATHOD!!!

Dimple has just been on a mission to find out about McFittie.

THE FACTS:

- ♥ He is 16.
- ♥ He is called Finan McCready.
- ♥ He's originally from Edinburgh.
- ♥ He used to live down south and was into surfing.
- ♥ HE IS SINGLE – YES YES YES YES YES!!!
- ♥ He is a Libra which is OFFICIALLY THE BEST SIGN FOR AN AQUARIUS LIKE ME ever.
- ♥ He is working at Bertie's because he wants to be a scuba diver.

Prediction: this will make Mum immediately not like him because he is not going to college! BRILLIANT!

Dimple says actually he seems really lovely and that he is very friendly. Oh, PLEASE PLEASE PLEASE let me go out with him. Perhaps Weirdo Jen can do one of her spells. Or can I COSMIC ORDER LOVE?

FRIDAY 23RD JANUARY

4.59 p.m.

My brother has heard I fancy McFittie and is now threatening to take some of my baby photos to show him the ones where I was a crazed podge-monster trying to eat an actual fork.

I'm going to see him tomorrow before my brother can do any damage.

7.02 p.m.

Just found McFittie on Facebook. He has 506 friends BUT IS SINGLE. YAY YAY and YAY!!!

7.05 p.m.

McFittie is a member of the Facebook group "I give my chips to the disabled seagull", so he is also very caring.

SATURDAY 24TH JANUARY

9.28 p.m.

OFFICIAL DEATH FROM EMBARRASSMENT.

MY GRAN ACTUALLY ORGANIZED A PROTEST AT MR PATEL'S SHOP.

I SAW IT WITH MY OWN EYES.

She and 5 friends from bingo had big notices and everything saying

> PLEASE THE OAPS

and

> BE FAIR TO PENSIONERS

Mr Patel came outside and offered them a free giant packet of Celebrations each as a "gesture of goodwill", but Gran shouted she could not be bought with out-of-date chocolate. Then the police turned up and threatened to arrest them for breach of the peace or something. Gran started shouting at the policeman saying that Derby was "full of drug dealers" and "shouldn't they be after them — not 6 women over the age of 60?". I didn't see what happened after this as I pretended not to know her when she shouted to me to help her. I know this is bad but I can't be associated with mental old people when I am in pursuit of my love.

Am I terrible for putting men before my gran? I'm sure she would understand. She did nick Grandad off her own sister.

Got to Bertie's and McFittie wasn't there. Rang Weirdo Jen, who said this was my karma for ignoring my gran. She said karma basically meant if you do bad things then bad things happen to you. This is complete rubbish because Miss Gorgeous Knickers at school is evil and she practically has her own Facebook fan page run by the boys who want to snog her.

Where are you, McFittie?

SUNDAY 25TH JANUARY

4.09 p.m.

My mum is officially crusty. This morning she said she was too tired to have a shower and just used half a can of Sure and a squirt of Romance by Ralph Lauren to be on the "safe side". Miss Gorgeous Knickers' mum won't even answer the door without a full face of make-up. Mum could at least put some lippy on. I hope crustiness isn't genetic — I've already got my mum's no tits — that's enough, thank you.

4.35 p.m.

Perhaps my dad left because my mum didn't wash? Maybe he's a clean freak and couldn't put up with her being the Queen of Grot?

Must stop thinking about him. Need to FOCUS on LOVE.

5.12 p.m.

It is actually disgusting that my mum expects me to have a tidy bedroom yet I have seen her dust the coffee table by blowing on it.

MONDAY 26TH JANUARY

11.19 p.m.

Was just having a MASSIVE chat with Weirdo Jen on Skype about McFittie when Mum flew in and threatened to take my laptop off me. She thinks I never get time away from my friends and I'm not getting enough "down-time rest". WHY DOES SHE WANT ME TO BE LONELY? I NEED TO KEEP UP WITH EVERYONE! If she wants me to get more rest she can tell Goose next door to stop singing everything at the top of his voice.

TUESDAY 27TH JANUARY

4.02 p.m.

Mr Patel's shop is closing. He's moving back to Kashmir in India, where he and his family originally come from. He says there is less trouble there and people do as they are told. His shop is becoming a Polish deli, which Gran is thrilled about as she loves their sausages. Gran didn't know much about Polish chocolate. I daren't tell Dimple – she loves Mr Patel – and if she can't get her hands on Dairy Milk at certain times of the month she could honestly kill.

WEDNESDAY 28TH JANUARY

6.36 p.m.

My mum always looks so tired and all she ever talks about is work. If she did more girlie stuff we could bond. Some girls at school go to spa days with their mums. The nearest I get to that is when my mum comes in to brush her teeth when I'm in the bath!

6.50 p.m.

I've been googling. Mum would really benefit from rediscovering her "inner woman", so I am going to talk to her about burlesque classes. Dita Von Teese says that burlesque is a celebration of the female body, and I know Mum thinks her body was partly ruined after she gave birth. I think this could bring us together, if you know what I mean.

7.26 p.m.

Just mentioned burlesque to my mother. She said, "Don't be ridiculous, Hattie – I haven't got time to have a decent bath let alone dance around in a diamanté thong and high heels."

I bet Dannii Minogue manages to have a bath, work, look after her kid and look good in a bikini. It can be done, Mum!

8.34 p.m.

Actually I don't want my mum to be sexy when McFittie comes round. She could turn into a cougar like Gran.

THURSDAY 29TH JANUARY

7.12 p.m.

Went to Bertie's straight after school. McFittie looked INCREDIBLE today – he even smelt TOTES amazing. Must be the sort of UBER expensive aftershave they keep behind the counter in Boots because everyone wants to nick it.

I even tried to start a conversation with him but I must remember NOT to order a latte because the frother machine noise makes that completely impossible. You can't be sexy when you're having to shout like Gran on one of her "deaf days".

I gave up in the end and just had to watch him like I always do.

9.18 p.m.

Dimple and Weirdo Jen have just been round. Weirdo Jen thinks she can help me get McFittie with magic. She's got loads of experience with spells and stuff and Mother Nature is her personal goddess or something.

She also reckoned if you light 2 matches, fuse them together and tap on 1 whilst chanting the alphabet, the matches will separate on the initial of the man who is destined for you. It's in her Wiccan handbook.

We did it 12 times. It kept separating on the letter C or D so Dimps and me think Jen may be talking actual crap.

FRIDAY 30TH JANUARY

6.09 p.m.

Went to Bertie's again to see McFittie and ordered a water. Was just about to say something and then — WHY DON'T PEOPLE FROM OFFICES ACTUALLY STAY IN THEIR OFFICES TO HAVE MEETINGS? — this load of people in suits came in and this big fat sales guy ended up ordering 12 cappuccinos, an Americano, 3 lattes, 1 hazelnut latte, 3 bits of carrot cake, 4 chocolate muffins and a piece of Victoria sponge. Poor McFittie was rushed off his feet. But he was a TOTAL miracle — he got it ALL right. And all the fat sweaty sales guy could say was "thank you". If that had been me I would have seriously filled out a customer satisfaction card thing and ticked the massively smiley "very satisfied" face.

6.37 p.m.

I didn't just remember the entire order, by the way. I nicked the bit of paper McFittie wrote it on. He's got AMAZING handwriting. Bet he writes songs. And plays the guitar.

8.42 p.m.

Weirdo Jen has been reading a book on love techniques for me. It's her mum's book (VOM!). Apparently food can be "powerfully erotic", and all men like to see a woman who "enjoys her food". Jen thinks I should go to Bertie's to try and eat something in a "seductive fashion" in front of McFittie. It's all about being "slow and meaningful" with the right "intense eye flicks". It could work. I need to rehearse though – I've never eaten sexily before. In fact I have never done anything sexily before. Unless I am naturally sexy and don't know it.

I think I would know if I was naturally sexy. I would feel more ... tingly.

9.23 p.m.

Just tripped over my actual own legs – not sexy.

10.14 p.m.

Just examined own legs. Leg stubble – NOT sexy. Why does it grow back so quickly?

SATURDAY 31ST JANUARY

5.05 p.m.

Been practising eating food in front of the mirror.

The following foods are NOT erotic:

* cornflakes
* crisps
* toast

---

* baked beans
* water biscuits
* Gran's fruit cake

The following foods COULD be sexy:

* Müller Light Fruit Corner
* dark chocolate Magnum
* banana

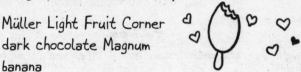

6.29 p.m.

Weirdo Jen says bananas are far too "obvious".

6.43 p.m.

Just tried eating another banana in the mirror. Jen is right.

SUNDAY 1ST FEBRUARY

3.29 p.m.

Asked Gran today why leg hair grows back so quickly. She says I'm a mental to shave and that they are doing cheap waxing at the college. I feel so sorry for the beauty student that sees the back of her legs. It would be enough to make her decide on another career!

Gran says she might have an eyebrow shape and a Brazilian as they are on offer too.

Gran having a Brazilian. I actually do now need counselling.

7.19 p.m.

Just tried to eat Gran's roast dinner erotically. She asked me if I had cramps. I don't think I am very good at this.

MONDAY 2ND FEBRUARY

4.27 p.m.

Showed Jen at lunch today how I intended to drink my coffee seductively. She said obviously she wasn't a boy but she thought I quite possibly could look quite good doing it. She told me I had to slow down though as it's the PACE of how you eat the food that really matters — NOT the actual food. You have to chew everything at least 36 times.

5.45 p.m.

How can you chew a Müller Light Fruit Corner?

6.43 p.m.

Goose came round to see my stepdad. He doesn't really count as a boy but I ate an orange in front of him to see if he would notice anything. He just carried on talking about being ripped off on eBay. HATTIE MOORE, YOU NEED TO BE MORE OBVIOUS. EAT SLOWER.

TUESDAY 3RD FEBRUARY

10.17 p.m.

I was late for school this morning as it took me 22 minutes to eat 2 Weetabix. Then at lunch Mrs Matfield asked if I was unwell as I was "meandering over my chips like an invalid". It's not easy learning to be sexy — I hope McFittie appreciates all this.

10.33 p.m.

Mum reminded me I have the dentist tomorrow afternoon — going to miss double Science — YES!!!

WEDNESDAY 4TH FEBRUARY

5.02 p.m.

TOTAL nightmare.

Just been to the dentist and he says I need braces — otherwise my teeth will end up sticking out like diving boards. I WILL NEED TO WEAR THEM for at least 12 months. Who is going to want to kiss a robot? The good news is for an extra £1500 I can have the ones which match the colour of my teeth!

10.24 p.m.

Mum says that I will have to have the cheaper version. Does she realize that I may now be single for the rest of my life?

10.38 p.m.

Asked Mum if I could contact my real dad to ask him for the money to pay for my braces. She turned into a mental and shouted, "Hattie, DON'T BE RIDICULOUS! He hasn't paid any child support ever and ... I don't even know where he is."

I BET SHE DOES! WHAT REALLY HAPPENED, MUM?
I DESERVE THE TRUTH!!!

I thought that but I didn't say it.

THURSDAY 5TH FEBRUARY

4.54 p.m.

OFFICIAL – I am having my braces fitted on the 16th
February. Please note this is 2 days after my birthday –
so I will start my 14th year on Earth looking craptacular
like never before.

I will NEED to go out with McFittie before then so he
can truly fall in love with the REAL me before I become
half-woman half-metal.

8.10 p.m.

Goose just texted me to say that braces "can look cool".

1. Why does my mum tell Goose's mum everything
   about my life?!
2. Why does Goose's mum tell HIM everything about
   my life? As a woman she should know I NEED
   PRIVACY.

9.35 p.m.

I've just listened to my fave song and I've decided I am
going to TOTALLY rock braces. I am NOT going to sit in
my room crying about it like a massive spoon. But first,
tomorrow is McFittie Day. I am going to go in there and
be the best woman I CAN BE. I AM GOING FOR IT!

FRIDAY 6TH FEBRUARY

5.26 a.m.

CAN'T SLEEP.

McFittie Day.

When I write here again I could be the girlfriend of someone gorgeous who gets free skinny blueberry muffins on a daily basis.

7.36 a.m.

Just had full MASSIVE bath with two LUSH bath bombs. Mum said, "You're up early." Yes, I am, Mum — as I basically have an appointment with Hotness after school.

I didn't say this, as she would go mental.

4.15 p.m.

Jen just did my make-up. My eyes are POPPING-OUT good and she let me borrow her lip plumper. I have officially the greatest friends in the world ever.

I'm going to go for it. It's time. McFittie BE MINE. Hattie Moore is ON A HOT LOVE MISSION TO CAPTURE McFITTIE.

11.35 p.m.

I think I would like to move to Spain and never come back.

I don't think I want to keep this thing any more either.

SATURDAY 7TH FEBRUARY

SUNDAY 8TH FEBRUARY

8.23 a.m.

This diary is looking at me. But I can't write it now.

10.34 a.m.

No, Mum, I am not getting up today. There is no point.

4.36 p.m.

Weirdo Jen says writing things down can make you feel better. So here it is. This is how my life ended.

I went to see McFittie in Bertie's after school and ordered a tea (you can make that quietly). While I was waiting I started a conversation.

Me:	How are you?
McFittie:	Fine. Would you like milk?
Me:	Yes. I like milk. I like music too. Who do you listen to? Do you write your own stuff?
McFittie:	Sugar?
Me:	No, thanks. My friend Dimple says sugar causes MASSIVE zits. You'd love Dimple. Her dad's a surgeon and she really likes bhangra.

(I know I was talking more than him but men don't talk a lot so I thought it was going really well.)

Next he offered me a biscotti and I bought it and sat at the table directly opposite him. Then I dipped my biscotti in my tea and tried to eat it sexily.

STUPID. STUPID. STUPID. Because a STUPID bit of biscotti went down my stupid useless throat the wrong way and I ended up nearly choking to death on it. My coughing got so bad McFittie ran over and brought me a glass of water and started patting me on the back. That didn't work.

Then stupid fat sales guy (who was in Bertie's for ANOTHER meeting) said, "I've got my first-aid certificate – stand her up and thump her between her shoulders!" This DID work but I ended up blowing bits of biscotti everywhere. And dribbling water down my top.

So just to sum up Hattie Moore's day of triumph – I nearly died because of a crumb, and the man I love saw me spit food all over the place like a STUPID fountain of spew. NOT SEXY. NOT SEXY. NOT SEXY.

I hate myself. And biscotti.

10.14 p.m.

My brother just heard me crying. He came in and asked what was wrong. When I told him he gave me a hug and said, "Perhaps he found it cute? You never know. And if he didn't there'll be other boys — even for an ugly like you." Then he winked.

Sometimes my brother is not evil and actually perhaps I will allow him to live.

10.36 p.m.
Perhaps the lovely part of my brother comes from my real dad. It certainly does not come from my mum.

MONDAY 9TH FEBRUARY

8.34 p.m.
Dimple agrees with my brother. She thinks choking on a crumb may make me seem "sweet" and that boys "like to look after you" and "be the strong one".

I love Dimple but I think she's just being nice.

TUESDAY 10TH FEBRUARY

7.34 p.m.
I have been waiting to use the bathroom for about 12 hours. I need to keep on top of my hairiness and zit situation so if I do bump into McFittie I am all gorgeousness.

My stepdad takes ages in there. I understand that he spends all day in his car, and BO is the fear of every driving instructor. But seriously — how long does a man need to make sure he doesn't smell?! He goes through two bottles of Lynx a week. How hard can it be to just sit there and tell people how to use a gearstick? He's hardly building up a sweat.

I've decided to give me and McFittie some space. I'm not going to go to Bertie's for a few days. Hopefully by then he will have forgotten about it.

10.45 p.m.

Who am I kidding? He's probably telling someone right now how he saved my life and what I looked like with biscotti all over my chin.

WEDNESDAY 11TH FEBRUARY

10.14 p.m.

We had the second meeting today of the Not Fair Protest Group.

* Invisible braces are to be free on the NHS. I am contacting the prime minister directly as he is in charge of this sort of thing.

Weirdo Jen has suggested that we combine NFPG meetings with a make-up masterclass. I think this may be the best idea in the history of the world.

* Teachers are NOT to wear make-up. If school isn't about looking glamorous then that should be for EVERYONE – including staff.
* Biscotti to be banned as they are actually dangerous and ruin lives.

THURSDAY 12TH FEBRUARY

10.19 p.m.

I've emailed the prime minister through the Downing Street website. It says responses cannot be guaranteed — but surely there are not many things more important than the nation's teeth?!

From: Hattie Moore <helphattienow@gmail.com>
Date: February 12, 09:23:12 PM GMT
To: <pm@number10.gov.uk>
Subject: Bad braces RUIN lives as much as the recession!

Dear Prime Minister,

I am writing to you today asking for your help.

I have been told I have to have braces but I cannot afford the ones that will actually stop me from looking like something from *Doctor Who*.

PLEASE, PLEASE, Prime Minister, can you make invisible braces free on the NHS to girls under 16? In the long run you will undoubtedly save money as people with bad braces always need counselling when they are older.

Looking forward to hearing from you. ← My stepdad told me to write this — apparently it means. "I want a reply".

He HAS to reply SURELY. I will be a voter soon!

10.57 p.m.

OMG — how good would it be to have the prime minister as your dad?! You could film him on the toilet and threaten to put it on YouTube — then he would do ANYTHING you wanted.

11.14 p.m.
For all I know my dad COULD be the prime minister!

FRIDAY 13TH FEBRUARY

7.56 p.m.
Goose said he had heard about what happened with McFittie (APPARENTLY THE WHOLE WORLD HAS) and he was really sorry and it was McFittie's loss as I was actually lovely and funny. WHAT IS THAT BOY'S PROBLEM? Does he actually enjoy reminding me of everything that is wrong with my life right now?

I told Goose that he should concentrate on his own life – like the fact his mum still calls him "Goosey Woosey" at the age of 15. LOL!!! Goose said he loved his mum and actually didn't care what other people thought.

Thinking about it, it is actually really sweet that Goose still feels that way about his mum. Wish I did.

11.36 p.m.
OMG – I FORGOT my Citizens' Advice Bureau appointment.

Can't believe I have let a near-death from a biscotti stop me from finding my dad.

I'll call them on Monday to re-arrange it.

SATURDAY 14TH FEBRUARY

12.09 p.m.
MY BIRTHDAY!

Got 6 birthday cards — but more to the point JUST got a VALENTINE'S DAY CARD. It has a massive picture of a battered old teddy bear on it with "Happy Valentine's Day" and then inside it says, "Valentine — I'd love you whatever you were."

PLEASE, PLEASE, let it be from McFittie. Dimple is coming round to examine it fully.

3.05 p.m.

Me and Dimple have been sniffing the card for the past 10 minutes and Dimps is convinced that she can smell caffeine. Also the message "I'd love you whatever you were" has to refer to me choking on a biscotti and ending up with drool on my face. Thinking about it, it SO could be from him.

Going bowling tonight for my birthday. Me, Dimple and Jen are going to work out a love plan.

9.23 p.m.

Just got in from Megabowl. We've agreed that Dimple is going to go into Bertie's tomorrow and basically ask McFittie if he likes me. If he says yes then I am going FULL-ON for action. If he says no — then I will die. But then at least I'll know and will be able to move on and continue to grow as a person.

SUNDAY 15TH FEBRUARY

7.32 a.m.

Just realized growing as a person is what Dr Phil says you should do. Once he is in your head he's very hard to get out.

My brace gets fitted tomorrow. Just taken a photo of my teeth on my mobile. Goodbye, naked white things. Hello, big metal gates on my face.

9.30 p.m.

Just spoke to Dimple. She said McFittie was really busy and they couldn't talk. Then she changed the subject to THE DENTIST!!! Why would I want to talk about my braces instead of hotness?! Anyway Dimple is going to see him again tomorrow. Whilst I am going through hell.

10.14 p.m.

Mum just came in to tell me that she's coming with me to the dentist! Apparently, according to her friend Paul it's the law. Err – yes, Mum, I am actually 14 now – I can dress and feed myself. I don't need you at the dentist.

But she's still coming!

MONDAY 16TH FEBRUARY

11.23 a.m.

Rang the Citizens' Advice Bureau. They now can't see me till the 21st April!

Half-term. In fact the worst start to a half-term EVER.

That's weeks away. Rob reckons it's because everyone is now going bankrupt, getting divorced AND having problems with anti-social behaviour.

AND NOW I'VE GOT THE DENTIST!!!

7.12 p.m.

I am in so much pain.

I've just had the afternoon from HELL.

We got to Mr Crawford the dentist. He numbed my mouth with about a million injections and then he started PULLING MY TEETH OUT. I thought, OMG – he's got the wrong patient! Like that guy on TV that had his arm chopped off because they mixed him up with his twin.

Then the dentist said, "Hattie, to fit your brace we need to take your Number 4 teeth out." ERR – MR MENTAL, YOU DID NOT MENTION THIS AT MY LAST APPOINTMENT! Apparently he did though and he even sent Mum a letter and that's why she had to be with me!

Next thing I know he is STANDING ON A CHAIR to PULL 2 TEETH OUT. There was blood everywhere – on me, on the dentist, on the big light thing above my head.

THEN he said, "Have a rest Hattie". He had a slurp of coffee and THEN started wetting himself at Steve Wright's "Factoids" on the radio.

WHY ARE DENTISTS EVEN ALLOWED THE RADIO ON? DOCTORS AREN'T!

AND THEN ... he glued my brace on.

My stupid, ugly, horrible, EVIL brace.

By the time he had finished I was even whiter than normal with crusty blood all over my lips. The only good thing was Mum looked SO WORRIED! HA! She DOES care! She said, "Hattie, you were great in there. I was really proud."

I have to be brave to prove that I am mature and capable of handling pain.

7.32 p.m.

I have decided I am not capable of handling pain. This is a nightmare. My entire face aches. I'm starving but I'm not actually allowed to chew. Mum has said she will "rustle me up something suitable for tea".

7.52 p.m.

Mum just brought me up some soup. It's the tin of Asda cream of mushroom that's been at the back of the cupboard FOR EVER. I ate it anyway.

8.32 p.m.

Just checked the tin in the bin. The "best before" date was 3 years ago!

Mum says mushrooms are rotten anyway so there's no need to panic. Thanks for your care, Mum!

Wonder how Dimple got on with McFittie... Even with MOUTH OF DEATH I still think of my gorgeous boy.

10.17 p.m.

Not heard from Dimple but she hates anything medical. She can't even have her eyebrows shaped without feeling sick.

TUESDAY 17TH FEBRUARY

8.01 a.m.

Texted Dimple and promised not to talk about anything dental. Told her I was desperate to hear what had happened with McFittie.

11.12 a.m.

Weirdo Jen came round today to look at my brace. She thinks I must have looked amazing with blood on my lips and thinks my brace is "ultimate geek chic". She wants a brace but her dentist says her teeth are perfect. When she is older though she says she might get her front teeth filed to look like fangs. Her mum won't let her at the moment because she doesn't want her daughter looking like the "Queen of the Undead" on her school photo. Jen has taken my teeth (Mr Crawford gave me them as a souvenir) as apparently they have immense magical properties and can be used for Wiccan magic.

I love Jen but she is a proper weirdo. However, if she can make a spell to make McFittie love me I may love her for ever.

She hasn't heard from Dimple either but I know she has a lot on and that her mum has been acting a bit weird recently. Dimps thinks she might be having a midlife crisis. This is apparently what all women have when their hormones run out — then you actually become a proper total mental. The good news is that you can get a patch you put on your arse that reduces mental symptoms.

Being female is SO unfair. Boys' hormones just make them snog machines.

2.12 p.m.

My brother just tried to hold up a load of fridge magnets to my face to see if they stuck to my brace. They don't.

3.12 p.m.

Keep looking in the mirror. I can't imagine kissing McFittie with this brace.

After every meal I have to pick half of my dinner out of it. VOM VOM VOM.

9.45 p.m.

Went round to see Gran tonight. She said you could barely see my brace, and when she started "courting" my grandad he had a broken ankle and a lazy eye. Gran thinks a bit of vulnerability is a good thing. Perhaps it is for men but boys only want perfect girls, Gran — we all know it.

If I could actually airbrush myself in real life I would.

Still nothing from Dimple. Sometimes you can't get hold of her. She left her mobile in a rabbit hutch once.

WEDNESDAY 18TH FEBRUARY

11.14 a.m.

Still no Dimple. Jen thinks she may be going through a period of "immense growth" and, like the caterpillar that is about to turn into the butterfly, she needs "space in her mental chrysalis".

Or her phone is broken.

4.15 p.m.

Now I'm worried. Been trying Dimple all day with no luck. No answer on her landline or her mobile. Her parents don't like people just "nipping round". Her dad works long, odd hours and the doorbell can make him slightly irritable when he's been on nights.

What's happening?!

THURSDAY 19TH FEBRUARY

7.23 p.m.

Weirdo Jen just rang. She said she didn't know how to tell me this BUT there's a rumour going round that Dimple is going out with McFittie. Obviously this must be totally craptacular, as a) Dimple's parents would not allow her to have a boyfriend at the moment, and b) Dimple is my oldest friend — she would NEVER do that to me. We have known each other since we were 4. We were wise men together in the nativity and everything.

9.24 p.m.

Been thinking. Dimple is gorgeous though. And boys do funny things to girls.

I don't mean in that way. I mean love can make you into a total cow from Planet Cowland.

Just need to speak to her to sort it out.

FRIDAY 20TH FEBRUARY

8.12 a.m.

Just tried to call Dimps AGAIN — no answer.

9.34 a.m.

Texted Dimple — no answer.

9.55 a.m.

Called again — left a message.

10.35 a.m.

Texted her — her phone might be off.

12.37 p.m.

Tweeted her but the last time she wrote anything was back in January moaning about one of the new Pringles flavours — so perhaps she doesn't check it very often.

1.14 p.m.

Facebooked her — perhaps her Internet is down.

Her Facebook relationship status says she is single.

2.15 p.m.

Her Facebook relationship status says she is still single.

2.55 p.m.

Just saw she wrote on someone else's wall 5 minutes after my message. Perhaps she just missed mine.

3.45 p.m.

I've run out of credit on my mobile. I am the only person left in the world on pay-as-you-go AND Mum has refused to give me an advance on my pocket money. DOES SHE NOT REALIZE THAT WITHOUT CREDIT I AM BASICALLY CUT OFF FROM EVERYTHING IMPORTANT IN MY LIFE?!

Have to ask my brother.

3.55 p.m.

My brother said he would give me £10 to top up if I performed "I'm a Little Teapot" with all the actions like I used to do when I was 3. Evil. But I am desperate, so I did it. Topped up. Texted Dimple 3 times. No answer.

4.15 p.m.

Sent Dimple a psychic message. Didn't feel any response in my head.

Where is she?

Will give her a few more hours to respond. She might be shopping or something. Don't want to look like a stalker mental.

8.12 p.m.

Asked Mum if I can go round Dimple's house – she said no as it was 7.45 p.m. – PATHETIC!!! That's not even late!

It's a Friday. There isn't even any school tomorrow. My life is falling to bits here and she doesn't care.

11.15 p.m.

Can't stop thinking about it. What if she is going out with him? Feel sick in my stomach.

SATURDAY 21ST FEBRUARY

11.43 a.m.

OMG!

Went round Dimp's house at 8 a.m. When I got to Dimple's room she looked really shocked and couldn't look me in the eye for some reason. Then I found out why.

ME: Dimps — there's a rumour going
         round that you are going out
         with McFittie.
DIMPLE: I'm not… But he did ask me out.
ME: DIMPLE!!!   ← I thought I was
         DIMPLE, HOW COULD YOU?   going to be sick.
DIMPLE: But, Hattie, I'm not. I wouldn't
         ever go out with him. You like
         him.

Then I just had to run out. HOW could she?! She's my best friend.

Can't stop crying. How am I meant to go back to school now?

7.32 p.m.

WHY DOES HE LIKE DIMPLE?

* She is beautiful.
* She is pretty.
* She has breasts.
* She looks good in a bikini.
* She is smart.
* All Miss Worlds come from India (except the ones that come from Venezuela).
* She can dance like a total goddess.
* Her dad is a surgeon and loaded.

WHY HE DOESN'T LIKE ME:

* I can't eat biscuits properly.
* I look like an ironing board in a bikini.
* I have a zit farm on my face.
* My mum runs a cafe and I probably smell of bacon too.
* I don't even know WHO my father actually is.

Dimple has texted me about 20 times. I can't speak to her right now.

I bet they end up married with babies. He probably loves her so much he'll become a Hindu.

SUNDAY 22ND FEBRUARY

10.19 a.m.

Mrs Rathod just rang Mum. She wondered if Mum knew why Dimple is so upset. Told Mum what had happened. Mum went mental.

She said, "Hattie, Dimple is not even going out with him. Don't lose a friend through jealousy. There's always going to be someone smarter or prettier than you (THANKS, MUM – that's nice of you). That's not to say you aren't smart or pretty – but don't lose a good friend because someone likes her, not you. That's not fair."

YOU DON'T NEED TO TELL ME IT'S NOT FAIR, MUM. I KNOW IT'S NOT FAIR.

McFITTIE WANTS TO SNOG MY BEST FRIEND. HOW IS THAT FAIR?!

12.32 p.m.

I know why Mum is so pro-Dimple. It's because Dimple always does her homework and is definitely going to university to do something super brainy, and she hopes it will rub off on me. NO WAY!

1.32 p.m.

Perhaps I am being unreasonable.

3.12 p.m.

I think I may have a problem with jealousy. I've googled it and it says:

1. I must EXPOSE myself to the problem.
2. I must DEAL with the problem.
3. I must ACCEPT the problem and MOVE ON.

The problem is Dimple.

7.12 p.m.

Oh God, I may have lost my best friend for the stupidest reason ever. She is not even going out with him.

I am a DOUGHNUT.

10.39 p.m.

Mum won't let me go round to Dimple's because it's 10.30 p.m.

PATHETIC.

10.45 p.m.

Texted Dimple inviting her to come round and "talk it through". I've also said sorry and admitted I am a stupid jealous cow. It was hard to write but it's true.

MONDAY 23RD FEBRUARY

10.34 a.m.

No response yet. I just want my friend back.

12.12 p.m.

Dimple just texted. She didn't see my message because she had her phone on vibrate and she'd left it in the toilet! She's coming round!!!

5.45 p.m.

YAY YAY YAY!

Dimple came round. I gave her a massive hug and said
how sorry I was. We have OFFICIALLY decided NEVER
to argue about boys EVER again and spent the whole
afternoon doing routines to songs. Dimple took it
Bollywood at one point and honestly we think we might go
on *Britain's Got Talent* as it was one of the best things I
have ever seen. But then Dimple said there was no point
because if there's a really clever dog or an old woman
singer there who looks rubbish but turns out to be quite
good they will beat anything. I agree — it's the same with
people who have had a terrible life. They always end up in
at least the semi-final.

6.35 p.m.

I HAVE had a terrible life! I don't know my dad for a
start. And I get tortured by my brother daily.

6.44 p.m.

Dimple says that's not enough.

There has to have been a really bad death or a terrible
disease.

I've had tonsillitis a few times but I don't think that
counts.

10.19 p.m.

I've decided I have to forget McFittie. I have to pretend
he never existed. I am just going to concentrate on my

friends, the Not Fair Protest Group and finding my real dad.

Back to school with my brace tomorrow and dreading it. Going to keep my mouth SHUT so no one sees. Mum says I will find that impossible – but I am determined to prove her wrong.

TUESDAY 24TH FEBRUARY

4.15 p.m.

Managed to keep my brace semi-secret. Pretended to have a sore throat and I didn't say much. It was hard but I don't want people to see my mess of a mouth.

Weirdo Jen finally got in to see Mrs Cob the head and told her about the Not Fair Protest Group and asked our question about why we can't wear make-up at school. Mrs Cob said she "appreciated our group" and "understood Jen's concerns", but make-up was "basically" dangerous. Mascara in particular was a "health and safety issue" as longer lashes could be easily caught up in a Bunsen burner.

WHY DO THE TEACHERS WEAR IT THEN?

Jen said, "But what about our human rights?" At which point total EVIL Mrs Matfield came in and said, "You don't actually have human rights till you are 18", and could Jen "stop bothering the headmistress with pathetic questions about long-established school rules".

Weirdo Jen says that now I am off McFittie and no longer need a love spell she may use my teeth for a dark spell against Mrs Matfield. That won't work, Jen, as Mrs Matfield is clearly the boss of witches and the goddess of TOTAL COW.

9.23 p.m.
I am not off McFittie by the way. I think about him loads but I'm trying to go cold turkey. That's what addicts do on Dr Phil and basically I am a McFittie addict.

WEDNESDAY 25TH FEBRUARY

6.23 p.m.
Today was a complete NIGHTMARE. At lunch Miss Gorgeous Knickers (don't want to even write her name – from now on MGK) and her gang noticed my brace when I was trying to eat some chips. At first MGK pretended to be really sweet and interested, asking all these questions about it. I told her it would have to be on for about 12 months and she said, "Oh Hattie, that must be really hard for you." But then she started saying, "A YEAR of wearing train tracks on your teeth – GRIM!!!" and laughing. Then Jen said there was a note going round in Science that said "Hattie Moore's breath is a weapon of mass destruction." I have licked my hand loads and smelt it and honestly it's not bad. Jen says Miss Gorgeous Knickers is a total bitch and she will have found another victim by tomorrow. I hope so.

THURSDAY 26TH FEBRUARY

7.34 p.m.

Just a HORRIBLE DAY. Miss Gorgeous Knickers and her gang have told everyone about my brace. At break a whole load of people started chanting "Tracks, Tracks, Tracks" at me, then MGK shouted, "The train now arriving at Platform 2 is Hattie." It wasn't even funny but everyone except for Dimple and Jen was laughing because they are all so scared of her. Just looked in the mirror – I am officially an UGLY. I hate this brace – I WANT IT OFF!

8.32 p.m.

Mum says the brace has to stay on and I'll be thankful when I am 20 and my teeth don't look like a beaver's. I didn't tell her about MGK as she would probably march up to the school and make everything a million times worse.

9.15 p.m.

I've decided – I'm not going to school. I can't face another day of it – I know my teeth are horrible. I don't need MGK to tell me.

I can learn loads of stuff from daytime TV anyway.

10.34 p.m.

Perhaps Weirdo Jen can use one of my teeth for an evil spell on Mrs Matfield and one for MGK.

Friday 27th February

8.15 a.m.

Told Mum I felt really bad. Then I rushed into the toilet, retched and poured half a cup of coffee down the loo. Sounded like a huge VOM. Mum looked suspicious but she said, "You'd better stay in bed today and get over it." YAY! Whole day of TV and no MGK!!!

12.32 p.m.

Jeremy Kyle was the most chav-mongous thing I have EVER seen. This woman with NO teeth (seriously made me feel better) had to get a DNA test done on her kid because she'd been sleeping with 3 different men at the same time. Jeremy was furious!

THEN after watching a couple more hours of daytime TV I can now tell you:

- ★ how to make a Tomato Seafood Symphony
- ★ how to deal with a gambling addiction
- ★ what Stephen Fry likes to keep in his shed

2.12 p.m.

OMG OMG OMG...

I had a bit of a headache so I was just looking in my mum's special drawer for some paracetamol, and right at the back behind a packet of furry Polos and a water bill (£569!!! It's only water!!!), there was:

- ➤ my mum's old passport (worst photo ever)

➤ a brochure about trips to "exotic" countries like Egypt, Kenya and Australia. (We can't even afford to go to Alton Towers!)

➤ a book called *The Italian Duke's Virgin Mistress* (PERV!!!)

➤ A SCRUMPLED-UP PIECE OF PAPER THAT SAYS THE FOLLOWING:

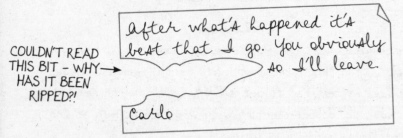

COULDN'T READ THIS BIT - WHY → HAS IT BEEN RIPPED?!

after what's happened it's best that I go. You obviously so I'll leave.

Carlo

I had to shove it all back as I heard Rob come in BUT WHAT'S THAT ABOUT? I was HONESTLY just looking for some headache pills.

2.54 p.m.

OK - I WAS having a nose around but I am entitled!

4.36 p.m.

Mum just got home and asked what I'd been doing all day. I said just watching TV.

I didn't eat anything for tea as I needed to look properly ill. Now I need to spend the whole weekend working out what the note is about. You know what I am thinking, don't you? I KNOW it's a massive coincidence but Weirdo Jen says sometimes if you really want something to happen, the universe actually listens.

7.14 p.m.

Actually I don't feel that well. Please let me have glandular fever — you get 6 months off school! I need more time off to go through the rest of this house to find out what else is being hidden from me. I KNOW there's something and I KNOW it's big. I have always known. It wouldn't surprise me if Mum wasn't my mum and I was actually an adopted Gypsy or something. OR perhaps I have been put into this house because I have special powers and the government is trying to keep me safe from terrorists or the forces of evil until I reach 18.

There MUST be a reason why that theory is in my head. Perhaps they wiped my brain before they put me here.

7.59 p.m.

Just realized that's basically actually what happens to Harry Potter — that's why it's in my head. LOL!

I could still be adopted though.

9.32 p.m.

So pleased it's Saturday tomorrow. Me and my brace can just hide from the world.

SATURDAY 28TH FEBRUARY

11.12 a.m.

Got up this morning, logged into Facebook and saw a message from MGK. I was nearly sick. I can't even get away from her in my own bedroom!

All the message had in it was a website link to
richardbluepaperproducts.com

I didn't get it at first. They are a company that make paper bags. Then I realized what she meant – I'm such an ugly I need a bag over my head.

Why can't she leave me alone? I've never done anything to her.

12.57 p.m.

Just went downstairs for some toast. My stepdad said, "Did you want that toast blended for easy eating?" He was just joking but I burst into tears and ran upstairs. Rob came after me and said, "Oh Hattie, I am so sorry – I was only kidding. Whatever is the matter?" I made him promise not to tell anyone then I blurted it out about MGK and the chanting and the Facebook message. Rob said, "Hattie, we HAVE to tell your mum." I said no, but he reckons it's her RIGHT to know and no one should have to live like this. OMG, I would rather just put up with it than Mum get involved.

5.15 p.m.

Rob told Mum. Now she is threatening to go up to the school. This will make it 20 times worse. Basically I will have to change schools, leave Dimple and Jen. I wish I could just go abroad like all the celebs do when they split up with someone. I know the paparazzi are not after me but Mum is – and that's worse.

SUNDAY 1st MARCH

7.23 p.m.

Goose came round today. I told him about being bullied. He asked if there was anything he could do. I said basically no, Goose. My life is about to end. My mum is going to go up to the school, make me look about 7 years old and ruin my entire life. MGK will then never leave me alone and I will be forced to be home-schooled like one of the girls you think are getting fatter but turn out to be ACTUALLY PREGNANT!

UNBELIEVABLY he then said that I should "trust my mum" and "get it sorted". Is Goose actually 86?! I don't want it sorted by my mum — I just want MGK to stop. I want to be able to go to school and not have everyone wet themselves at my metal head. I HATE THIS LIFE.

Then I told Goose about the note — but I didn't tell him what I thought — and he thinks EXACTLY the same thing. IT MUST BE MY DAD. IT MUST BE!!! CARLO? CARLO?! Goose said he must be on the Internet somewhere but when we googled Carlo 🔍 it came up with 62 million results. Goose agreed we need to narrow it down a bit. I can't ask Mum because she will know I've been through her drawer but I might casually mention the name to Gran.

11.47 p.m.

Just remembered one good thing — Goose said that all the boys thought MGK was a total doughnut slagbag and it's hilarious she wants to be a glamour model because she has no breasts. This has made me feel slightly better.

11.52 p.m.

Bet MGK gets the best boob job ever. And marries someone famous. And has her wedding in *OK* magazine. In fact I can actually guarantee that this is going to happen.

MONDAY 2ND MARCH

2.05 a.m.

I can't sleep. So worried about everything and keep thinking about MGK's celebrity wedding. She will have mini cupcakes and a Cinderella carriage-thing.

3.19 a.m.

She won't have bridesmaids unless they are all fat and make her look even better. The Beckhams will be there and Elton John – if he's still alive.

I can't believe MGK is actually getting millions for her wedding – it just sucks.

6.34 a.m.

Think I got a bit carried away but I know it's going to happen. When it does I am showing everyone this to prove I am never wrong.

7.12 a.m.

Mum just said, "Hattie, either you go to school or I will." When I begged for a couple more days off she just shouted, "Me or you!" Well Mum, it's you then – go and make everything 20 million times worse. Thanks. Ruin my life.

Weirdo Jen texted. She told me she loved me and said she is trying voodoo on MGK but needs some chicken legs. This is difficult as both her parents are vegans. It's sweet she is trying though.

10.10 a.m.
Jeremy Kyle has got a drug dealer on. Well he did have – he just told him to "get off my stage". Might ring Jeremy Kyle and get MGK on. He will sort her out AND be nice to me.

10.37 a.m.
Oh GREAT. You have to be 16 or over to be on Jeremy Kyle. Craptacular. Of course none of us under-16s have any problems at all. Bullied, and WHO IS MY DAD?! Can't even do a DNA test, Jeremy, as he is nowhere to be seen!

1.43 p.m.
Mum just rang. She has been up to the school. She was there before 9 – OF COURSE! I HAVE to go in tomorrow. They couldn't go into detail with my mum BUT they have started their anti-bullying procedure and are going to talk to MGK today. They want to talk to me tomorrow about "the situation". I could vom. Now I've dropped her RIGHT IN IT she will make me pay. I can't get out of it though. Mum is walking with me to school like a mental.

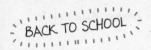
BACK TO SCHOOL

6.32 p.m.

Me and Mum went in just after 8. It was weird walking through the empty playground into Mrs Cob's office. When we got in there Mrs Cob's secretary made me and my mum A CUP OF TEA. It was really freaky. Then Mrs Cob said that she was very sorry that I didn't feel that I could talk to her about what had been going on. In line with the school's anti-bullying procedure she had spoken to MGK. She said she couldn't discuss what MGK had said BUT she would be speaking to her parents.

Mrs Cob then told us that ANY bullying would not be tolerated at school and that prolonged abusive behaviour would result in a suspension that could severely affect a pupil's career plans (though I don't think you need GCSEs to get your breasts out for money, Mrs Cob).

Basically if ANYONE ever takes the pee out of me again, I am to go straight to Mrs Cob who will take "immediate action".

After that I went to double Art and MGK didn't even look at me! She just carried on doing her craptacular clay model of a Hermès Birkin bag. I AM FREE! I AM FREE! It was SO good to see Dimple and Weirdo Jen again and they gave me a massive hug — until Mrs Matfield went mad at us and said school wasn't "for hugging".

Why can't the school start its anti-bullying procedure against Mrs Matfield?

Can't tell you how much better I feel. I have been so worried about things.

6.46 p.m.

Just realized Mum actually really helped me. Might go downstairs and thank her.

6.59 p.m.

Thanked Mum. She looked upset and said in a huge strop way, "Hattie, just tell me things – I've known that girl's mother for years, you know. I can help. I'm on your side. Please don't bottle stuff up." If she is on my side, then:

1. Why doesn't she tell me about my real dad?
2. Why is EVERYTHING I do wrong?
3. Why am I the only girl of my age that has been banned from wearing actually decent knickers?

Wednesday 4th March

5.12 p.m.

MAXMARVELLOUSNESS day at school.

MGK is STILL ignoring me and all her gang just stay right away from me. THEN Danielle Lance revealed the following:

* Danielle's mum still lays her clothes out for her every evening and helps her out with "difficult sleeves".

---

* Her mum also has never actually been sick — she just swallows it.

LOL! Perhaps my mum isn't so bad after all.

Then went to see Gran and told her about the bullying. She was really offended that I hadn't told her too but when she threatened to give MGK "just what the prissy little madam deserves" I was glad that I hadn't! Gran really, REALLY hates her. It's FANTASTIC.

Then I had to find a way to casually ask Gran if she knew a Carlo, so I just slipped into the conversation the question "What's your favourite Italian men's name?" I don't think she was suspicious. Gran said, "Giuseppe."

When I said Carlo Gran looked ever so slightly weird, turned her back and said, "Isn't he the bloke who owns that restaurant in town?" Then there was a massive gap and she started talking about her bunions. She always talks about those when she wants to change the subject.

THURSDAY 5TH MARCH

8.32 p.m.

I think I may actually be the new Gordon Ramsay. In Food Technology today I made the finest apple crumble in the history of modern desserts. I think Jamie Oliver may actually want to marry me and let me do the cooking. Mrs Angel said it was "first class" and she can't wait to see what I can do with a frittata next week.

After school we went shopping and I asked Mum if I could get the ingredients for a beef Wellington with a horseradish cream as I'd seen it on *Masterchef* and I thought I could recreate it from memory. Mum said, "Hattie, we are having oven chips and drumsticks tonight – I want my dinner at 7 p.m. not 11 p.m." So I stayed outside in a mood. If she is not willing to encourage my talents I'm not going to help her do a big shop.

10.14 p.m.

Just googled frittata 🔍. It's got loads of eggs in it. Eggs will be banned in my restaurant. You don't really need them for cooking anyway.

10.55 p.m.

OMG – frittata! Carlo! Perhaps great Italian cooking is in my genes.

FRIDAY 6TH MARCH

5.13 p.m.

Realized this morning that while I was waiting for my mum outside Tesco's last night I put my apple crumble down and forgot to pick it up again. Marv to think that my crumble is currently being enjoyed in someone else's house. It's totally like being famous.

6.19 p.m.

UNBELIEVABLE! Mum has gone mental about me losing an apple crumble. She says we have to ring Tesco's manager and ask (AND SHE IS SERIOUS) if anyone has actually handed in an apple crumble!

7.35 p.m.

Rang Tesco's customer services. They said no apple crumble had been handed in and even if it had been it would have been destroyed immediately as a contamination risk. Is it the mission of all adults to make me feel craptacular?

SATURDAY 7TH MARCH

10.26 a.m.

MUM IS STILL MENTAL about the crumble. Is her life so empty?!

I said, "Mum if someone found my crumble they would just eat it and keep the dish." Mum said, "Call the local police. Perhaps someone handed it in!" When I refused she went completely LOON and said, "Hattie – you are calling them."

Apparently I HAVE to find the dish because it's a family heirloom that Gran's mum had and has been passed down through generations.

1. How can a dish survive that long?
2. Think of all the manky food that has been in it. ERRRGGHH!
3. Other families have jewellery and paintings that they can take on *The Antiques Roadshow*. Why have we got an oven dish?!

SUNDAY 8TH MARCH

2.25 p.m.

Called the police. UNBELIEVABLY someone has handed in my crumble. The policeman was laughing his head off saying, "Yes, we have apprehended a stray crumble in the vicinity of Tesco's. It is currently being detained in a holding cell in our fridge!"

Oh LOL, NOT.

MONDAY 9TH MARCH

6.34 p.m.

After school we collected the crumble from the police and the address of the person who handed it in. Mum is making me write a thank you note. According to her, "Dear Mrs Crisp, thank you for saving my crumble" is not sufficient. What am I meant to say?!

I am having to spend time on an APPLE CRUMBLE rather than investigating MY OWN HUMAN GENES.

I have decided though that I actually DO want to be a celebrity chef.

8.17 p.m.

Just spoke to Dimple on my mob. She pointed out that I will be following in my mum's footsteps if I get into cooking. I went up like a mental: "Dimps, I want to be a celebrity chef, not cook fry-ups in a cafe!" Dimple said I would probably have to start somewhere small then work up. ER,

NO!!! Did Jamie Oliver start his career cooking bacon sarnies?! Dimple reckons he started in his parents' pub!

9.23 p.m.
Been on Wikipedia — Dimple is right. Bet it's a posh pub though and builders and their bums are banned.

TUESDAY 10TH MARCH

6.24 p.m.
Dimps has just texted. She's invited me round for her festival of Holi tomorrow. Now religiousy things are usually completely boring. EVEN more boring than the "quiet birthday party" Danielle Lance had when she was 6. BUT at Dimple's house there is always tons of her mum's food, which is utterly DELISH. Basically I can just ignore the God stuff and focus on the samosas.

I'm not allowed to tell Weirdo Jen I am going as she is banned from Dimple's house. She once did Mrs Rathod's tarot cards and told her she would benefit from a new relationship. Mr Rathod went mental.

WEDNESDAY 11TH MARCH

9.42 p.m.
OMG. Weirdest day EVER.

Dimple and I never get serious about world things but I actually think my best friend might be a Nazi.

Basically I went round Dimple's house and there was a MASSIVE Nazi swastika symbol thing on her front doorstep. Everybody there was acting totally normally but it was there. In bright colours. HUGE. And when I think about it, Dimple's uniform is always perfect — and Nazis ALWAYS looked dead smart. AND at school she always does as she is told. PLUS her dad is really tough. He says there is never any excuse for someone not to be working — unless they are dead or in intensive care.

My best friend is a NAZI!!! WHAT DO I DO? And I can't even call Jen and ask for advice because that big Nazi party that just happened was not meant to have happened.

Have to speak to Dimple tomorrow. I feel actually dead angry with her.

10.09 p.m.
But less angry than when I thought she had nicked McFittie off me. Does that make me shallow?

10.13 p.m.
Just realized I haven't thought of McFittie in ages. Yes, I am officially shallow. And fickle.

THURSDAY 12TH MARCH

12.16 p.m.
Tackled Dimple at break. She is NOT a Nazi. Apparently Hindus had the swastika first and Hitler just hijacked it. What a relief!

4.45 p.m.

That sucks for Hindus though as I bet loads of people think they are actual mental Hitler lovers. OMG, in fact perhaps Hindus are losing out on loads of full-on love action because who wants to tongue a nutter?!

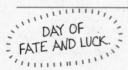

DAY OF
FATE AND LUCK.

FRIDAY 13TH MARCH

5.12 p.m.

Weirdo Jen brought her runes into school today. They are these fortune-telling stone things. She did mine – there was absolutely no mention of men. She said she couldn't see any men on the horizon, just a focus on "maturing" and "growth"! That MUST be about finding out who my dad is.

Dimple got loads of love stones, but we couldn't finish because Mrs Matfield saw us playing with them and confiscated them as "school is not about messing with the occult". Weirdo Jen said that Mrs Matfield did not know what she was messing with and she had awakened Nature's forces. Mrs Matfield gave Jen a lunch detention and said she wasn't scared of anything that wasn't actually holding a machine gun.

She is a PURE EVIL mental. She should not be allowed near young people. Or any people in fact.

8.37 p.m.

Keep thinking about "growth". I HAVE to ask Mum about Carlo. I just need to find the right time because she'll pretend to be busy. Or ill. Or she'll turn away so I can't see the mental twitch she gets when she is majorly lying.

SATURDAY 14TH MARCH

7.12 p.m.

Dimple, Weirdo Jen and me just met at Bertie's for the third monthly meeting of the Not Fair Protest Group. I hadn't been there since the social death biscotti incident but it didn't matter because McFittie has left! GONE! Good — he came between me and my best friend and I cannot allow that to happen. Apparently he has gone back to Cornwall to surf. IT'S MARCH! I hope he freezes his stupid quiff off that I used to love so much.

Anyway, the things to make fair were the following:

1. More people to realize that Hindus had the swastika first and not Hitler. (Is it a bit tragic that we are trying to sort out a God thing?)
2. Police to IMMEDIATELY destroy any food that they find, as a) it's a security risk, and b) it's an embarrassment risk.
3. Mrs Matfield to make a list of everything that "school is not about". We agree that this is a HUGE job and will be impossible to do. Hopefully that might make her realize how craptacular it is that she uses it as an excuse for EVERYTHING.

The problem with all of these is that we don't quite know how to actually fix them. Jen suggested we set up a website called theswastikaisnotjustnazi.com but that will cost a fortune. And as for Numbers 2 and 3 how do you make the police or Mrs Matfield do anything?! We spent FOR EVER trying to work it out and we are going to sleep on it and see if we come up with anything. Jen is eating some cheese before she goes to bed as sometimes it gives her answers in dreams.

We've also decided we need to make the NFPG more flexible — we need to tackle injustice as it happens. So we may not have a monthly meeting any more. Anyway, by the time we had worked out that we couldn't make things fair we had run out of time for our make-up masterclass so Jen and Dimple are coming here tomorrow.

Sunday 15th March

4.14 p.m.

We all slept on it and we have agreed that we just have to accept that there are some things we cannot fix. Jen said her cheese just gave her a nightmare — she was naked in the Westfield shopping centre and Mrs Matfield was chasing her with a massive sausage. That sounded rude to me but I didn't say anything.

THEN we had a MARVTASTIC make-up session. Jen gave me and Dimple smoky eyes!!! No one does eyes like Jen — she made me look like this bedroom's next top model. Jen got bored though and wanted to go experimental so she put the "Toffee Waffle" lipstick she got free with a magazine all over her face. It looked well weird. Trouble was, it wouldn't come off. Not even with Clearasil and half a bottle of No. 7 Microdermabrasion stuff.

Jen wasn't bothered though. She said it reflects other tribal cultures but I think in Derby it just makes you look like an actual doughnut.

MONDAY 16TH MARCH

4.13 p.m.

Mrs Matfield used ALL her portable Nivea wipes on Jen's face today and it was STILL toffee waffle. Jen got another lunchtime detention for wasting cow-face Matfield's "time and money". Jen is now OFFICIALLY the coolest person in our year. MGK even spoke to her this afternoon and lent her a *Vogue*. Jen gave it straight to me. I am going to read it, spit all over it and then give it back to her. LOL!!!

4.32 p.m.

I mean give it back to MGK not Jen. I love Jen.

8.17 p.m.

God, I hope MGK doesn't take Jen off me and Dimple.

TUESDAY 17TH MARCH

6.12 p.m.

Jen just told me and Dimple that she would never be part of the MGK clique as all they ever talk about is boys and shopping. We talk about all that — but other important stuff too.

8.34 p.m.

I would never say this to Jen and Dimple but a lot of the other "important" stuff is actual dullster von dullster. If I am being honest I would rather read about whoever's had liposuction this week than earthquakes. That's bad, isn't it?

9.22 p.m.

Actually I am not that bad as we did do a sponsored silence and raised loads for somewhere once. We have never raised any money for anyone in *Heat* magazine.

WEDNESDAY 18TH MARCH

7.34 p.m.

UNBELIEVABLE. OFFICIALLY MY LIFE IS TRAGIC.

Came home tonight to see that Mum had washed my sheets but had put a Barney the Dinosaur duvet cover on my bed from when I was about 5. When I went mad she said, "Hattie, what's the problem? No one is going to see it." I said, "Mum, that is not the point. I am making the transition from girl to woman, and it's important that my femininity is encouraged. Having a big purple Tyrannosaurus rex on my bed does not help my femininity — even if he is a friendly one!"

Mum says it HAS to stay as there are no other covers available and with no cover a duvet gets filthy.

THURSDAY 19TH MARCH

5.45 p.m.

Couldn't get the thought out of my head today that if MGK knew I had a dinosaur duvet cover on my bed my life would not be worth living.

7.23 p.m.

My brother has just poked his head around the door and started singing the Barney "I love you, you love me" song. He is 17. Why can't he MOVE OUT?!

8.46 p.m.

Oh dear, Mum. I have just accidentally on purpose spilt a glass of Ribena all over Barney. I will have to change it immediately. LOL!

8.54 p.m.

Mum says as Barney is the same colour as Ribena I can just keep the cover on. Why can't Barney be pink like Barbie? Now I've got a soggy bed AND a T-REX.

FRIDAY 20TH MARCH

LAST DAY OF SCHOOL THIS TERM

6.37 p.m.

Mrs Matfield said we should use the school holidays to catch up on any work that we had missed in the term and do some revision for our exams. Dear Mrs Matfield – NOT A HOPE IN HELL, BABY!!!

ANYWAY, THE BIG BREAKING NEWS: there is a rumour going round school that if you attach a vacuum cleaner to a funnel and put the suction on your breasts it actually pulls them out and encourages them to grow. It's got to be worth a try, SURELY? I, Hattie Moore, would like to proclaim that the school holidays are officially OPERATION BOOB GROWTH AND IS CARLO MY ACTUAL DAD?!

SATURDAY 21ST MARCH

10.56 a.m.

Just got the Hoover out. Mum is thrilled that I found the Dyson and says could I clean out the fridge too. Sorry, Mum – cleaning out the salad drawer will not make ANYTHING grow.

11.12 a.m.

We are the only family in the history of the world that does not have a funnel. I will have to go round Gran's. I haven't been to see her in ages but she'll understand.

4.56 p.m.

Gran was not very happy at all that I had not been to see her. She started saying, "I won't be around for ever, Hattie." I wish she wouldn't say that – it makes me want to cry and never stop. I didn't say that though. I just asked her if she had a funnel and of course she does! Gran has everything as she doesn't throw anything away. Her house should be on *Cash in the Attic*.

Anyway, I'm doing it tomorrow. Get ready for a BREAST EXPLOSION.

Sunday 22nd March

9.34 a.m.

LOL! I just accidentally vacuumed up an entire toilet roll!!! It shot up the nozzle sheet by sheet!

10.19 a.m.

I have just Dysoned each breast for 3 minutes. They've just gone all red. Perhaps it's like the redness you get before a spot grows. PLEASE LET THAT BE TRUE. Perhaps they need rest. I'll leave them overnight.

10.43 a.m.

They don't look like they've grown.

10.53 a.m.

Still NO change.

11.12 a.m.

Decided I can't treat my breasts like my mum treats me — watching every move they make and nagging them. Things cannot grow when they are being watched. I am going to forget about them till tomorrow.

7.13 p.m.

Just had to clean my room so Mum doesn't get suspicious.

7.33 p.m.

Cleaning my room has made my mum suspicious anyway. I can't win.

11.38 p.m.

HAVE TO LOOK. Breasts just a bit red. Not bigger.

MONDAY 23RD MARCH

7.23 a.m.

Just measured my breasts.

NO bigger. Just red.

I'll do it again later.

11.24 a.m.

Just did it again. I haven't got a lock on my door so I moved a chair against it. If my brother came in I would die from embarrassment and he would take the pee out of me till my actual death.

My breasts are just red again.

12.53 p.m.

Perhaps I should forget even trying to vacuum them and just do what Gran said she used to do – bunched-up toilet roll in each bra cup. She reckons it looks completely natural and men absolutely can't tell the difference unless you get caught in the rain or go swimming.

1.01 p.m.

Just remembered I Dysoned the spare toilet roll up yesterday! Going to have to go downstairs and get something else.

1.10 p.m.

Plenty kitchen paper towel may be able to wipe up loads with one sheet but it makes RUBBISH breasts. I look like I have textured tits!

1.19 p.m.

Flash Wipes are also craptacular for looking like boobs —
they make your bra soggy and you smell lemon fresh in a
bad way.

I'm going back to the Dyson.

6.36 p.m.

Perhaps I am doing it at the wrong time of day. Might
try doing it later at night when my boobs are calmer and
more relaxed. Trouble is I need an amazing excuse for
vacuuming after 9 p.m.

9.54 p.m.

Just smashed an old Elmo from *Sesame Street* glass
on my bedroom floor! It's everywhere in the carpet.
Mum came to investigate and even she said I definitely
need the Dyson. She offered to help but I put her off
by saying, "I made the mess — so I'll clean it up." This
gives breast growth solo space AND makes me sound
MASSIVELY mature. I, Hattie Moore, am an actual mum-
managing genius with ever bigger boobs.

10.23 p.m.

Late-night breast-vacuming completed! I quickly cleaned
the broken glass too. Sorry, Elmo — but you died to make
my breasts bigger.

11.57 p.m.

I am getting REALLY mad now. There is no movement in my
breasts AT ALL. I wasn't going to tell anyone what I was

doing but tomorrow I will go and see Dimple. She's from a medical family. She understands breasts.

TUESDAY 24TH MARCH

8.12 a.m.

Just cut my foot on a massive piece of glass (Elmo's eye!). And my breasts are NO BIGGER. So I now have small boobs and deformed feet!

4.36 p.m.

After I made Dimple swear on her life that she wouldn't breathe a word to A SOUL ON EARTH, I told her about the breast growth machine. She said it was utterly craptacular and she couldn't believe I fell for that. OK, OFFICIALLY I AM A DOUGHNUT but I am desperate. My breasts are holding me back!

Dimple reckons the only way to increase breast growth is to a) have implants (I AM TOO YOUNG – I HAVE CHECKED), or b) do some exercise that encourages "definition of the muscle tone" (?).

Anyway we have decided to go to Bikram Yoga at the community centre as Dimple thinks it will be good for my breasts and good for her mind. You do it in a really hot room so you sweat LOADS.

8.37 p.m.

I think Dimple may be more mature than me.

9.12 p.m.

Just took the Dyson downstairs. Never want to see it again.

9.45 p.m.

I want to be more like Dimple. I think I need to think about others more. I've decided to make a book about school rumours so other people don't end up hoovering their breasts for no reason.

WEDNESDAY 25TH MARCH

3.12 p.m.

Dimple and me are a bit worried about Weirdo Jen. She isn't answering texts and she hasn't been on Facebook for 2 days. It's like she's died. We are going to her house tomorrow to check on her.

10.23 p.m.

I've been working on this all day and I think I've included everything!

Not Fair Protest Group's Craptacular List of School Rumours

- Vacuuming your breasts will not make them grow.

- Putting toothpaste on spots just makes your face minty.

- You cannot repair split ends with Flora – your hair just looks totally greasy.

- Chocolate does not cause zits – so you can have ← YAY! 1,000 Kit Kats if you want.

- Going to bed with your iPod on does NOT make you a better singer in your sleep. ← MGK spread this whe[n] she was trying to get on *The X-Factor*.

- You CAN get pregnant on a boat. ↰

MGK says you can't – DOUGHNUT!!!

When we get back to school I think I might put this on the noticeboard. It will be the most interesting thing on there – LOL!

THURSDAY 26TH MARCH

9.35 p.m.

Dimple and me went round Jen's house.

She's been busy writing a book!!! It's a zombie romance called *Really Dead Love*. We said, "Jen, how the hell can a zombie kiss? Their lips would fall off!"

Jen says her zombies are special members of the undead who NEED to be in love or they start to disintegrate – they are basically kissing maniacs. Her main character – called Jennifer (it's based on her) – meets a boy and he begs to be snogged or he will lose his arm. Then all these other zombie boys turn up in Derby, desperate to be kissed, and they are all TOTALLY gorgeous.

Wish it was true. I WISH IT WAS TRUE. I am in a love drought. I need a boy shower of hotness.

10.01 p.m.

Sometimes I sound like such a mahoosive dork.

Bikram Yoga tomorrow. We did invite Jen but she says she is at an important stage where her main character has to choose between snogging a zombie and a werewolf.

10.17 p.m.

I think Jen's book is actually just *Twilight* but with zombies.

11.23 p.m.

Just been on YouTube to look at zombies. Feel sick.

FRIDAY 27TH MARCH

2.14 p.m.

AND THIS IS WHY THE NOT FAIR PROTEST GROUP MUST CARRY ON!!!

Dimple and me went to the Bikram Yoga class. WE ARE OFFICIALLY TOO YOUNG TO TAKE PART. We aren't allowed to do the pole-dancing class either.

Don't they realize that we need to work on our bodies now?!

Dimple thinks we should just do it at home anyway, so she is coming round tomorrow to mine while Mum and Rob are at work and my brother is at YET ANOTHER job interview. We would do it round Dimple's house but middle-age hormones have turned her mum into a complete mental now. She cries at cat food adverts and won't eat anything but cheese on toast and Chupa Chups.

BIKRAM
YOGA DAY.

Saturday 28th March

8.12 a.m.

I haven't got any decent exercise clothes so I borrowed
my brother's Jimi Hendrix T-shirt. He will go mad if he
finds out! MARVELLOUS!!!

5.12 p.m.

Dimple came round about 2. She brought her mum's ancient
yoga DVDs. I tried to make the living room MASSIVELY
hot so we put the gas fire on and boiled the kettle in
the living room to get it steamy. We were really getting
into it when Mum decided to come home early (WHICH
SHE NEVER DOES) and went LOON about her Julien
Macdonald wallpaper being affected by heat! ERR, MUM –
what's more important? Your lounge decor, or my ACTUAL
breast definition?

6.34 p.m.

And she embarrassed me in front of Dimple.

6.47 p.m.

And her wallpaper is craptacular anyway. Gran said she had
the same thing in the 1970s and it didn't cost £27 a roll.

Right. I am going to ask her about Carlo. TONIGHT IS
THE NIGHT.

8.37 p.m.

OMG!!!

Just cornered Mum in the kitchen. She is always in a
better mood after dinner – and we'd had Thai chicken

curry then a Tesco's Finest tiramisu. It's the ULTIMATE in MumMoodFood. So I went for it.

Me:	Mum, have you ever known someone called Carlo?
Mum:	Why do you ask?
Me:	Just wondering...
Mum:	Has someone been talking to you, Hattie?
Me:	No.
Mum:	Gran is getting old, you know. Sometimes she gets confused.

Still calm but TOTALLY panicking — I could tell.

All COMPLETELY casual

OMG — Gran may be a mental but she NEVER gets confused! Plus she does at least 2 crosswords a day and never misses *Countdown*. She gets at least 3 conundrums a week!

Me:	Seriously, Mum, Gran has said NOTHING.
Mum:	No — I don't think I've ever known a Carlo, Hattie. Why do you ask anyway?

This is not a lie!

And TOTAL DIBBO me! I hadn't even worked out a reason why I was asking her, so I said:

Me:	Oh — someone rang here asking for him. Must have been a wrong number.
Mum:	What time was that?

OMG — MASSIVE pause — hadn't even worked out what the HELL to say!

Me:	Earlier.
Mum:	When earlier?
Me:	Oh — I think it was around 2.
Mum:	Must have been a wrong number, Hattie.

BUT then she MASSIVELY stared at me and I heard her go into the lounge and say to Rob, "Hattie just asked me about..." THEN she must have whispered because I couldn't hear anything.

NOW I 100% KNOW THAT SOMETHING IS GOING ON.

Sunday 29th March

9.34 a.m.

Told Goose about yesterday. He says when the trail goes cold you have to keep on high alert for any clues. Goose says we need James Bond. He can stop deadly viruses and nuclear bombs and solve MASSIVE threats to the world in a matter of hours — finding my dad would basically be a tea break for him. Goose ALWAYS makes me laugh.

10.23 a.m.

My brother just burst in and wanted to know why his T-shirt smells of Impulse — LOL!

I am so bored. School holidays ARE boring. Might try meditating and getting in touch with my inner woman.

12.43 p.m.

Can't find my inner woman. Think she may actually be dead.

5.47 p.m.

Just had a wardrobe overhaul. You should do it every 6 months.

My wardrobe contained the following:

* 2 pairs of jeans
* 2 Primark tops
* 1 actually gorgeous Topshop shirt (thanks, Gran)
* 7 tops from Tesco's
* NO high heels
* 1 pair of sequin pumps
* a hoodie with **YES!** written on it in massive pink letters (VOM!!!)
* a Shrek sweatshirt

No one could rock a Shrek sweatshirt.

I would like to overhaul my wardrobe but I can't as I have no money.

6.33 p.m.

Just asked Mum for some money for a wardrobe overhaul. She said she needed to tax the car this month (BORING!) and that my wardrobe could wait.

My wardrobe always has to wait. It is the most patient wardrobe IN HISTORY.

Monday 30th March

3.12 p.m.

Asked my mum where my real dad was and could he help with any money. Apparently there is more chance of "Simon Cowell paying for new clothes". Why can't HE be my dad? He's MAHOOSIVELY rich.

Tuesday 31st March

9.45 p.m.

I am very confused about men. I don't seem to actually fancy many of them. I haven't been actually in love since McFittie and at 14 I should be IN LOVE. I don't fancy girls AT ALL either. I have checked this weekly by looking at my brother's FHM magazine. I am 100% non-lesbic. Jen is coming round tomorrow — she has had a boyfriend. I'll ask her how she actually got a man.

Wednesday 1st April

9.24 p.m.

Jen told me today that if you want to find your true love, ask a fox after midnight but before 2 a.m. The myth is they all get powers of speech and can tell you who you should go for.

It sounds MENTAL but it HAS to be worth a try. I NEED to find someone.

THURSDAY 2ND APRIL

12.32 a.m.

Nicked some of my stepdad's wafer-thin turkey sandwich filling as bait. BUT no fox. Just Goose's STUPID cat Colin, who ate it instead and then tried to attack me.

Will try again tomorrow.

FRIDAY 3RD APRIL

1.10 a.m.

Mum just went MENTAL and asked me what I was doing in the garden at "past midnight". I just said, "Err — looking for something." She then FORCED me to come in.

9.45 a.m.

Just rang Weirdo Jen to see if she had any fox-catching tips. She then told me that it was an April Fool's joke and she had forgotten to tell me.

Not happy. At all.

SATURDAY 4TH APRIL

12.45 p.m.

Can't believe I fell for a talking fox.

5.23 p.m.

I'm not the only doughnut. Dibbo Hannah totally believed MGK when she told her Victoria Beckham was designing our new school uniform. LOL!

Wish she was. She would NEVER put anyone in turd brown.

6.12 p.m.
I just laughed at an MGK joke. OMG, I hope I am not maturing into a total cow.

SUNDAY 5TH APRIL

10.32 a.m.
My brother has gone for an interview at Lord of the Burgers – please, PLEASE let him get the job. It will mean he'll be in the house less AND it's a craptacular job!

5.24 p.m.
Decided to try to find my inner woman in the garden as my gran reckons that fresh air can help everything. Goose came out of his house to ask me why I had been in the garden over the last few nights at midnight. I said, "Were you perving?!" and he said, "Err NO, Hattie, you doughnut. I actually thought you were a mass-murderer or a stalker." Goose has been a bit mental ever since he watched *Jeepers Creepers* at age 11. This is Derby – there are no murderers!

7.34 p.m.
Just googled Murders in Derby 🔍. Wish I hadn't! There have been loads of mentals killing people! And loads of the crimes are unsolved – including one from 1907 when a man was killed with a pitchfork through his head!

11.34 p.m.

Can't sleep. Would a pitchfork through your brain hurt? An unsolved crime means a murderer is actually walking round Derby RIGHT NOW.

11.45 p.m.

Mum just came in to ask why I wasn't asleep. Told her about the pitchfork murderer and she reminded me that if the murder happened in 1907 the person who did it was dead anyway. Then she said the only crime being committed in this house was my crime of being a "total doughnut".

Thanks, Mum, for your sensitivity.

MONDAY 6TH APRIL

7.12 p.m.

Weirdo Jen says we all have spirit angels and we need to thank them for everything in our lives. You have to be grateful — then more good things will happen to you. Here goes:

- ✔ My zit farm has decreased in size.
- ✔ My socks are super warm.
- ✔ I am thankful for my duvet cover which no longer features Barney the Dinosaur.
- ✔ Dinner tonight was edible.
- ✔ The pitchfork murderer is dead.

Surely that is enough?

9.30 p.m.

My brother got the job at Lord of the Burgers! Jen is right!!! I will be grateful every day!!!

6.24 p.m.

I was chilling in the garden this afternoon when Goose decided he was going to do some work on his BMX at the same time. Goose said he was making the most of the sunshine. There was no sunshine at all. The boy is a mental. His mum told me he ate a whole tube of toothpaste at age 3 because he thought it was liquid sweeties! This explains A LOT.

I have got loads on Goose and he must NEVER forget it.

I AM GRATEFUL FOR ... carrots – as they do not ming as much as broccoli.

11.34 a.m.

Just realized that actually Goose could destroy my entire life as he knows the following:

* That I used to be scared of toilets because I thought they could suck you in when you flushed them (MY BROTHER'S FAULT).
* That I used to think my toys came to life when I was asleep and that if I was nasty to them they would gang up and kill me. (MY BROTHER'S

FAULT AGAIN – HE TOLD ME *TOY STORY* WAS BASED ON A TRUE STORY.)

* That I used to think horses laid eggs. (Not my brother's fault – I just assumed – LOL!)

7.32 p.m.

I AM GRATEFUL FOR ... breast implants. I don't have them but it's good to know they exist.

THURSDAY 9TH APRIL

6.54 p.m.

My brother has started working at Lord of the Burgers.

Mum has called him a traitor but after he told her what he gets an hour she said she wished she could join him. The best thing is that his costume is designed to look like a wizard. LOL!!!

I AM GRATEFUL FOR ... craptacular uniforms that torture my brother.

FRIDAY 10TH APRIL

7.42 p.m.

Just asked my brother if he could magic up some dinner for me and save me from the dark forces of meat. He turned into a mental and tried to tear my decent Topshop shirt. Mum had to get involved and obviously took his side. She said this is a difficult time for him so I should stop winding him up.

Mum, it's not my fault he couldn't manage Business Studies and now has to pretend he is Gandalf with extra fries.

I AM GRATEFUL FOR ... having a brother who is suffering after years of torturing me.

SATURDAY 11TH APRIL

7.15 p.m.

My brother has quit Lord of the Burgers. My mum said she understood as it's a dead-end job. UNBELIEVABLE!!!

If I did that she would LOSE IT BIG TIME. Even when I stopped Brownies after I failed my Entertainer badge she said I gave in too easily. I didn't want to stay there after I hadn't passed the easiest badge in history – even Doughnut Hannah got hers for doing a craptacular dance to the theme from *Emmerdale!*

9.34 p.m.

Why IS my mum so nice to my brother? What does HE know that I don't?

10.13 p.m.

Prediction – it is something to do with my real dad. It MUST be. I'm going to ask my brother if he knows who Carlo is.

I'll ask him tomorrow.

10.34 p.m.

I AM GRATEFUL FOR ... nothing – as it doesn't work.

Sunday 12th April

9.38 p.m.

Went round to see Gran today. I found her in the lounge looking slightly mental.

She said, "I am entering EVERY competition in ALL these magazines, Hattie. Doreen Dixon from bingo won an all-inclusive holiday to Mexico with *Woman's Realm* and SHE still gets the £100 question wrong on *Who Wants to be a Millionaire.*"

I said, "Gran, this is mental. You are 67. Why do you want to win a 'Gluety Booty buttock exercise machine'?"

Gran gave me a massive death-stare and said, "I may be older, Hattie, but I still think about my bum. I've always been proud of my backside — in 1972 I was 'Rear of the Year' at Butlins in Skegness. Now help me with this wordsearch. We have to find 23 types of garden vegetable to win a fortnight at an *Eco Green retreat* in Swansea, cleaning out a river."

Eco Green retreat?! My gran has told everyone at the pensioners' club that global warming is a lie. She thinks it's an excuse for "silly greeny" people to not work, not wash and live in trees.

She is making me go round tomorrow after school to help her.

10.13 p.m.

Just asked my brother if he remembered our dad. He was older when he left! Nathan got really narky and said, "No, Hattie. Now DO one!" Then when I asked him if he knew a Carlo he said, "Hattie, our dad must be a waste of space as he hasn't bothered with us in YEARS. Get over it. He doesn't care about either of us."

So I said, "Perhaps Mum has banned him from keeping in touch and he currently has a cupboard full of birthday and Christmas presents waiting for us that he can't send!" Then Nathan went MENTAL and shouted, "DREAM ON, Hattie – you just want an iPhone and you hope that he'll buy it for you!" Then he stormed off.

That is SO NOT TRUE. I want to find my dad for emotional and personal growth reasons only.

11.35 p.m.

Dr Phil says he wants me to "get excited about my life". It's very hard, Dr Phil when your life isn't about parties and YUM boys but actually about doing a wordsearch for your gran and trying to find out who your dad is because no one else will tell you.

MONDAY 13TH APRIL

6.34 p.m.

Back to school. It was BORING and UNBELIEVABLE all at the same time. Mrs Matfield is trying to ban pencil cases as they can be used to hide "illegal items".

She wants us to carry stuff around in transparent sandwich bags. Me, Jen and Dimps already know Matfield is a mental but she has gone beyond that. From now on she is officially classified as the INTERNATIONAL PRESIDENT OF TOTAL EVIL COMPLETE LOON MATFIELD.

9.45 p.m.

Went to see Gran. She said she was off to a Boxercise class at the community centre. Apparently they have a two-tier Boxercise system: the young people run and punch, "mature" people are allowed to sit on the floor and punch the air. Gran likes it because she can pretend she is lamping people she doesn't like.

She asked if I would like to go. Yes, I would – I might invite MGK to come too, and be my boxing partner. LOL!

Instead I said no – but asked Gran if I could just stay at hers while she was out. I said it would give me some peace and quiet to do some of her competitions. Gran said yes. So I spent the next 2 hours looking through her drawers for anything CARLO-related. I know it's bad but it's totally what any of the detectives she watches would do.

Anyway there was NOTHING, except for old bills and out-of-date coupons for washing powder and something called "Coffee-mate".

WHERE IS THE TRUTH? WHEN WILL I KNOW THE TRUTH? WHERE IS MY DAD?!

Tuesday 14th April

5.37 p.m.

Dimple, Jen and me had a FULL conversation at lunch about what we are going to wear for the Geography trip to the Peak District tomorrow. I am going for jeans with my Topshop shirt and my only pair of a bit glam shoes. Dimple has proper walking boots as her dad thinks an idle body makes an idle mind. She looks good in them though. Like she looks good in everything. She would be an uber cow if she wasn't so lovely.

9.12 p.m.

Mum is MAKING me take my patterned wellies too just in case it's muddy. She also wants me to take my **YES!** VOM hoodie as it will be cold. NO WAY. I would rather die of the freeze than die of terminal geekness.

School trip to Dovedale.

Wednesday 15th April

10.32 p.m.

I HAVE JUST HAD THE MOST BRILLIANT DAY OF SCHOOL FOR THE FOLLOWING REASONS:

1. Me, Dimps and Jen all sat together on the bus – which meant THE best game of truth or dare ever. Jen admitted that she had once had a crush on Jeremy Kyle! It only lasted for 2 days but it is OFFICIALLY the worst crush on a person ever in history.

2. THE PLACE WAS SO FAR OUT WE COULD NOT GET SIGNAL on our mobs!!! If we got

lost we would basically be lost there for ever. Then Weirdo Jen said we might have to eat one another to survive. ALL of us decided that Miss Gorgeous Knickers dies first. LOL!

3. Miss Gorgeous Knickers came in her MASSIVE lap-dancer high heels and ended up twisting her leg on a cattle-grid. Mrs Cripps went mental and said they were not suitable footwear for hill walking and examining crop rotation and maybe she would like to borrow some of her flats. LOL! MGK had to wear a pair of right granny frumpsters! (Hate to say it, but Mum was right about the wellies. My shoes would never have been the same.)

4. MGK basically cried all the way home and said when she had fallen she had "pulled everything out" as she was "delicately balanced like a ballet dancer". PLEASE let her have to wear a neck brace as it will give her 440 double chins.

5. We didn't learn anything, but on the way home we were all having a MASSIVE singing session until MENTAL Hitler Matfield (Why did she come? She is Art!) told us to be quiet as we were disturbing Brian the driver. But Brian the driver said he was "quite enjoying it", and it made a difference from the "crap people usually sing". Matfield looked mentally mad but could not do a thing as Brian the driver is an actual adult and doesn't have to do what she wants. LOL!!!

Basically it was MARVELLOUS!

11.12 p.m.

Just remembered one mental thing. We saw a pig and her piglets. Dimple says her mum is so middle-aged hormonal she can't look at ANYTHING pregnant at the moment as it makes her cry for hours. Poor Mrs Pig looked so tired ... AND the dad was NOWHERE to be seen.

TYPICAL.

THURSDAY 16TH APRIL

4.22 p.m.

Unbelievable!!! Gran has won a 40-inch flat screen TV from a competition in the local paper. I asked her if she really needed it (HINT). She said she did think it was a bit big for her front room but she was going to give it a try.

5.56 p.m.

Gran just watched *Big Cat Diary* in HD. She said she has never seen anything so amazing in her entire life and you could see EVERYTHING when the lions brought down a buffalo. She says that watching her fave film *Titanic* in HD will be like a dream come true. It'll be wonderful to be able to see right up Leonardo DiCaprio's nose.

10.13 p.m.

Why has my gran got an HD TV when we have to hold the remote control in a funny place to make ours even work?

FRIDAY 17TH APRIL

4.27 p.m.

NOW my mum has joined Facebook. This proves that she actually is a complete MENTAL. No, Mum, I will not be your friend! I am NOT giving you a licence to stalk me under any circumstances!

8.38 p.m.

FarmVille?! No time to put a face on or tell me who my dad is but you have got time to look for a golden sugar cane on *FarmVille*!

I have a gran with a flat screen and a mum on Facebook. This has to stop.

SATURDAY 18TH APRIL

7.46 p.m.

I was hunting around today in the "important drawer" to have a look at the Carlo note again. IT'S GONE!!! Anyway I ended up raiding Mum's make-up bag and found the following:

- 1 eyeshadow in "Ocean Breeze"
- 1 lipstick in "Tanzanian Sunrise"
- 1 cover-up stick marked 95p from the Body Shop. Now I know for a fact that the same thing

today would cost her £4.50. My mum has make-up that is older than me – VOM!

SUNDAY 19TH APRIL

7.34 p.m.

Mum asked me if I had been going through her personal things. I denied it, but then she said she knew I had as she leaves things in very specific places.

She asked me what I was looking for. When I said "stuff", she said, "Hattie, I've noticed you are starting to get an attitude. I don't want it. Sort it out. While you're under this roof you respect my privacy – I am your mother."

Yes, Mum, but I want the truth. I want to find out who the hell I am and where the hell I come from. No, I didn't say that – but I thought it.

I am OWED the truth.

MONDAY 20TH APRIL

4.23 p.m.

We had a discussion today at school – "What do you hope to be doing in 20 years' time?" Weirdo Jen said she just wanted to be "staining the white radiance of eternity".

Jen is not called Weirdo Jen for nothing.

Tuesday 21st April

5.36 p.m.

Florence Morse – TOTAL REBEL – wrote on her exercise book: "Virginity is like a balloon... One pop and it's gone for ever!" Instead of going mental Mrs Cob kept her after class and gave her the most embarrassing sex talk ever. We were listening at the door.

Mrs Cob was saying stuff like: "Making love is actually a beautiful thing", and "It's the ultimate expression of devotion that shouldn't be cheapened by graffiti..."

Florence was DYING. Worst punishment in history!

6.12 p.m.

Sorry – that should have been "One prick and it's gone for ever!"

6.45 p.m.

Just want to say I do actually know how sex works.

Wednesday 22nd April

5.35 p.m.

Just picked up a message from the Citizens' Advice Bureau. I missed ANOTHER appointment. WHAT IS WRONG WITH ME?!

Now they can't see me till the 8th of June. THAT'S 7 WEEKS AWAY!!! I asked Rob why again. He thinks it's because everyone is still having problems with bankruptcy, getting divorced and anti-social behaviour. OR they are thinking of going abroad for cheaper dental care and want to know if Thailand is "good for teeth".

OMG – why didn't I think of THAT? I could have got invisible braces AND a holiday.

7.35 p.m.

Suddenly Goose out of nowhere has invited me to watch him play football. He is in goal. I have nothing else to do so I might as well go along. At least there might be some fit boys there.

I invited Dimple too but she has got a Bollywood dance class. Weirdo Jen refused to come as she and her family think all sport is pointless and that it has "undermined British culture"(???). Though this has not stopped her mum using a key ring that says "Mrs David Beckham".

THURSDAY 23RD APRIL

7.37 a.m.

I wish Rob wouldn't do his crap driving instructor jokes – like when I bump into him on the landing he always says, "Mirror, signal, manoeuvre, Hattie." This is not funny and totally annoying as is the way he always says, "Hattie, make me a cup of tea, would you? Proceed to the hallway and then take your first available exit."

I wonder what kind of funny my real dad is. Hope he is Russell Brand funny.

5.34 p.m.

Mr Halston has given us a "special" History project — we have to write a poem about Joan of Arc. It's ridiculous — we are 14, not 6! In some countries we could be married with 3 children by now.

I am glad we're not in those countries, but that is not the point!!!

FRIDAY 24TH APRIL

6.36 p.m.

Have to write this STUPID poem — but I am craptacular at writing stuff. Texted Goose. He is coming round to help.

8.27 p.m.

Goose has helped me write the poem. I think I may get heavily told off for it but I am still handing it in.

> Joan was in a field
> It all happened quite by chance
> A voice came out of nowhere
> And said, "Go and fight for France!"
>
> Joan dressed up like a boy
> It wasn't accidental
> People wouldn't listen to a girl
> They would just think she was a mental
>
> Joan fought many battles
> She beat off all the rest

But then she was captured by the English
'Cos we are the best

The English said, "Joan – you are the enemy
And you are a liar
You dress up like a man
It's time for death by fire."

Joan on the wooden stake
The flames oh they did dazzle
And when they finally did die down
Joan was just a frazzle

Saturday 25th April

9.25 a.m.

Just woke up. Had a dream about Mrs Matfield putting me in a toaster. Joan of Arc has given me nightmares so deserves a craptacular poem.

Football today. Goose is coming round at 1.30.

10.10 a.m.

OMG – does this make me a WAG?

7.01 p.m.

That football match was as boring as hell BUT I have seen my destiny. I have seen the man that I want to BE with and kiss and EVERYTHING.

Basically on Goose's team was a load of Toky-OK-ers except for this just perfect man. He was utterly perfectamundo – his eyes were LUSH.

And his bum was like chiselled marble. He IS the Taylor Lautner of Derby. I am in love. Epic, pulsating, passionate love.

His name is Zachary and he is the most beautiful man I have ever seen. I don't normally go for blonds but he is just MASTERCHEF YUMSTER! He is like a really young David Beckham. And HIS BODY – he must work on it because IT IS SEXUAL. Even at half-time he refused an orange segment and did press-ups instead.

At the end of the match Goose came over and said, "Did you enjoy it?" I said, "Not the match, Goose, but the talent. TELL ME ABOUT ZACH!"

Goose looked a bit pissed off (probably because he was covered in mud). He said, "Yeah, Zach is OK – bit in love with himself, but he's OK." Goose reckons he plays every week, and some league clubs have been interested in him. LEAGUE CLUBS!!! He is going to be famous. Right, I am coming to football every week.

10.56 p.m.

Forgot to say Goose saved about 17 goals and was man of the match. He gave me his prize, a tin of Roses, which was nice of him!

I saw a sign on the clubhouse:

> TRAIN WITH THE FOOTBALL SQUAD
> EVERY WEDNESDAY – CALL STAN

I think I might give it a try. Mum will let me because it is exercise and she will never guess I am doing it for full-on LOVE ACTION.

Sunday 26th April

4.56 p.m.

Apparently girls are not welcome at football training! Stan the coach said he is with Ron Atkinson (whoever he is). He thinks that "Women belong in the discotheque and the boutique but not on the football pitch".

I told Stan that I was a member of a group that was dedicated to making unfair things fair. Stan said, "Listen, Love – women can't keep up with men on the pitch and no bird I've ever known wants to do a header. It's got nothing to do with fair – it's just a fact of life."

Are men like this actually allowed to breathe? The Not Fair Protest Group needs to STAMP OUT STAN. OMG – that is actually a brilliant phrase.

5.24 p.m.

Rang Dimple – she agreed that it was wrong but her Bollywood dance class is just for girls so she can't really complain.

6.34 p.m.

Texted Jen – she replied by saying that all sport should be banned.

Sometimes I think I am the only one who really cares about our group. I am basically a lone crusader for JUSTICE and LOVE.

I'm training on Wednesday. NOTHING will stop me. Not even Stan.

7.01 p.m.
Just realized I don't have a sports bra.

7.03 p.m.
Just realized I don't need a sports bra.

MONDAY 27TH APRIL

6.36 p.m.

NIGHTMARE at school.

Mr Halston in History said he found my Joan of Arc poem a "total disgrace", and it was "inappropriate to mock the death of a saint and true feminist". I now have a detention tomorrow where I have to write a proper essay about Joan of Arc's achievements.

I don't care — I am in love.

9.23 p.m.
Been praticising headers all night for football practice with a bathroom sponge. Now I'm worried. I look stupid trying to do it and Stan is right — it DOES hurt. Even with a sponge.

9.45 p.m.

Just tried a header with a loofah. That hurt too.

9.56 p.m.

My brother came in. He thinks I should try headers with a sharp knife.

10.02 p.m.

I will never take the pee out of Premiere League footballers again. They go through torture doing this with an actual ball. They definitely deserve £250K a week.

If they ask me to do headers on Wednesday I'll just say I would like to be in goal. Then you basically just have to stand there.

TUESDAY 28TH APRIL

7.45 p.m.

Did detention. Actually Joan of Arc was quite cool. And she cropped her hair and had the pixie look YEARS before everyone else.

Been thinking all day about Zach. If we did get married I could help change the way WAGs are seen. Don't get me wrong, I would always make sure I looked amazing, but I would also have my own career. Basically if I became a celebrity chef I could do TV with Jamie Oliver during the week and then still go and see Zach play at weekends. I am sure Jamie would be fine with that ... especially if I brought more viewers in.

I'd be TOTALLY GORGEOUS just with a spatula.

WEDNESDAY 29TH APRIL

7.23 a.m.

Told Gran how much I hated the way I looked. Gran said I was pretty, and like a fine wine I will mature and grow more beautiful.

Gran thinks her perfect partner is Stephen Fry — she is not to be trusted.

7.34 a.m.

Actually Stephen Fry would be ace doing a speech at the wedding.

8.06 a.m.

OMG — I would LOVE Stephen Fry to be my dad. THAT WOULD BE MAGNIFICENT. EVERYBODY would want to come round my house. I would be the Queen of TOTALLY Popular. Plus we'd NEVER lose the PTA's annual trivia quiz EVER again. He would know the capital of Uruguay and how to tell the sex of a budgie. Unlike Rob.

8.12 a.m.

I do love Rob though. He'll just never be my real dad if you know what I mean.

Football training tonight. Can't wait to show Zach how much I love football AND HIM.

4.53 p.m.

Got my outfit sorted for tonight's training. I've borrowed Jen's Hello Kitty shorts. I thought they looked like they were for 7-year-olds but Jen says they are "Japanese Harajuku fabulous". I agreed but I'm going to have to google it later because I honestly don't know what the hell she means. She also lent me a GORGEOUS yellow vest top that makes my breasts look slightly big.

I'm going to feel cold but look HOT.

Goose is picking me up at 7.

10.23 p.m.

Football training – the good things:

- Zach looked AMAZING and before training smiled at me. Sort of half a smile. A flirting smile, I think!

- I actually managed to join in a conversation about football. Goose asked everyone who they thought Chelsea's new manager was going to be and I said, "Oh, it's bound to be someone good." I don't know ANYTHING about it but it must have been right because no one argued. They all just went quiet and walked off! Result!

- I managed to keep up mostly with the warm-up. I got a stitch on the second run down the pitch but I did the first one!

Football training — the bad things:

- I can't dribble.
- I especially can't dribble through traffic cones. Have you EVER seen David Beckham dribble through some traffic cones mid-game? No. It is POINTLESS.
- I can't shoot.
- I can't catch anything in goal. The balls come too fast and sting your fingers.
- Stan didn't use my name once — he just called me the "little lady".
- NO ONE would pass the ball to me.
- I am still covered in mud.
- There were NO refreshments.
- I was so cold I got headlamp nipples.
- NOT ONE of the boys looked at my headlamp nipples when I did have them.

I am not going again to train. Just to watch. At LEAST Zach noticed me tonight.

11.01 p.m.

Just googled Harajuku 🔍. Thanks, Jen. I looked like a massive doll dork. Who couldn't dribble.

THURSDAY 30TH APRIL

6.36 p.m.

My brother caught me practising my celebrity chef-ing today. I was talking into Mum's little mirror pretending it

---

was a camera. He was standing at the door for ages. I told him if he told anyone I would tell everyone about the time I caught him singing to his Katy Perry poster in his underpants.

7.35 p.m.

Just asked Goose if I could come to football again. He looked really pleased and said, "Of course you can, Hats – love you to."

TOMORROW IS TOTALLY ZACH DAY.

7.28 p.m.

MARVELLOUSNESS DAY BEYOND MARVELLOUSNESS.

Got up early and changed about 5 times. Went for skin-tight jeans and good Tesco's top. Actually looked sort of good, I think.

Goose asked why I had dressed up so I told him about the Zach love. He must be going through a bad patch as he seemed a bit annoyed that I was coming just to see Zach.

ANYWAY I stood at the side of the pitch and it was a dead boring game, BUT THEN AT THE END – HEART ATTACK AND TOTALLY MIGHT VOM EVERYWHERE – Zach came over and said, "Do you want to go out for a pizza?" I said, "Love to," I think. I can't REALLY remember as I COULD NOT PHYSICALLY BREATHE WITH THE BRILLIANCE OF IT ALL. Then Zach said, "Give me your number and I'll call you."

10.45 p.m.
Can't believe this has happened. Is this actually my life?

10.57 p.m.
I haven't made it up. It IS my life. My life could be hotness.

SUNDAY 3RD MAY

7.24 a.m.
After a boy has asked you out, when should he call? Think it's too early now.

9.34 a.m.
PLEASE call ZACH. PLEASE, PLEASE, PLEASE CALL.

2.46 p.m.
It's nearly been 24 hours. WHY HASN'T HE CALLLED?

5.36 p.m.
The Not Fair Protest Group will make it a crime for a boy to say he is going to call then NOT CALL.

6.14 p.m.
Or you HAVE to call within 12 hours. Or text to say you are not interested.

8.13 p.m.
I hate boys. ALL MEN in fact.

9.37 p.m.

Except for Stephen Fry.

10.12 p.m.

And Jeremy Kyle. And Rob. All other men are craptacular.

(Bank Holiday Monday)

MONDAY 4TH MAY

7.32 p.m.

ZACH JUST RANG!

BUT disaster.

I left my mobile in the kitchen and ROB ANSWERED IT!!! AND HE ANSWERED IT BY SAYING, "Happy Dragon Takeaway" in a crap Chinese accent. Zach hung up and tried again and I got to the phone first this time. FULL epic conversation:

Z:	Hello, Hattie — it's Zach.
ME:	Hi, Zach. Great day for football and doing your washing… ← WHY DID I SAY THIS?!
Z:	Err yeah. Pizza Express OK next Sunday?
ME:	Yes — I don't like eggs though.
Z:	Well, most pizzas should be fine and we will share some dough balls.
ME:	Brilliant — share some ← WHY DID I SAY THIS?! x 4 BILLION balls — like you share … balls on the pitch!!!
Z:	Yeah — see you next Sunday then.

And if that wasn't bad enough — and here's a tip from Hattie Moore — when you press the red button to end the call, and say, "That man is pure hot SEX!" just make sure you actually HAVE pressed the red button.

I hope he didn't hear.

9.38 p.m.
I HAVE A DATE NEXT SUNDAY. MY INNER WOMAN HAS BEEN FOUND.

TUESDAY 5TH MAY

5 days till date!!!

4.15 p.m.
Goose has been rushed into hospital. He could barely walk with the pain.

I said to Mum that I hoped it wasn't his testicles. Mum said, "Hattie, why on Earth would you think it would be?" and the truth is, I don't know why I said that.

OMG — am I a sex perv?

5.39 p.m.
Just realized why I said that — it's because Jen's friend's cousin who lives in Blackpool woke up in agonizing pain because 1 of his balls got twisted. They had to remove it because it was basically in a knot. I will never moan about periods again.

6.12 p.m.
Actually that is a lie as sometimes I have a period that makes me into a mental.

WEDNESDAY 6TH MAY

4 days till date!!!

8.01 a.m.

FULL DRAMA – Goose has appendicitis. Apparently it's a rubbish part of your stomach that you only need if you are a rabbit that eats grass. Goose's got infected and they have to take it out. He's having the operation later today.

It's not serious but like all operations he could actually die.

6.43 p.m.

Dimple came over after school to sort out what outfit to wear for the date. We went through EVERYTHING in my wardrobe and decided on Dimple's black skirt, Dimple's striped jacket, Dimple's mini clutch and Dimple's Converse.

So just to confirm – I have actually NOTHING to wear for a date.

8.12 p.m.

Goose survived his operation. Feel bad that I was stressing about clothes when he was near death.

3 days till date!!!

THURSDAY 7TH MAY

9.33 p.m.

Went to see Goose in hospital. He had about 4 nurses round him in the children's ward and he was making them all laugh. They must be desperate.

While we were there Bob the Builder came round – well a man dressed up as Bob the Builder. I was well embarrassed but Goose just asked him where Pilchard the cat was. Goose just doesn't seem to care what people think of him — it's actually quite worrying.

10.12 p.m.

Googled <u>when you don't care what people think of you</u> 🔍. This makes you a sociopath, which means you have a very high chance of committing some sort of mass murder. Great! And there's only a very thin wall between us normally.

2 days till date!!!

FRIDAY 8TH MAY
7.46 p.m.

Went to see Goose the sociopath again. He was helping a 5-year-old make a Lego crane. I asked him why he was in the children's ward. Apparently you are classed as a child until you are 16 years old! This is completely mental. I have texted Dimple and Jen and the NFPG is going to write to the person who runs all the hospitals to demand that teenagers get a separate ward.

9.21 p.m.

The person who runs the NHS is the prime minister. He didn't reply last time — AND craptacular braces are more important!

10.58 p.m.

Forgot to write — I asked Goose why Zach hadn't texted. Goose thinks he might be on pay-as-you-go and is trying to save money! DOUBLE YAY!!! There's a good reason for him not texting and it's another thing we have in common!

SATURDAY 9TH MAY

1 day till date!!!

5.34 p.m.

My brother just told me the worst date story ever. This GORGEOUS girl went on a date with a guy she had liked for AGES when she had a bit of a cold. Everything was going fine until she laughed at one of his jokes and ended up firing 2 massive bogeys – one out of each nostril – straight at him. He went RIGHT off her and everyone knew her as "Snotty" from then on. My brother said whatever you do make sure you clean your nose before you go.

7.45 p.m.

Ever since my brother told me the bogey story I have been sniffing every 5 seconds to make sure my nose is clear. I am sure I can feel stuff up there.

8.14 p.m.

Checked again – nothing there but it feels like there is! Texted Gran. Gran says put salt water up your nose to clear it.

8.43 p.m.

Think I might be sick but I am bogey-free.

9.02 p.m.

Mum says I am sniffing all the time – what is the matter – have I got hay fever?

10.47 p.m.

Mum has just been on the Frank website, where it says that sniffing is a possible sign of cocaine use. I have

NEVER been near drugs except for paracetamol and Night Nurse! I am not a drug user. I just have BOGEY PHOBIA.

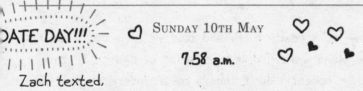

DATE DAY!!! ♡ SUNDAY 10TH MAY ♡ ♥ ♡
♡ ♥ ♥

7.58 a.m.

Zach texted,

C U @ 6 outside Pizza Express, Irongate.

Bet he just woke up and thought of me – YUM!!!

1.09 p.m.

Right – have to start getting ready. Will be back later with FULL DATE EVENT ACTION.

10.12 p.m.

OMG OMG OMG OMG OMG OMG OMG OMG!

I HAVE JUST BEEN TONGUED!

CAN'T WRITE...

LATER...

11.38 p.m.

So I met Zach outside Pizza Express and my stomach was doing flips. I felt actually sick, so we ordered dough balls. He had 9 of the 12 that you get, because a) I WANTED TO VOM WITH NERVES, and b) he is a sportsman and needs carbs.

Then he asked if I was having pizza or salad as usually thin girls like me never ate a lot! I told him that I was having a Quattro Formaggi and he WINKED and said, "It's good we are both eating garlic." and I thought, OMG, I think he wants to kiss me!!!

Anyway he is really funny and told me all about what his future plans were. I didn't get a lot of chance to talk but to be honest I don't think I am as interesting as him. He is hoping to get signed by a BIG club – if not, he thinks he'll just become a plumber. TBH I don't know if I will like him as much if he fixes toilets for a living, BUT I can tell he is just going to be HUGELY famous.

Anyway he walked me home and said, "Thanks for a great night" – then he LUNGED at me and said, "Shall we share some garlic?" and we had the most amazing snog EVER. Only I didn't know where to put my hands so I just shoved them on his magnificent bum and turned my tongue around his a bit.

IT WAS PHENOMENALTOTALAMAZENESS!!! IT WAS A SNOG!!!

Then he just said, "He shoots, he scores. I really like you, Hattie. I'll call you."

Then Rob came to the door (hope he wasn't watching) and offered Zach a lift home. Zach said he was going to get a bus, which I was DEAD relieved about as I knew Rob would either play level-crossing roulette or pretend he had no brakes. NEITHER is funny AT ALL and could result in the death of Zach – and he can't die now as I HAVE TASTED REAL MAN AND HE IS MY BOYFRIEND.

MONDAY 11TH MAY

12.45 a.m.

BTW went to the loo 3 times in the restaurant to check for bogeys. None.

3.12 a.m.

Zach, PLEASE call – even though it's 3 in the morning.

5.23 p.m.

At school told EVERYONE about Zach. Dimple and Jen were really happy for me but apparently MGK told Rachel who told Sophie who told Charlotte who told Doughnut Hannah that I was "hardly WAG material". Dimple said, "Just ignore her – she's jealous." IT WAS AMAZE!!!

Then in French, Monsieur Très Gros, the fattest French teacher in the history of Europe, said, "What am I doing with my bra?" He meant bras as in French for "arm" but I wouldn't be surprised with his man boobs if he had to wear one!!! LOL!!!

7.27 p.m.

Just thought – Monsieur Très Gros probably has more reason to wear a bra than me. This is depressing.

10.17 p.m.

Zach hasn't called.

TUESDAY 12TH MAY

4.23 p.m.

REALLY weird in English. Florence Morse did a book report on *The Very Hungry Caterpillar*. She just wrote, "It was a hungry caterpillar. It ate stuff. It turned into a butterfly. Then someone probably trod on it because life is cruel. The end."

Dr Richards said she had great economy with language and that it made a refreshing change from the 450 reports on *Harry Potter and the Deathly Hallows* he had read in the last year. You would think that Florence would be happy but she looked well pissed-off.

9.36 p.m.

NO CALL AGAIN. WHERE IS HE?!

Do you think I was a bad kisser? Perhaps I flicked my tongue too fast.

10.45 p.m.

Just tongued my hand. Think I am too frantic. Perhaps I've put him off with my mad mouth.

Shall I text him and apologize for my kiss? I'll ask Dimple.

11.09 p.m.

Dimple must be asleep. CRISIS!!! Don't put your mob on silent at the most vital point of my life, Dimps!

WEDNESDAY 13TH MAY

4.56 p.m.

Disaster! Showed Dimple in the loos at break what I did with my tongue. Lily Richardson saw, then she did an impression of me to Ruth Palmer, who showed MGK. MGK has now spread it that I kiss "like a mental".

5.12 p.m.

OMG – that sounds as if I snogged Dimple!!! I didn't. I just stuck my tongue in the air!!!

7.46 p.m.

Still no call. Called BT – landline is fine. Called Orange – mobile is fine.

Just texted him with

> Hi R u ok? x

Dimple said to put just one kiss as more looks desperate.

10.14 p.m.

No response. Have I been dumped?!

THURSDAY 14TH MAY

6.23 p.m.

Went round to visit Goose, who is back home. He looked really pleased to see me until he realized I only wanted to use his Facebook login to spy on Zach. I'm not even his friend yet!

Anyway TOTAL AMAZE... It said,

> **Zachary** is liking a certain girl right now

IT MUST BE ME!!!

Goose said, "It's OBVIOUS he likes you, Hats. Just boys don't text as much as girls. Oh, and by the way, I am fine now I am out of hospital – thanks for asking."

Goose is a bit sensitive. He has to realize I am actually in a relationship and this takes up a lot of my time.

FRIDAY 15TH MAY

6.52 a.m.
Why hasn't Zach been in touch? He says he likes me on Facebook – WHY CAN'T HE JUST TEXT?!!

6.32 p.m.
Went round to see Gran after school. She says that I should "treat them mean to keep them keen", because "men like bitches".

Gran always "operates by The Rules", she says. "The Rules" say you should not accept a date for a Saturday on a Tuesday. So basically if Zach asks me out now I should say no. Attention, Gran – that is SO not going to happen!

7.01 p.m.
Gran "always operates"?! VOM – GRAN IS DATING. Bet bogeys are the least of her problems. She hasn't even got her own teeth.

Actually I wonder if snogging with no teeth is better. Your tongue can just go straight in and thrash about without fear of being bitten.

I need to snog more before I am past it – RING, ZACH, RING!

SATURDAY 16TH MAY

7.47 a.m.
FINALLY A TEXT!!! YAY!!! YAY!!! YAY!!! Just got it:

Hatz – c u at footie

Must start getting ready. Haven't shaved my armpits or my legs.

10.34 p.m.
After football Zach took me to his house with a load of his mates. We sat there playing *Grand Theft Auto* on the Xbox. I was actually brilliant at it and his mates said, "Zach, your girlfriend (YOUR GIRLFRIEND!!! YES!!!) is a pro."

Weird – Zach didn't look very happy that I was amaze at *Grand Theft Auto*, but I've been playing it with my brother since I was about 4 – so I am bound to beat everyone!!! MY BOYFRIEND said I was a woman of many talents. OH YES, ZACH, I AM. MY LOVE TALENTS ARE HERE FOR YOU.

Then Rob pipped his horn outside and I had to go. Zach wouldn't kiss me in front of his mates but I'm sure that now I am OFFICIALLY his girlfriend, there will be LOADS OF SNOGGING.

I am someone's girlfriend.

I need to read Dr Phil's "Healthy Relationship Guide".

SUNDAY 17TH MAY

3.19 p.m.
Dr Phil says to "keep communication open between you and your partner" — so I am texting Zach with how I am feeling and what I am doing.

5.45 p.m.
I've had no reply but that's fine.

6.32 p.m.
Actually it's not fine at all. I've sent him 14 texts today and got NOTHING.

8.40 p.m.
ZERO, ZACH!!!

MONDAY 18TH MAY

7.54 a.m.
Perhaps if I pretend I've left something at his he'll call me.

1.10 p.m.
Texted him at break and told him that I've bought him the new *House of the Dead: Overkill* game. I haven't but he MUST be interested now.

4.24 p.m.

Checked phone straight after Science. STILL *NO TEXT.*
Texted him with the slightly pissy

> Any chance you can text me
> before the end of the year
> perhaps?

I am not playing it cool because I cannot play it cool. I am
HOT with passion and *NEED!!!*

TUESDAY 19TH MAY

5.23 p.m.

Weirdo Jen thinks I shouldn't have been so
good at *Grand Theft Auto* – as boys don't
like women being better at boy stuff than
them!

I have texted Zach apologizing for
mullering him at *Grand Theft Auto.*

WEDNESDAY 20TH MAY

3.45 p.m.

Dimple thinks I need to be more assertive.

I have texted Zach telling him he is coming to dinner at
my house on Saturday after football.

THURSDAY 21st MAY

8.23 a.m.

Zach hasn't texted so he must be coming round for dinner on Saturday. If he didn't want to come surely he would tell me?

7.32 p.m.

Just told Mum I am bringing Zach round for dinner on Saturday and gave her this list:

* no crap jokes
* no baby photos
* no asking what he intends to do with his life once he leaves school
* no asking what his parents do
* no asking what he does in his spare time
* no mention of me being frightened of donkeys at the seaside
* no mention of me being frightened by the Angel Gabriel in the school nativity when I was 4
* no mention of me before the age of 13 in fact

Mum asked where did I get off inviting people round without asking her first? Rob said, "Oh, come on, darling – it's fine – Hattie just wants to show us off."

Please note – it's my stepdad who takes my side, NOT MY OWN MOTHER!!!

Friday 22nd May

9.56 p.m.

Today I smeared *Blu-Tack* on my eyebrows then ripped it up the wrong way – many hairs have detached themselves from my head. I may have discovered a new beauty technique.

10.04 p.m.

No, I haven't. I now look as if my eyebrows have been sprinkled on.

Texted Zach to tell him with a LOL!!!

Saturday 23rd May

Don't care about the time. Just got this:

```
Hatz - been really fun but
not ready 2 commit right now.
Football comes first.
```

WHY CAN'T I GO OUT WITH SOMEONE ACTUALLY NICE?! WHAT IS ACTUALLY WRONG WITH ME?!

10.45 p.m.

What IS wrong with me? SERIOUSLY?!

Sunday 24th May

7.32 p.m.

I know EXACTLY what is wrong with me. I've just looked through this and on the actual 14th January I said that girls who don't know their real dads pick rubbish men! AND NOW IT'S HAPPENED.

So I NEED TO FIND OUT WHO MY DAD ACTUALLY IS SO I CAN FIND A BOY THAT LOVES ME. Mum HAS to tell me the truth about Dad NOW as she is ruining my actual life.

She's at the cinema tonight with Rob, but tomorrow I am TELLING HER. IN FACT I AM ORDERING HER.

MONDAY 25TH MAY

8.45 p.m.

Just STORMED downstairs to tackle Mum and LOST it.

I said, "RIGHT, MUM — I am picking rubbish boys to go out with and it's TOTALLY your fault. TELL ME WHO MY DAD IS!"

Mum said, "Hattie — not now..." so I said, "It's NEVER NOW — I have had enough."

And I was so mental I smashed her You Are the Weakest Link mug. She looked REALLY shocked but I just carried on and said, "Mum — it's my right!" and then Rob came in and said, "Hattie — please calm down." And I said, "SHUT UP, ROB — YOU ARE NOT MY REAL DAD AND NEVER WILL BE."

 And then Mum started to cry — which is her typical rubbish tactic. She won't be upset about me — she'll be upset that I've broken her precious non-hilarious mug.

AND THEN, GET THIS – ROB SHOUTED AT ME TO GET UPSTAIRS. ERR – WHO ARE YOU EXACTLY, ROB?! WHO?!!

They are BOTH CRAP. CRAP. CRAP.

9.12 p.m.

Just texted Dimple. She says she understands I am upset but I should respect my mum as she works hard and loves me very much.

Sometimes Dimple is too Indian.

9.47 p.m.

Just texted Weirdo Jen – she agrees that I need to get angry, as "gaps in your identity" lead to "spiritual stunting of the soul". Plus resentment blocks your arteries in your heart with special "bad vibe" fat.

Sometimes Jen is too weird.

TUESDAY 26TH MAY

7.12 a.m.

Rob just came up and apologized for shouting last night. He really made me angry because he was so quiet and kind, which is just ... ANNOYING. He said he knew he wasn't my real dad but he felt like he was, and loved AND liked me very much.

I said, "I know that, Rob – BUT I need to know the truth."

He just looked sad, and said he wanted to explain – but there would soon be a time when they would tell me everything – they just need to get some things in place first.

WHAT DOES THAT MEAN?!

Before I could ask, Rob said he thought I should say sorry to my mum.

Suppose I will have to. I ALWAYS have to say sorry first.

8.12 a.m.
Just said sorry to Mum before school. She grunted OK.

Like all this is MY fault!!!

7.34 p.m.
Mum is acting like nothing has happened. But it has.

The BROKEN *Weakest Link* mug in the bin is the symbol that something HAS happened and lies have been smashed!

8.12 p.m.
That last bit made me sound like a bit of a doughnut, didn't it?

WEDNESDAY 27TH MAY

4.13 p.m.
Just went round to see Goose. Wish I hadn't bothered.

He heard the shouting through the wall. He says he would love to have Rob as a dad as he's a sound bloke. I tried to explain to Goose that not knowing my dad is causing me to pick rubbish men.

Goose looked at me and said, "Hattie, it's your fault you have no taste. Perhaps you are missing decent men that are right before your eyes."

ERR, GOOSE, I WATCH *DR PHIL* — I understand how things work.

Goose says he'll help me find out who Carlo is if I'm nice to Rob. But he promised me that last time, and all we did was google the name! It's like every time I go to look for my dad, something happens in my life to stop me — boys, school, the NFPG or my gran being a mental. It's like my actual life is against me.

Goose says I need to get a grip, have patience and gently try to find out more from Gran.

Goose is very harsh.

5.32 p.m.
I think actually Goose might be very right. I need to try something new.

I am going to try patience.

THURSDAY 28TH MAY

6.23 p.m.
Went to see Gran to try to get some more info. But as usual she didn't want to talk about anything but herself.

She was very excited because her and her friend Denise had been "trevving". When I asked her what that was, she said her and Denise went round in the car and every time they saw something they didn't like they shouted rude stuff out of their window. This included couples kissing ("The pavement is for walking on – not for sticking your tongue down someone else's throat!"), gangs of youths ("Bound to be drinking or up to no good") and people in Motability cars ("Half of them are just fat and lazy, not disabled").

FRIDAY 29TH MAY

9.45 p.m.

OMG – Gran and Denise were pulled over by the actual police for trevving.

The policeman said mature ladies shouldn't be spending their time bullying youngsters who were behaving in a law-abiding way. Gran has been given a caution so she has to behave.

Seriously. And I am still expected to do well at school despite the fact I come from a family of TOTAL mentals.

Dad, wherever you are, come and save me.

SATURDAY 30TH MAY

7.12 p.m.

Gran had an argument today with Mum about trevving.

Gran said that Mum had forgotten how to have fun and needs to get back in touch with her inner child (she had seen that on TV). Mum said she didn't have time for her inner child — she was too busy looking after all the children around her and anyway she had to grow up fast when "what happened, happened". Then they both shut up.

I must have patience.

Even though I actually want to go totally mad right now.

SUNDAY 31ST MAY

10.56 p.m.

Weirdo Jen says sometimes you just have to give up wanting and searching in order to find what you truly want. She thinks that "desperation leads to desolation", and that you have to "set what you love free — then it will return to you".

I need to google constantly with Jen — she uses stupid words.

I asked her if she could prove this. She said yes. Apparently she once had a pet wasp that broke away from the "slavery of the nest". She fed it on M&Ms for 2 days, and then let it go. Jen reckons it came back to see her.

Unfortunately Jen's mum then swatted it with a copy of the *Guardian*, but that was perhaps "karma for the wasp ruining someone's picnic".

Jen IS weird.

She might have a point though. Perhaps I should use this holiday to revise, and then the universe will reward me with the real knowledge of my real dad.

HALF-TERM

MONDAY 1ST JUNE

11.12 a.m.
I will start revising after lunch. I'll just watch a bit more TV then I will honestly start.

1.43 p.m.
Might just go for a walk as it's a well-known fact that your brain needs oxygen to function correctly.

5.23 p.m.
No point starting now – it's nearly dinner time – and your mind doesn't absorb information at night.

TUESDAY 2ND JUNE

8.02 a.m.
I will honestly start revising tomorrow, BUT I have to go round and see Dimple as I haven't seen her for a few days and I don't want her to forget me.

Friendship comes before exams.

11.34 a.m.
Dimple's mum said Dimple had gone to the library to revise. I love her but not enough to walk all the way down there. Especially in drizzle. I'll get the frizz.

WEDNESDAY 3RD JUNE

12.12 p.m.

I can't concentrate on my revision. NONE of it is going in. I'm going to text Jen to see how she is getting on.

1.54 p.m.

Jen has done ALL her History, ALL her Geography and even some of her French!!! I told her I have done NOTHING. Jen thinks my "subconscious mind" (googled it again!) is too full to take on more information, and I need to clear my head of things that are bothering me.

Texted back:

> Jen, HERE IS THE PROBLEM. The thing that is most bothering me is my dad, and NO ONE WILL HELP ME!!!

Jen thinks I need to "explore different avenues of assistance".

What I need are the REAL experts in finding people.

THURSDAY 4TH JUNE

12.35 p.m.

Just rang the BBC. Apparently they only have celebrities on *Who Do You Think You Are?* But the woman there was dead nice and suggested some people called the Salvation Army.

5.12 p.m.

Mum just asked how my revision was going. I lied and said, "Good."

I'll call the military people tomorrow. I am surprised the Salvation Army offer that service considering they are fighting wars all over the place.

FRIDAY 5TH JUNE

2.24 p.m.

OMG – the Salvation Army are an actual church!

The woman there was dead lovely too. Unfortunately she said that they didn't trace fathers of children "born outside of marriage" (I think that's me), and even if they did she would probably need a little more information than "He might be called Carlo."

Still at least she didn't tell me to shut up. In fact complete strangers are nicer to me than my own family.

5.53 p.m.

Goose has just been round. I told him the trail had gone cold again.

Then he came up with the best idea EVER: HIRE A PRIVATE DETECTIVE!!! IT IS GENIUS!!! We are going to research it fully tomorrow over some KFC.

Goose is officially MYHERO.COM.

7.12 p.m.

Mum has been up again to ask me what I had revised today. I said "stuff". I think she fell for it.

SATURDAY 6TH JUNE

4.15 p.m.

Goose and me have spent all day looking into private detectives.

It seemed really hopeful at first because we found a company that had a 95% success rate in finding missing people. BUT when we read more on the website, that's only if you have their full date of birth AND a last known address. I don't have any of that. Plus it costs £200. We can't afford that! Goose and I are so skint we had to share a two-piece meal at KFC!

Anyway Goose gave me a hug and said, "Hats, we will find your dad – I promise." Then he gave me one of these intense stares he does sometimes and it all went a bit weird.

So weird I had to say the first thing that came into my head, which was: "Do you think it's true that Victoria Beckham just eats boiled eggs to stay thin?" Goose thinks she probably just watches what she eats and has a fast metabolism.

He's good with girlie things.

8.12 p.m.

My gran rang. She has bought a Nintendo DS. She is 67 years old.

8.34 p.m.

Please note: I can't afford a KFC Bargain Bucket or a private detective, BUT my gran CAN afford a DS.

SUNDAY 7TH JUNE

7.53 p.m.

Went round to Gran's for dinner. She was excited as she had just discovered that Super Mario could shoot things from his head. I'm actually worried that she might become a games addict.

9.12 p.m.

I have done no revision, I have not found my dad BUT I have helped my gran get to the 2nd level on *Mario Kart*.

My life is TRAGIC.

BACK TO SCHOOL AND CAB MEETING.   MONDAY 8TH JUNE

7.32 a.m.

Telling school I have a dentist appointment but I'm seeing the Citizens' Advice Bureau at 9.30 a.m.

1.34 p.m.

The woman at the CAB was MAHOOSIVELY LOVELY. She was called Sylvia and she used to be a lawyer until she retired. Then she got sick of watching daytime TV and now she works at the CAB for FREE! MENTAL!

Anyway she suggested a lot of things that I've tried already (the Internet, Salvation Army), THEN she said

AND I CAN'T BELIEVE I HAVEN'T THOUGHT OF THIS BEFORE: "Have you looked at your birth certificate? Your father should be named on it."

OMG – GENIUS. EVERYONE has a birth certificate and Sylvia reckons if I have a passport (I do!), there is probably a birth certificate in the house.

Sylvia ALSO said, "I wish you all the best, Hattie. You seem like a smashing young woman."

Yes, Sylvia – a smashing young woman who is going to find her birth certificate AND her dad.

Now I have to work out when the right time is to ask Mum.

4.13 p.m.

MAGNIFICENT at school today!!!

Loads of us haven't done any revision and we all know that we are going to get the most craptacular exam marks ever. So we have OFFICIALLY set up a Cheat Club. It's me, Clare, Dibbo Hannah, Charlie and Becca. We are going to work out a way to get through the exams without doing any work.

5.32 p.m.

Mum just got in. She didn't get a delivery of tea bags to the cafe this morning – 10 pensioners threatened a sit-in, as a "Big Brew" is advertised as part of her special OAP breakfast meal deal – AND GRAN WAS LEADING THE PROTEST!

Now is NOT the time to ask about my birth certificate.

7.45 p.m.

Jen just texted – she is worried that the Cheat Club doesn't fit in with the values of the NFPG. I have told her that really exams are a completely unfair way of testing your brain, and the Cheat Club is partly about trying to find fairer tests. She is going to text Dimple.

8.34 p.m.

Jen just texted – her and Dimple agree that the Cheat Club is basically OK but must be kept separate from the NFPG. I have agreed.

It's all right for Jen and Dimple – they know who their dads are, so they can actually revise. In the Cheat Club 3 of us have never met our actual fathers. That's why we are actually craptacular at concentrating.

TUESDAY 9TH JUNE

7.32 a.m.

Mum is still livid. I know her bad moods. This could last a week. I'm not risking asking and ruining a good chance to get the truth. I'll just focus on getting through my exams.

5.02 p.m.

The Cheat Club has a plan! Clare is going to pretend to sleepwalk into the staffroom and try to get the exam papers. It's brave but it may just work. Clare was the lead in the school play last year so she is an amazing

---

actress and does occasionally sleepwalk. She says she needs time to "get into the role".

We have given her tonight to get herself ready.

WEDNESDAY 10TH JUNE

8.01 a.m.

Clare is going to do it today at lunch — she says no one can tell her off as the doctor has told her mum she shouldn't be woken up at any point.

MY mum is OFFICIALLY not speaking to Gran because of Tea-Gate. Living with her is like living with an anger bomb.

4.23 p.m.

Cheat Club FAIL. Clare walked into the staffroom, but Bitchface Matfield didn't know you weren't meant to wake someone while sleepwalking, and started blowing a whistle in her actual ear. Then Matfield found a "Cheat Club ROCKS" piece of graffiti on Dibbo Hannah's pencil case. Dibbo Hannah has cracked under pressure and told her everything. Mrs Cob now wants to see us tomorrow.

We have to think of something else.

THURSDAY 11TH JUNE

6.32 a.m.

Gran just rang Mum to apologize. Mum told me that she said sorry and blamed it on "tea dependence". She told

Mum that when you're geared up for a cup of PG and it doesn't come it can send you over the edge.

7.34 p.m.

Mrs Cob said she thought the Cheat Club was disgusting, and that "cheating in exams went against the very ethos of the school". She said she would be monitoring our exam results very closely.

We are screwed. I have basically got to revise EVERYTHING this weekend.

FRIDAY 12TH JUNE

5.12 p.m.

Mrs Matfield made all the members of the Cheat Club stand up today in Art. She then said, "Today we are going to paint 'deceit'. What do you think deceit looks like? I think it's very ugly and will get nowhere in life."

This actually makes no sense but she got her point across. COW.

SATURDAY 13TH JUNE

5.02 a.m.

This is a nightmare. It's TOO early but I have to revise.

7.10 a.m.

Just revised glaciaiation.

7.15 a.m.

It's "glaciation". I can't even spell the subject!

9.45 a.m.

Just did 2 hours of the Tudors. I like the Tudors. I watched some of the TV show on YouTube. King Henry was all GORGEOUSNESS when he was young.

12.36 p.m.

Gran just rang – she has won a 2-week holiday in Portugal. She must take the holiday between 14th October and 1st November and pay a non-refundable £175 administration fee. All she has to do is listen to 3 4-hour presentations on a great opportunity to share in a property in the Algarve.

I think it may be a scam.

1.37 p.m.

I can't revise any more today – my head is full. Plus I need to go round Gran's and look after her. She could sign up to anything. Protecting the vulnerable is more important than passing exams.

5.12 p.m.

Had a brilliant afternoon. Watched loads of TV, ate Doritos and, most importantly, protected Gran from scammers.

I have a feeling that Gran may end up living with us, which will be the greatest thing ever, as a) she LOVES me wearing make-up, and b) she ALWAYS takes my side.

I might tell Mum she seems a bit confused so she moves in quicker.

SUNDAY 14TH JUNE

1.12 p.m.

Told Mum about Gran. She said Gran could look after herself, and how was my revision going?

If she ever finds out about the Cheat Club I am actually dead.

Maths tomorrow. You can't revise Maths. You can either do it or not.

MONDAY 15TH JUNE

5.12 p.m.

You CAN revise Maths. I couldn't remember how to do fractions or percentages.

I am going to write very little here this week. Once I have revised, updated my Facebook status AND tweeted, I actually haven't got time to write.

TUESDAY 16TH JUNE

7.35 p.m.

History.

No questions about Henry VIII's snogging!

UNBELIEVABLE.

Failed that.

WEDNESDAY 17TH JUNE

5.35 p.m.

Geography.

I think global warming is the same thing as glaciation – so I wrote about that.

6.12 p.m.

Just checked with Dimple. It's not.

Failed that.

THURSDAY 18TH JUNE

4.12 p.m.

R.S.

MARVELLOUSNESS! Florence – ultimate rebel – wrote "I Love You" on her eyelids and kept opening and shutting her eyes to Mr Hopkins the trainee RS teacher during the exam!

Questions on Hindus!!! YES!!! My best friend is one. I know she doesn't eat beef. I may have passed that.

FRIDAY 19TH JUNE

5.32 p.m.

English and French oral.

Haven't read *To Kill a Mockingbird*, and I accidentally told Monsieur Très Gros that I came to school on a horse as I couldn't remember the word for walking.

And then he asked me what my dad did for a job. I think I said in French, "My dad is lost."

6.02 p.m.

Checked with Jen – I actually said in French, "My dad is a pear." No wonder Monsieur Très Gros quickly asked me about my hobbies.

7.23 p.m.

Goose just came round. Apparently Zach is going out with another girl.

Apparently she is not as "full-on" as me. Goose says Zach is an idiot and I deserve better.

WHY CAN'T I JUST BE BORING AND BEAUTIFUL like that pretty woman who reads the news? Then boys would like me!

9.01 p.m.

Just tweeted:

> I have had the most craptacular week ever.

Out of my 34 followers no one has asked me why.

9.12 p.m.

Someone called "Sportswear Dudes USA" has tweeted that they can give me 25% off a home gym and some protein shakes.

Great!

I only stay on Twitter so I am easy to track down if someone wants to find me.

SATURDAY 20TH JUNE

7.12 p.m.

Went round to see Gran. She has given me another "not fair thing" that she would like me to fix. Due to "bloody shoplifters" her Cathedral City cheese now has a "bloody security tag". It's cheese – not gold bullion!

I complained to Gran about how shallow men are, and asked if she thought I needed to be quieter? Gran turned mental:

"REAL men like REAL women with personality, and boys who don't always have small ... egos – and you shouldn't be going out with them anyway. The best thing a woman has is herself, Hattie. Never pretend to be something you're not for ANYONE. You're a lovely-looking girl with a great mind and a lovely figure. If boys don't appreciate it now, MEN will."

Which is all very well but it doesn't help me now, does it? I can't wait for boys to mature to find love. I NEED LOVE NOW.

SUNDAY 21ST JUNE

8.23 a.m.

What I actually need is a proper dad NOW. BIRTH CERTIFICATE, where are you?

4.12 p.m.

AND a time machine so I can go back and do some revision. Exam results tomorrow.

MONDAY 22ND JUNE

1.23 p.m.

Exam results.

Failed everything except French and RS (thanks Dimple).

I am going to be in such craptacular crap with my mum. I'm not going to tell her till she actually asks, and then I will be telling her it's completely her fault.

OMG — better ask her for my birth certificate before she finds out.

4.19 p.m.

I should have known.

Just asked Mum for my birth certificate and she said, "I'll just nip upstairs and get it."

She brought it down. For father, it says UNKNOWN.

Not even my birth certificate knows who my father is.

I knew it was too good to be true. Like my Dyson grow-some-breasts machine.

Depressed now.

6.12 p.m.

Weird – Mum hasn't asked about my exams yet. Perhaps she knows I'm gutted about the birth certificate.

6.55 p.m.

Goose just came round. He understands how upset I am about the birth certificate but he thinks I should put it out of my mind. He ALWAYS says stuff like this. I think he thinks he is Dr Phil.

7.12 p.m.

Dimple texted. She agrees with Goose. I think she thinks she is Mrs Dr Phil.

7.32 p.m.

They are both right. Of COURSE my birth certificate wasn't going to tell me ANYTHING. That would have been far too easy in MY life.

7.52 p.m.

Mum still hasn't mentioned my exam results. Beginning to think she has forgotten.

8.55 p.m.

STILL no mention – I KNOW she will explode any minute though.

10.12 p.m.

I am officially worried now. It's like living with a volcano. She seems really worried about something.

Tuesday 23rd June

5.23 p.m.

I LOVE MY BROTHER – he has saved my life!!!

My brother is considering going in to the army. Rob thinks it's a great idea but Mum just burst into tears and said, "Doesn't he ever watch the bloody news?"

Nathan says that there wasn't a lot else to do for someone like him with average GCSEs and no real other skills, and that he did not want to be serving Mega Cheese Elf Burgers for the rest of his life. Mum said she would rather him be fed-up than maimed for life – or dead.

My exam results are just so not important now.

Wednesday 24th June

7.13 p.m.

I won't miss my brother. He used to play hide the baby with me and try and put me in the dishwasher when Mum wasn't looking. Plus once he pretended he had hypnotized Mum and she played along and he said, "You are under my control..." and Mum said, "Yes..." and he said, "Give the baby away!!! Give the baby away!!!"

Everyone finds this funny except me.

THURSDAY 25TH JUNE

8.46 p.m.

My brother came in tonight. We actually just had a half-decent conversation:

HIM:	Hello, Zitty — how's it going?
ME:	Are you really going to join the army?
HIM:	Hats, it might be a real opportunity to do something actually amazing with my life.
ME:	But you could get killed!
HIM:	You could get killed by a bus every morning.
ME:	But the difference is that mental suicide bombers aren't actually aiming the bus towards you.
HIM:	I am going to the recruitment centre tomorrow. Wish me luck.
ME:	Good luck … and thanks for making Mum forget about my exam results.

Then he winked at me and left. I think I may like my brother.

FRIDAY 26TH JUNE

4.12 p.m.

My brother can't go in to the army because he has asthma! LOL!!!

6.21 p.m.

My brother has just asked my mum how I did in my exams.

6.33 p.m.

My mum has gone mental. I didn't even tell her the actual results. She said she knows they are bad because I haven't told her. I have to go round Gran's tomorrow to weed her garden and I am banned from seeing Jen and Dimple outside school for a week. Don't care. I can Skype! Mum is so last century. Her punishments are RUBBISH.

SATURDAY 27TH JUNE

5.32 p.m.

My back kills. Weeding hurts. My mum is a torture queen.

Then I went to wash my hands and OMG – Gran has got a Paul Smith towel! Gran said it was a free gift with some perfume she bought. But why has she got something designer, when my life is Primark, Primark, Primark?

6.09 p.m.

I must not be shallow. I must not be shallow. There are girls my age fighting wars. I must remember that.

6.16 p.m.

In fact Mum always says that to me, but where exactly do 14-year-old-girls fight wars? Adults have to remember that we have information at our fingertips these days. We cannot be lied to like the old days, when people believed in the tooth fairy until they were 19!!!

6.58 p.m.

I wish I hadn't googled that. I now officially feel totally depressed. There are children fighting wars everywhere. Especially in parts of Africa.

I am a cow with actually no problems.

SUNDAY 28TH JUNE

7.32 p.m.

Just Skyped Dimple and Jen (Dimple was round Jen's house).

The NFPG have decided there's nothing we can really do about child soldiers, but whenever we hear someone moaning about something crap and stupid we are going to say, "At least you're not a child soldier". It's our new phrase. It reminds people that even though life isn't fair here, it's even less fair in other places.

MONDAY 29TH JUNE

4.49 p.m.

At school today Bitchface Matfield was moaning at us that we hadn't done our homework. When I said, "At least you're not a child soldier," I got a detention for being cheeky.

I suppose this is what happens when you try to alert people to all the injustices and terrible things that happen in the world. People don't want to hear it. We at the NFPG know that we will have to suffer to get our point across, and we accept that.

TUESDAY 30TH JUNE

7.46 p.m.

Gran said the queue for her pension at the post office was stupidly long because they don't even bother with a decent amount of staff these days. I told her at least she wasn't a child soldier in Africa. Gran said, "Hattie, I bet they look after their bloody old people there!"

That's not the point, Gran, but never mind!

WEDNESDAY 1ST JULY

7.56 p.m.

CRAPBLOODYTACULAR BALLS!!!

Mum just dropped a TOTAL BOMBSHELL.

I HAVE to go on holiday with her and Rob to STUPID Sicily at the end of this month. My brother is allowed to stay at home, but I'm not. WHY?!

I cannot believe this — I am being forced to go on holiday because I am apparently too young to stay with my brother. I went MENTAL and all Mum could say was: "At least you're not a child soldier!"

YES, MUM, I know. But she kept smiling. No one EVER said she could use an NFPG slogan!

8.15 p.m.

I've checked and Africa is nowhere near Sicily, which is a good thing. I can't fight a war — anyone with a gun could see the braces on my teeth shining from a mile off. Mum has made me a sitting target by not letting me have the expensive nice ones.

THURSDAY 2ND JULY

8.12 a.m.

Why are we going to Sicily anyway? Why can't we be like normal families and go to Disneyworld?

9.34 p.m.

OMG OMG OMG.

Goose has just been round and when I told him we were going to Sicily he said, "Hattie, think about it. Sicily? Italians? Italian men? CARLO!!! Your mum could be taking you to meet your real dad."

O M G !!!

It DOES makes sense because why else would you go to Sicily?

10.12 p.m.

OMG!!!

From now I am counting down till OFFICIAL DAD DAY. D-DAY is on its way.

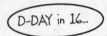

6.37 p.m.

Told Jen today about the Goose Sicily theory. She thinks he's right — at least I think that's what she said. She's had her tongue pierced, and it's difficult to understand her. Jen says it's so sore it hurts to say certain words. So she is communicating mainly through nodding and texting. If her mum finds out she'll go mental.

Then, OMG, Jen said, "What are you wearing to the prom?"

THE PROM!!!

Because of TOTAL heartbreak, child soldiers, revision, helping Gran with *Mario Kart,* bad exam results and trying to find my ACTUAL REAL DAD I'd forgotten about the prom!

AM I A MENTAL??

I now only have about 10 days to get ready. I know for a FACT MGK had her outfit sorted in March and has been building up a Fake Bake tan since December last year! I AM DEAD.

10.32 p.m.

Been on eBay for 3 hours looking for a dress. Just sniped at last minute to win a prom dress — it's AMAZING! It's strapless black with red detail it's GORGEOUS and it only cost 27p! The seller is from

China but I'm sure it will be fine. Going to use Mum's PayPal to pay for it. Even she won't mind 27p!

11.14 p.m.

Just noticed postage is £35. It's still cheap.

11.46 p.m.

Texted Dimple – she thinks it will be touch-and-go whether it gets here or not. Craptacular Hattie strikes again.

D-DAY in 15...   SATURDAY 4TH JULY

11.32 a.m.

Asked the postman today how long things take to get from China to the UK. He laughed and said, "Depends, duck – anything from 7 days to 10 weeks. That's if they send it at all. Bye!"

Stupid letter-box-loving dork machine. And he wears shorts in winter. Hope the mad chav-mongous dog 3 doors away gets him one day.

PLEASE let it get here.

1.01 p.m.

Spoke to Gran about the prom dress disaster. She said, "No problem, Hats – I can run you up something on my Singer." Then she took me to the spare room and showed me this ANCIENT sewing machine that would probably be worth a bomb. Turns out Gran is basically Versace and used to make her own clothes ALL the time. Apparently

Mum LOVED her dresses and people begged her to make stuff for them.

ATTENTION, WORLD — I AM GOING TO BE ALL GORGEOUSNESS! YES, MGK — some of us ARE BASICALLY COUTURE. My real Sicilian dad will LOVE that — the Italians TOTALLY invented style.

2.34 p.m.

OMG what if my real dad is Roberto Cavalli the designer?! Victoria Beckham stays on his yacht. She could be my BFF!

Except for Dimple and Weirdo Jen. But they could come too.

3.55 p.m.

Just told Mum about Gran's offer. She went white with this mad stare and said, "Hattie, I've got something to show you. You must never talk of it to anyone or EVER mention it to your gran or it could kill her."

She went upstairs and came down with a photo. It took me a while to realize who it was. It was Mum when she was about 15 in the MOST craptacular dress you have EVER seen. It was navy blue and white striped with gold wonky anchors stitched all over it. Plus it was long at the front and back but short at the sides. She stared at me and said, "Your gran made this for the most important school disco of my life. I'd been chasing Andy Crouch for 3 terms. She thought it was 'trendy' and 'experimental'. People laughed at me from the night I wore it till I left school. Everywhere I went people sang 'What shall we do with the drunken tailor?'. Under no circumstances, Hattie, let Gran make you any clothes. EVER."

She then just walked off. She actually looked like she was about to cry.

4.12 p.m.
Texted Gran and told her not to worry as Dimple was lending me something. Gran rang me IMMEDIATELY and said, "Are you sure, Hats? I've got some lovely print with mini pansies." I said I was sure.

4.34 p.m.
Thanked Mum for saving me. She just half-smiled. I think this afternoon brought back some terrible stuff for her. Oprah would definitely recommend counselling.

Mum has just saved me from social death. I am going to make her a cup of tea without her even asking. If the dress isn't here by next Friday I will start to panic.

8.32 p.m.

VOM!!!

Jen thinks her tongue may have gone septic — as there is (I MAY BE SICK) a yellow crust round the edges of the stud. She is going to have to tell her mum. She has been trying to hide it from her parents as her mum thinks piercings are the worst kind of modern tribal enslavement and have no place in a body that is truly free. Sometimes

I think Jen's mother is so clever her brain may actually explode.

D-DAY in 14...

SUNDAY 5TH JULY

4.23 p.m.

Googled <u>exploding brains</u> 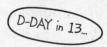. Found out that some people spontaneously combust. This means one minute you are sitting there watching *EastEnders*, the next you are on fire and there is NOTHING you can do to stop it. And it mainly affects women.

MONDAY 6TH JULY

D-DAY in 13...

4.17 p.m.

No dress.

Felt a bit hot today. Got a bit worried then just took my cardie off and I felt fine.

6.23 p.m.

Hot again. Please, God, don't let me spontaneously combust. *Not before I've found my real dad.*

9.12 p.m.

Jen said there is more chance of being abducted by aliens than spontaneously combusting. I think she was trying to make me feel better, but now I'm worried about aliens.

Tuesday 7th July

D-DAY in 12...

7.32 a.m.

No dress.

Apparently there is this massive place in America full of captured spaceships but it's TOP SECRET. WE NEED TO KNOW so we can avoid being taken by aliens.

ARE THE PEOPLE RUNNING THIS WORLD TOTALLY MENTAL?!!

7.54 a.m.

I'm emailing the American president — he looks kind on TV and the first thing he did when he was elected was buy his daughters a dog. ARE YOU TAKING NOTE, MUM? YOU say you are too busy for a pet. The president runs half the world and he has got time.

You can email the White House and tell them what you think.

From: Hattie Moore <helphattienow@gmail.com>
Date: July 7, 07:03:42 PM GMT
To: <president@whitehouse.gov>
Subject: I know Buzz Lightyear and Wall-E are nice BUT

Dear Mr President,

I am part of an organization called the Not Fair Protest Group. We try to make things fair for all — which I know you totally agree with. I am asking you to please, PLEASE make everything you know about aliens public. We need to know what we are dealing with so if a massive jelly thing with black eyes comes to experiment on us we can tackle him.

Thanks,

Hattie Moore

BTW – please tell the First Lady that she dresses really well for someone middle-aged. MUCH better than my mum.

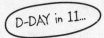

WEDNESDAY 8TH JULY

6.24 a.m.

No dress.

OMG – perhaps my dad got abducted by aliens? You can't write from Mars!!!

That's tragic – it's 2 million per cent more likely that he can't be arsed. This is Hattie Moore talking out of her Uranus – LOL LOL LOL!!!

6.26 a.m.

That joke was UBER craptacular.

10.43 a.m.

Jen's tongue is in a super bad state. And she says she feels really hot. I'm worried that it might be a sign that she's about to spontaneously combust but she says there's nothing to worry about as it's much more likely to be a flesh-eating superbug.

11.25 a.m.

Jen has just been to the school welfare officer. She showed her her tongue – she's been sent straight home and told to go to the doctor IMMEDIATELY.

She must be totally ill. Normally all you get off the welfare assistant is 2 paracetamol and a lecture on how to use a hanky properly.

4.10 p.m.

Jen had to tell her mum. She went MENTAL.

Why do mums overreact to EVERYTHING on Earth? A piercing does not mean you are having actual sex or anything.

THURSDAY 9TH JULY D-DAY in 10...

7.12 p.m.

STILL NO DRESS (from tomorrow I will officially totally be in a panic).

Jen's mum went down to the piercing shop to complain about them piercing a 13-year-old girl. "Big Mick" said it was difficult to tell the ages of people these days and many of them had fake IDs. He said she was lucky that Jen couldn't afford the big butterfly she wanted tattooed on her shoulder.

Jen's mum is now threatening to check her body every day for tattoos. Jen says when she does have one she is going to have it tattooed on her heel because no one will ever look there.

9.54 p.m.

Jen just texted — her mum heard her talk about the heel tattoo. She is now checking her every day for "permanent ink body vandalism" — and verrucas.

D-DAY in 9...

FRIDAY 10TH JULY

5.23 p.m.

OFFICIAL TOTAL DRESS PANIC!

Everybody is now talking about the end of year prom ALL THE TIME. I am NOT for the following reasons:

- I've got nothing to wear as my dress is currently in Beijing.
- I've not got a boyfriend.
- MGK will look gorgeous.
- Even when she doesn't bully me with words, MGK can bully me with stares and craptacular laughing.
- Unless I have major surgery my breasts will not grow 4 sizes in 4 days.

I think I like making lists. It seems to make things easier to cope with.

6.12 p.m.

Tried to call the post office. They close at 5.30 on a Friday. Probably because all their staff are getting ready to go to parties wearing dresses they've nicked from the mail.

7.23 p.m.

My brother just came in and said, "Poor Cinderella has nothing to wear to the ball. Sorry – not Cinderella – her ugly sister." QUESTION – WHY IS NATHAN SUCH A TOTAL PIG DORKFEST?!

8.35 p.m.

Total prom FAIL. Total postal FAIL. Total lack of dad fail. Total LIFE FAIL.

SATURDAY 11TH JULY

D-DAY in 8...

9.23 p.m.

OMG.

My mum knows I have no money and has offered to get me something for the prom. She seems to think she understands what would suit me better than I do. Plus if she's paying for it, she says she's choosing it. AM I ACTUALLY 7?! Rob said I should let her as it's her attempt to "connect" with me, and I need to trust her.

I know she saved me from Gran "thinks she's Chanel" HELL but...

Reasons why I think this is the worst idea EVER:

1. Mum had a perm when she was a teenager — yes it was the '80s, but that's no excuse.
2. Mum thinks that you don't need make-up and that men appreciate the natural look (MENTAL).
3. Mum thinks that Kate Moss looks scruffy. Kate Moss is a goddess. She has no breasts either and it has never stopped her.
4. Mum only buys *BBC Good Food* magazine and never even looks at a fashion magazine. I CANNOT WEAR A NICE QUICHE.

I think I am going to have to say no.

10.46 p.m.

Actually Mum knows better than anyone that if you look stupid at a prom it will be talked about for years and years. AND all the celebrities have stylists that pick their clothes for them.

Plus I can always not go if it's really bad. I'll just say I've got a stomach bug or something.

SUNDAY 12TH JULY

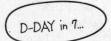

8.32 a.m.

Just a week before I meet my dad.

Mum is going shopping tomorrow. Perhaps I can wear my prom outfit to meet him.

I have given her a list of total NOs:

- anything brown
- frills
- animal print (yes I did love my zebra print coat but I was 5 then)
- anything pink

I said, "Please, Mum, I am also too old for Dora the Explorer." Mum snapped, "Yes, obviously, Hattie!"

But is it obvious, Mum? You still ask me if I have cleaned my teeth every morning, and it's obvious that I would –

just in case a rampant SNOG machine wanted to kiss me right there and then!

MONDAY 13TH JULY

D-DAY in 6...

5.23 p.m.

Mum has come back from shopping. She is going to unveil it after tea. She says it comes from Miss Selfridge, which is actually a really positive sign.

7.34 p.m.

OMG!

Mum has actually bought me something ... good!

It's like a dress with a sheer top with a camisole underneath — it sounds rank but it's quite daring. Plus with my Wonderbra I look like I have actual tits.

Going to the PROM, BABY!!! Hope it is JAMMED FULL OF BOY LOVE MANIACS WHO WANT TO FEAST ON MY LIPS.

TUESDAY 14TH JULY

D-DAY in 5...

8.23 a.m.

Wish Rob would GET OUT OF THE CRAPPING BATHROOM. I NEED TO START GETTING READY.

Actually shouldn't moan. Bet Sicilian men take longer.

9.26 a.m.

Just borrowed Mum's Chanel perfume and put it on my wrists.

10.12 a.m.

Also just put some on my neck.

10.34 a.m.

And the back of my knees. Weirdo Jen told me they were an erogenous zone.

12.01 p.m.

Right. I am going into GET READY MODE. Will write after the prom.

11.46 p.m.

PROM.

Can't write.

D-DAY in 4...   WEDNESDAY 15TH JULY

5.22 p.m.

Being at school today was like being at the centre of massive smirk and whisper storm. TOTALLY CRAPTACULAR.

6.13 p.m.

My mum is officially evil. She may yet get her wish. I may never go out again and may die alone.

How could she have known? She must have asked. It's the only way.

7.34 p.m.

Mum has been up – but I don't want to talk to her. She says she thought she was genuinely buying me something nice and stylish (SHE SOUNDS OLDER THAN GRAN), and that how was she meant to know?

She knows. I can read her like a book.

8.13 p.m.

Dimple called my mob. She said it wasn't that bad. I said that if it wasn't that bad why did Miss Gorgeous Knickers nearly choke on her Diet Coke with laughter and why did everyone – including the teachers that were there – POINT AND LAUGH?!

9.23 p.m.

Teachers who laugh at pupils should be sacked immediately. They could easily scar me for life. I wouldn't mind but NONE of them have a clue how to dress – Dr Richards came in once with WHITE SOCKS AND SANDALS.

And Mrs Bitchface Matfield once wore a catsuit. A catsuit when you are ancient is plain wrong – especially after two children!

D-DAY in 3...

THURSDAY 16TH JULY

4.01 p.m.

Everyone was STILL talking about me at school today. I know how Kate Middleton feels now.

5.14 p.m.

At least my real dad will never get to hear about this. It might put him off me for life.

6.23 p.m.

Dr Phil says sometimes writing things down can help the healing process.

Everything was going good till the man on the decks (who was ancient) started to play with his new £70,000 special effects machine. First there was smoke, which would have been the best snogging fog ever had I got that far with a man. Then there was this strobe thing that made us all look like we were dancing in slow motion, and then he put on this ultra-violet light that made everything white look VERY, VERY bright.

Including my VERY white padded bra.

Because mum had bought me a sheer top, EVERYONE could see EVERYTHING.

I ran out of the school hall, but by that stage it was too late and what's worse the DJ refused to turn the light off as he said he was practising for when he got a residency in Ibiza and what was my problem anyway — girls like to show off their bras?

Yes — when there is something in them. Now the whole world knows I have NO TITS.

7.32 p.m.

Just said that to Mum. My brother overheard and said it's been apparent to the world for many months that I am breastless.

8.23 p.m.

Goose has just been round. Apparently I am now a TOTAL LEGEND as the boys at school know me as the girl who flashed her bra – this apparently makes me cool.

Yeah, Mum – so your plan to keep me caged has gone horribly wrong. My underwear has become the star!!!

FRIDAY 17TH JULY

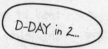

D-DAY in 2...

4.12 p.m.

BREAK UP!!!

MARVELLOUSNESS!!!

Rumour is that MGK's boyfriend asked her if she could get a top like Hattie Moore's as I looked "really sexy". Dare I believe that I, Hattie Moore, am actually a sex symbol, and boys in their heads are doing rude things with me right now?!

That said, ALL clothes should be correctly labelled if they are likely to go see-through. I will bring it up with the NFPG!

5.37 p.m.

I hope no geekazoids are doing rude things with me.

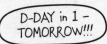

D-DAY in 1 – TOMORROW!!!

SATURDAY 18TH JULY

5.23 p.m.

Done my packing – I've decided to take my see-through tit top, obviously. I have also taken some semi-smart clothes, as when I meet up with my dad I want to look sophisticated. I need him to know I am mature enough to cope with ALL the issues which are (I have googled all these):

*   abandonment
*   parental sabotage of a relationship with another parent
*   loss of self-esteem due to absence of a parent
*   infidelity (probably – my mum)
*   immature maternal figure
*   parent favouring eldest male child as he presents "no threat"

7.36 p.m.

Goose has just been round to wish me luck with my dad. He's told me not to be disappointed if it doesn't work out, as I was "actually great". When I said, "WHAT DOES THAT MEAN?" he just said, "TEXT ME." Then he gave me one of his long looks.

Bet my REAL dad would love Goose. Everyone loves Goose.

NEXT TIME I WRITE THIS I WILL BE IN ITALIA, BABY!!!

OMG – will I have to call my dad "Papa" or something?!!

SUNDAY 19TH JULY

7.14 p.m.

Hotel Prego
Prego, Sicily.

NIGHTMARE FLIGHT.

I got sandwiched on the plane between these girls who were singing "Paparazzi" by Lady Gaga very loudly in weedy voices and two men having a conversation about an Air France crash — they kept saying this is the same model of plane and they've never found out what caused it to crash!

Ended up nearly puking with TOTAL FEAR, and even then Mum wouldn't let me have a mini bottle of vodka to steady my nerves. French children are allowed wine when they are 3!

Now we are at the hotel, which is slightly Chav City — I have already seen about 7 fake Louis Vuitton bags. And there's a teen club called "Chico Bambino" that Mum is FORCING me to join.

I'm not here to make friends. I'm here to meet my dad.

MONDAY 20TH JULY

8.23 a.m.

OMG, there's karaoke tonight. PLEASE, PLEASE don't let Rob do his version of "The Court of King Caractacus".

Just off to Chico Bambino. If they make us do any craft activities with pasta shapes I may actually die.

2.42 p.m.

Chico Bambino may be the finest club ever invented.

There are only two members — me, and an Austrian boy called Jürgen Weber. He speaks English brilliantly and likes emo (Jen would go MENTAL for him). The club consists of a room with unlimited Internet access! TRIPLE YAY!!! Jürgen said he would love to help me find my dad as he enjoys a "superb relationship with his farter" (I know he means "father" but I am not correcting him – LOL!). Jürgen hates just sitting on a beach (like me!), hates karaoke (like me!) and would like to spend the rest of the week "assisting me" and looking at stuff on YouTube.

We both have to go to karaoke tonight though. Our parents are forcing us.

Misery caused by parents is international.

11.23 p.m.

Night of TOTAL SHAME. Rob's "The Court of King Caractacus" got a standing ovation. Even the waiters were doing the actions. Then Jürgen's dad got up and did "Sex on Fire" by the Kings of Leon!!! And the worst thing was he got Jürgen's mum up on stage and sang it to her – VILE!!!

FATAL EMBARRASSMENT caused by parents is also international.

TUESDAY 21ST JULY

9.23 p.m.

Spent all day with Jürgen and HE spent ALL DAY telling me how cool my parents were. Apparently my mother is "kinda hot" (???) and my stepdad is "funny".

I said, "YES, JÜRGEN, BUT he is not my REAL dad – SO LET'S FIND HIM."

Jürgen says we should go into the town tomorrow and look for Carlos. I agreed but we are not doing this until I have put on some fake tan. My actual dad is going to meet his REAL daughter when she looks REALLY brown.

11.12 p.m.

I can hear my mum and Rob coming back from the bar. Mum is STILL singing. PLEASE tell me she didn't do karaoke in front of everybody.

WEDNESDAY 22ND JULY

9.23 a.m.

Apparently Mum was the star of the show last night. Perhaps if I put on loads of fake tan I can actually change my identity and pretend she is not my mother.

10.12 a.m.

Apparently I have to exfoliate before I put fake tan on. They always say stuff like that. I will just have a good wash – that will do.

10.43 a.m.

This stuff stinks. I smell like a melon AND I have to be naked for 20 minutes.

11.26 a.m.

It's drying a bit weird. Like more brown in some parts than others.

12.15 p.m.

OMG – I actually look stripy.

1.01 p.m.

I AM OFFICIALLY A TIGER. Craptacular. My real dad has a daughter that looks like she should be in a safari park.

1.05 p.m.

Jürgen just knocked – told him to come back later.

2.12 p.m.

Just HAD to let Jürgen in. He doesn't like being late. Apparently that's very Austrian. He says no dad would turn his daughter away for looking like a big cat. He obviously hasn't met my real dad who hasn't bothered with me since I was born and turned me away because I was born a baby.

He's just gone back to his room to get his hat. Will write more after we've looked round town.

4.25 p.m.

OMG.

Walked round the town for ages. Saw lots of Italian men playing with their kids. ALL of them could have been my dad. Felt totally depressed and was about to go home when we saw it — a tiny barber's shop called ... "CARLO'S". OMG. OMG. OMG. BUT IT WAS CLOSED!

The good news is, they open again tomorrow at 10 a.m. AND Jürgen can speak Italian. Not going to tell Mum about it OBVIOUSLY — but SO excited. What if it IS him?! What shall I say? I hope Jürgen's Italian is good enough to say, "Dad — why did you abandon me as a baby? Is it because my brother is actually a total Satan and you couldn't stand it any more?"

7.12 p.m.

Jürgen says he might need to refer to his phrase book as the only Italian he knows he learnt in his dad's ski shop and it's about padded jackets, snowboards or sex.

He is actually really mature. Much better than British boys.

7.43 p.m.

No, Mum, I do not want to come with you to watch you make a fool of yourself on karaoke. I am going to watch *Pirates of the Caribbean* in Italian and think about Dad.

8.12 p.m.

Can't understand what the hell Johnny Depp is saying so just texted Goose about Dad and Jürgen. Told him Jürgen was helping me and that he was LUSH.

8.45 p.m.

Just got this back from Goose:

> Hats - don't get your hopes up.
> Gxx

Pissy or what? No mention of Jürgen and totally NEGATIVE. Must be on his boy period!

Anyway I can't worry about Goose — he'll always be around. My dad hasn't been.

9.13 p.m.

Feel sick with nerves.

10.01 p.m.

Still feel sick.

THURSDAY 23RD JULY

1.23 a.m.

Now I can't sleep AND I may VOM at any time.

4.32 a.m.

Have listened to music now for nearly 3 hours. I am so bored of Adele. Yes, you should give up, stop rolling in the deep and GET OUT OF MY ACTUAL LIFE.

7.36 a.m.

Told Mum I didn't fancy breakfast. She asked if I was anorexic. I MISS 1 MEAL and she thinks I have an eating disorder. Everyone knows you have to miss at least 3 weeks of food AND faint in 2 PE lessons before the school nurse will let you even see the counsellor.

8.21 a.m.

Feel like vomming but hungry at the same time. This is what pregnancy must be like.

8.59 a.m.

Jürgen will be here in 1 minute. Here we go. My heart is really bumping.

12.53 p.m.

Goose was right. AND I KNOW WHAT YOU ARE THINKING — "we knew that was going to happen." Yes WHATEVER. BUT you have to keep trying. If you didn't know your real dad YOU WOULD. And yes I am upset so just ... JUST JUST JUST...

4.56 p.m.

How many times do I have to write things down before everything becomes better?

Basically we got to Carlo's and went inside. It was packed with men but I saw this middle-aged guy who really, really honestly did slightly look like me.

Jürgen was brilliant — he just went right over and said, "Carlo?" and this guy just burst into tears. I thought, OMG, he has been waiting for this moment. He knows!!! BUT then he said something that sounded like "Papa morto" — and pointed to a photo of this really old man above one of the big dryer things.

Basically Carlo died a couple of years ago at age 91. He's not my dad.

I really can't see my mum doing it with a massively old man. Rob is younger than her and everyone knows you shouldn't have sex when you are over 60 as it could kill you.

Anyway we made a man cry and I didn't find my dad. Craptacular-est day of all days.

Jürgen kept saying sorry and stroking my hair.

That was the only thing that wasn't craptacular.

7.23 p.m.
Mum just asked me if I had been crying. I told her I had got Factor 30 in my eyes and to just go to karaoke and leave me alone.

So she did. Thanks, Mum – thanks for your support.

8.12 p.m.
Just thought: why is someone whose dad died 2 years ago still crying?

What AM I MISSING OUT ON?

Friday 24th July

9.14 a.m.
Mum just came in and said, "Hattie, stop MOPING!!! Get out, have some fun and get some sunshine!"

Whatever, Mum – I actually LOVE my bed right now and I am staying here.

10.01 a.m.
Jürgen just knocked. I've told him to come back at 1.

1.01 p.m.
Jürgen must be camping outside my door because he turns up at 1 o'clock TO THE SECOND. Must be as bored and lonely as me.

7.43 p.m.
Spent all afternoon with Jürgen. He wanted to google more Carlos but it's like looking for a Prada bag in Primark. TOTALLY IMPOSSIBLE and pointless.

Jürgen keeps stroking my hair. It's nice.

9.34 p.m.
Texted Jen. She texted back and said that baboons stroke hair and groom each other to show sexual interest.

Dear Jen – I am not a baboon and I do not have a big red arse.

SATURDAY 25TH JULY

9.34 a.m.
Me and Mum just had a hugemongous row. She was furious when I told her about the barber.

She screamed, "GET CARLO OUT OF YOUR HEAD. YOUR DAD IS NOT CALLED CARLO and doesn't LIVE HERE!!! We've come here because I have always wanted to visit Italy. YOU NEED TO FORGET ABOUT YOUR DAD and concentrate ON THE NOW!!!"

So I shouted, "BUT, MUM, here are the facts — while you are pretending to be Madonna every night I actually NEED A REAL FAMILY."

And THEN Mum said, "I have NEVER done a Madonna song at karaoke" — like that is IMPORTANT!!!

She stormed out like she ALWAYS does. I'm not even upset any more — just angry and pissy and OVER IT.

Jürgen will be here soon. To stroke my hair. Like a monkey.

6.23 p.m.
I think Jürgen might fancy me. I can't imagine snogging someone from another country. Except for Taylor Lautner and he's American so not technically foreign.

10.03 p.m.
According to Jürgen, who heard it from his parents, Mum didn't sing anything at karaoke tonight.

Why do I always end up feeling guilty about hurting her even when I have a really good point?

SUNDAY 26TH JULY

9.11 a.m.
Jürgen's mum just asked Mum at breakfast why she didn't sing last night. Mum said she didn't feel like it, and looked at me.

Jürgen has invited me to a water park this afternoon. I usually hate swimming because of my lack of tits BUT I like slides, and Jürgen, so I am going to put my breasts out of my mind.

Like I have to put everything important to me out of my mind.

7.24 p.m. ♡ ☀

OMG – DAY OF TOTAL HOTNESS! ◎

I can't believe what's happened. Jürgen and me were having a real laugh at the water park. Then as we were both soaking wet wearing just our swimming costumes he said something in German and STARTED TO KISS ME.

We had this amazing wet snog that went on for ever. And Jürgen was putting his wet hands all over my wet back and it was like something out of a film. TOTALLY EROTIC!!!

He says we shouldn't tell anyone yet but that we should go to the water park again tomorrow. LOL – oh yes, we should.

10.34 p.m.

Just been to karaoke. Actually quite enjoyed it – mainly because Jürgen kept winking at me.

11.13 p.m.

Keep smelling my arms. The smell of chlorine is such a turn-on to me now.

MONDAY 27TH JULY

8.34 p.m.

Jürgen and me got told off at the water park today for getting too "heavy" with each other in a public place. Jürgen said we must have been very, VERY heavy, as the Italians basically invented sex. What has happened to me? I'm like a Hotness Goddess. Texted Dimple – she was really happy for me but asked me to be careful.

I'm not going to have sex or anything, Dimple!!!

TUESDAY 28TH JULY

4.12 p.m.

Jürgen and I have been dry snogging all day today. It's not as good.

Jürgen also told me that lots of Austrian girls lose their virginity early on. I told him I am not Austrian.

WEDNESDAY 29TH JULY

7.01 a.m.

I think Dr Phil would say I am snogging away my inner pain over my dad. Dr Phil you are probably right but I am still going to the water park for UBER wet hotness.

6.34 p.m.

I feel bad writing this but I got a bit bored with wet snogging today. In fact I went on the mega-splash super slide 5 times while Jürgen watched. I think he might be slightly more into me than I am into him.

THURSDAY 30TH JULY

9.18 a.m.

Jürgen has told his parents that we are seeing each other. They are dead relaxed about it. I have told him that my parents would go mental so he has sworn his parents to secrecy.

10.34 p.m.

Jürgen's parents got drunk tonight at karaoke and ended up telling Mum and Rob that we'd been kissing by the pool. Mum was furious.

They called her up to sing "Moves Like Jagger" by Maroon 5 but she refused just so she could sit at the table and tell me how disappointed she was that I couldn't confide in her. LOL!

I said, "But, Mum, I didn't think you were that interested in my life." She went mental at this but I couldn't hear what she was saying as Jürgen's dad was doing his version of "Umbrella" by Rhianna.

FRIDAY 31ST JULY

9.42 p.m.

Mum has just given me a lecture about how my relationship with Jürgen is going nowhere and how I shouldn't let it get serious.

In what can only be described as the best thing I have ever said, I told her I knew that it couldn't go anywhere — but I was just enjoying the physical side.

This is not strictly true as I am bored of wet snogging BUT I knew it would wind her up.

She said that once we were home we had to have a serious chat. Tell you what, Mum — you tell me about my dad and I will tell you about my hotness.

SATURDAY 1ST AUGUST

11.13 p.m.

Last day with Jürgen. We did some more snogging (my lips are actually chapped now), and then he did Katy Perry's "I Kissed a Girl" at karaoke and dedicated it to me.

Mum was cross at him till Jürgen's mum said, "Would you prefer it if Hattie sang it?" Mum didn't say anything, but later on she mentioned to Rob that she didn't want to keep in touch with the Webers as she thought they were "a bit continental". And she quite fancied Cornwall next year.

SUNDAY 2ND AUGUST

5.23 p.m.

BACK HOME.

Well I still haven't met my dad. BUT right now, near Vienna, a boy is thinking of my hotness.

Jürgen was in tears when we said goodbye. He said, "Will I ever see you again?" I said yes — but I don't know if it's even possible, or if I even want it.

Surely if a relationship is going to work you can't be bored of kissing them after less than a week?

7.12 p.m.

Goose has just been round. He was sorry about my dad but all he wanted to know about was Jürgen! When I said I didn't think it was going anywhere, Goose said, "Yeah – he doesn't sound right for you."

And Goose is basing that on WHAT?!

12.13 p.m.

Dimple and Jen came round. They both think Jürgen sounds gorgeous and I should probably think long term about him.

2.13 p.m.

I think there IS a way that we can keep our love alive. I have found out that a cheap airline actually flies to near where Jürgen lives – you can get a ticket from just 2p. It might be destiny that we are meant to be together.

2.43 p.m.

Just worked out if you include airport taxes, airline taxes, green taxes, the fee for luggage (I will need to take some clothes) and toilet taxes, a single fare comes to £328.47.

I think destiny is against us.

Tuesday 4th August

4.12 p.m.

Went to see Gran. Told her about Jürgen.

She said it was a classic holiday romance and I shouldn't take it seriously. She reckons she had one with a waiter in Torremolinos in 1975. She nearly left Grandad for him.

When I asked why she didn't, she said, "When I saw the amount of olive oil he put on his potatoes, Hattie, I knew it never could have worked."

That has to be the most rubbish reason ever for not having a relationship.

6.01 p.m.

Actually I didn't like the way Jürgen dipped bread in his hot chocolate.

6.43 p.m.

Or the way he ate oranges.

7.01 p.m.

The small things do affect a relationship. Jürgen and me are just going to be Facebook friends.

Wednesday 5th August

4.32 p.m.

Mum hasn't said much to me since we've been back but today she asked if I still wanted to be a celebrity chef.

When I said yes, Mum said she'd decided that I am going to be helping her in the cafe. I know why she has made this decision:

- It gives me less time to investigate my dad.
- My wet snogfest has worried her.

When I said I shouldn't even be working at my age she just shouted, "Hattie, do you want 20 extra pounds a week?"

Answer YES. So OFFICIALLY I am now being used for slave labour. And it starts TOMORROW.

THURSDAY 6TH AUGUST

5.13 p.m.
OMG. I have to wear a hairnet when I am preparing the sandwiches. When I complained that this was mental, Mum said, "Be thankful you haven't got a moustache — or you would have to wear a moustache net too."

7.05 p.m.
Was that Mum trying to tell me I have got a moustache?!

I do fear facial hair.

9.32 p.m.
Just texted Dimple to ask her if I had a moustache and she said no.

FRIDAY 7TH AUGUST

4.43 p.m.

Dimple just rang to ask if me asking her if I had a moustache was actually my way of saying that she had a moustache. I was like, "NO – seriously, Dimps, you have NO top lip hair. I asked because my mum mentioned that people working in a cafe with a moustache have to wear a moustache net, and I thought she was saying I had a moustache."

Dimps said, "Isn't that weird? I thought you were saying that I had a moustache because you thought your mum was saying that you had a moustache when she told you about people who do actually have to wear a net because they have a moustache."

5.12 p.m.

I think that may have been the most boring conversation ever written in a diary.

6.01 p.m.

I have had the most boring day ever – that's the problem.

SATURDAY 8TH AUGUST

6.12 p.m.

I hate to agree with Mum but it's true. After working all day you don't feel like doing anything. Even looking for your REAL dad.

SUNDAY 9TH AUGUST

4.13 p.m.

Asked Mum if she would consider putting on some of my Gordon Ramsay-inspired specials:

- goat's cheese salad
- fresh hummus with crudités
- tomato and courgette frittata with a tomato ketchup coulis (actually it's just tomato ketchup but a coulis makes it sound better)

Mum said that she didn't think that builders would really go for any of those — but if I liked I could try the tomato frittata tomorrow.

MONDAY 10TH AUGUST

7.23 p.m.

I have decided all builders are total rubbish — ONLY ONE OF THEM went for my tomato frittata. They all just stuck to boring old bacon sandwiches and burgers. No wonder all men die of heart attacks at age 40 — ALL of them eat rubbish.

Goose came in and Mum gave him some of my frittata for free — it's unbelievable what that boy gets away with!

Mum says I can try the goat's cheese salad tomorrow but I can only make two of them. Great.

TUESDAY 11TH AUGUST

5.12 p.m.

Tyler, who ate my frittata yesterday, ate my goat's cheese salad today. He said it was nice and sharp. He is 17. I think I might like him. I know I've only just finished with Jürgen – but he was just a fling.

WEDNESDAY 12TH AUGUST

2.13 p.m.

Told Goose about TYLER. HE SAID ALL BUILDERS WERE THICK and that I could do better. Goose is down on anyone I remotely like. It's weird.

THURSDAY 13TH AUGUST

4.13 p.m.

Tyler came in and asked if I had any specials on. When I said no, he said, "That's a real shame."

He likes my food – he MUST like me!!!

6.23 p.m.

Marrying a builder would be magnificent. He could do EVERY job in the house. Mum has been waiting for Rob to do the tiling on the shower for about 5 years. Driving instructors can't help you with anything – except your parking. And then Mum just picks a parking space that has 2 free spaces either side so she always fits.

7.35 p.m.

Goose reckons that while I am busy working he will keep on hunting for my dad. He thinks technically you can get to the end of Google and all the information in the world. Basically unless my dad is from outer space Goose thinks he can find him.

It's really sweet of him but only one person can really help me find my dad. And she's too busy at the cash and carry.

FRIDAY 14TH AUGUST

5.43 p.m.

Sat with Tyler at lunch. He is the most boring, BORING man in the history of boring men. He just talked about *Top Gear* for 2 and a half hours. I don't care if Jeremy Clarkson smashed a train into a people carrier, and how "cool" it was.

And THEN he said, "You don't have a lot to say for yourself, do you?"

NO, I DON'T. BECAUSE YOU DON'T SHUT UP.

If all boys are going to go on about is cars then I would rather NOT have a boyfriend.

7.12 p.m.

Goose has found nothing new about my dad. But he did find a great video of an antelope crashing into a cyclist.

I don't think I want any boys who are friends either.

SATURDAY 15TH AUGUST

8.39 p.m.

Went to see Gran today. She says boys can wait. Anyway she thinks I should marry a royal. She thinks that I would be great at "regal duties" and she would really enjoy living with us, as the queen can afford to have a walk-in bath put in.

10.02 p.m.

Texted Dimple. She thinks I would be quite a good princess.

10.34 p.m.

Texted Jen. She says it's fine for me to marry someone really posh but she is still coming emo to the wedding.

SUNDAY 16TH AUGUST

8.23 a.m.

Can you actually marry a royal if you don't know who your dad is?

9.12 a.m.

Even Goose doesn't know. He has just found something on eHow called "How to Marry a Royal". He is bringing it round tomorrow for us to go through.

Goose doesn't think I should go for a royal, and that "happiness could probably be found closer to home". Goose, you might want to stay in Derby all your life but I want some GLAM! AND I want a tiara.

7.12 p.m.

Called Gran. I told her that I probably was a bit too moody to be a royal wife and that I would need to tell the queen who my dad was. Gran said she "had gone right off the idea too" because she "wouldn't have a private life any more and that would play havoc with her bingo schedule".

8.32 p.m.

Just realized my gran went off me being a royal when I mentioned my dad again. I will have to get married one day, everyone, and then I HAVE to know.

Monday 17th August

8.34 p.m.

Goose's eHow article was useless. I can't find my own father let alone discover some noble bloodline. The only thing I can do on the list is "act with indifference and contempt". That's easy — I will start with my brother. LOL!

Tuesday 18th August

5.45 p.m.

Acting with indifference and contempt in a cafe just gets you in trouble.

Tyler complained to my mum that I just "bloody threw his burger at him". Then Fat Dave the foreman said that I had "an attitude problem" when delivering his brew, and that he had "enough surly women to cope with at home without having to deal with a right little madam while he was at work".

Can't wait till these people have to be nice to me and I get my breakfast made for me.

6.36 p.m.

My mum is not buying her mother of the bride outfit from Primark. The queen will go mental.

7.01 p.m.

All royal marriages end in divorce anyway. Wish I could divorce my brother. And my mum!

7.16 p.m

OMG — you CAN divorce your mum. You can divorce your parents. Found it on eHow. Why didn't Goose find this?!!

Perhaps that's what I'll do. That's what they always do in soaps. Threaten someone who loves you with divorce and they do WHATEVER YOU WANT! If I said, "Mum, we're through!" I know she would TOTALLY tell me about my dad.

7.26 p.m.

That is SO an *EastEnders* ending. You can even hear the "dum dum dum der der der DUM DUMS!!!"

7.34 p.m.

Goose thinks divorcing my mum is nasty and stupid. Well, not telling me who my dad is is nasty and stupid too, Goose.

Wednesday 19th August

7.54 a.m.

Just told my mum I wanted a divorce from her due to our "toxic relationship".

MUM:	(MASSIVE LAUGH) Who do you think you are, Hattie? Macaulay Culkin?!
ME:	(CALM BUT SLIGHTLY PSYCHO) Tell me who my dad is and I'll call off the divorce.
MUM:	(REALLY LAUGHING) Only American film stars divorce their parents.
ME:	That's not true! An American gymnast did it too.
MUM:	Hattie, I will tell you about your dad when it's the right time. Not when you threaten me with something stupid.

9.37 a.m.

Rang the council and asked if they give financial assistance to people who have divorced their parents. The woman laughed and said no. Neither can you get a flat or a clothing allowance. What is wrong with this country?!

11.45 a.m.

Who IS Macaulay Culkin anyway?

12.11 p.m.

Macaulay Culkin is the little boy from *Home Alone*. Only he's about 40 now. Probably with kids of his own he actually speaks to.

THURSDAY 20TH AUGUST

12.01 p.m.

Postman knocked this morning. It was my prom dress from China.

Sometimes EVERYTHING is crapbloodytacular.

1.12 p.m.

OMG – my PROM dress is spectacular! I can't believe it cost 27p (plus the postage). EVEN I THINK I LOOK GOOD. I'M KEEPING IT ON ALL DAY. MAYBE ALL ACTUAL YEAR.

1.25 p.m.

Texted photo of me in dress to Dimple and Jen. THEY LOVE IT. Jen thinks I look like Bella Swan in it. YES, EDWARD CULLEN, COME AND SNOG ME!

1.29 p.m.

But don't bite me and make me into a vampire as I actually like the day time.

2.23 p.m.

I know Edward Cullen is lush and everything but what's the point of a boyfriend you can't go on holiday anywhere nice with? Bella hasn't thought that through. When she's in Florida he will be sat at home with the curtains closed.

2.45 p.m.

Jen says living in a cloudy place is a small price to pay for an all-consuming, eternal and passionate love.

3.12 p.m.

Rob just brought me up a random Jaffa Cake and said I looked AMAZING. Feel bad now. I wish he was my dad. But he's not, is he?

FRIDAY 21ST AUGUST

6.54 p.m.

Had a Facebook message from Jürgen:

> Hatz,   22 minutes ago
> I am kissing a girl called Gerda. She is hot.
> Stay cool,
> Jürgen

1. I don't care.
2. I don't actually care.
3. "Stay cool"? GEEK.
4. Gerda sounds like a type of yoghurt.

Bet she gets bored of kissing him too.

SATURDAY 22ND AUGUST

8.23 a.m.

Just had a text from Gran – it says I have to go round there urgently as she's had a "life-changing" email.

OMG – it could be my dad.

4.32 p.m.

When I got round to Gran's she made me swear a vow of total silence. She said she didn't know how they had managed to get hold of her email address, but she had been sent this. I've printed it out:

From: <princecokerokoyeandmikethedog@hotmail.com>
Date: August 20, 14:53:15 PM GMT
To: <glamgran@netscape.co.uk>
Subject: Nigel chase me! Help me and my dog will give you millions!

Dear Friend,

My name is Prince Coker Okoye. I used to live amongst peacocks and friendly tortoises in a palace they call "Very Nice Palace". Then my dog Mike bit a Nigel. He cross at Nigel for riding giraffes. Nigel get angry and Mike and me come to live in bungalow in the Gambia. I weep now with poor. Mike eats Moths. Sadness is all over my sofa. And in my trousers.

Because we had to flee fast I have left $20 million US in a bank account in Nigeria. I am unable to collect this money as if I return to Nigeria my dog Mike forced to work in a diamond mine until his tail becomes a droop. He may even be sold to bad chefs and end up in a sauce. My tortoises are already a curry.

If I return I certainly will fail to feel alive and may even have my hair toes and fingers trimmed with a very big gun.

I beg of you, friend, you can help me release my money. Please send me $1,000 so I can pay for international bank fees to transfer my money from Nigeria to Gambia. In grateful for this I will give you 5% of my earnings. If you send me your bank details I will do this immediately when my money arrives.

Please keep this transaction absolutely secret. Tell not even your beloved partner or pet for fear I will be captured and fed to the madness of Nigel's elephants. If your interest is mine I would want you to contact me immediately through my email address: princecokerokoyeandmikethedog@hotmail.com

Thank God she told me. I explained it was a scam to get money off her. Gran didn't believe it at first till I said, "How many people do you know with a dog called Mike?" Gran shouted, "Goose has got a cat called Colin!" But I said, "Just read it through again – why would a prince contact a senior citizen from Derby?"

Gran agreed that thieving scams like this were wicked, but admitted that when Mum was little and when she didn't have much money she regularly took vegetables from farmers' fields. Gran as a thief?! I cannot believe it. She thinks people who overfill their wheelie bins should get life. She could see that I was shocked. She said, "Poor people will do desperate things, Hattie – never forget that. Be grateful that your mum can and does work hard to afford nice things for you."

I am grateful to my mum but when I try to tell her it comes out wrong. Like when I said the top she got me recently was "really nice – especially considering it came from Dorothy Perkins".

Sunday 23rd August

11.32 a.m.

Gran just called me to thank me for saving her from "scum scammers". I may actually be a hero and this hero will be spending Sunday doing nothing.

12.45 p.m.

OMG – I have just had the biggest shock ever looking in Rob's paper.

I have just seen a photo of Daniel Radcliffe – now when he was Harry Potter he was dweeb central – but now he's TOTAL HOTNESS. He's wearing a tux and looks like an actual proper guy. There is no way you would think he was ever a small geeky wizard with a pet owl!

5.32 p.m.

I have OFFICIALLY got a massive crush on Dan Radcliffe. Dimple and Jen have seen the photo and they think it's fine as now he is clearly a real man.

Monday 24th August

9.21 p.m.

I swear – working in the cafe is easy when you can think about Daniel Radcliffe in his tux ALL DAY. I made 8 ham and tomato rolls without even having to engage my brain. This must be how everyone gets through having to work — THINKING OF HOT SEX!

TUESDAY 25TH AUGUST

5.12 p.m.

My brother has heard about my love for Dan.

Now he is calling me Hermione and asking where my wand is, because "he knows where Daniel's wand is". He thinks he is Captain Hilarious — he is not. He is Flight Lieutenant Not Funny At All, and I wish he would go on an unarmed mission somewhere very dangerous.

He is also TOTALLY OUT OF DATE. DAN IS A MAN. HARRY POTTER IS GONE!

7.52 p.m.

Just told my brother he might find a nice little place in Afghanistan to stay in if he fancies moving out.

He said, "Oh, Hattie, you are so hilarious — you should be on *QI*."

8.13 p.m.

Actually I think I should be on *QI*. They never have women on there, except for Jo Brand. I know my mum loves her, but she's not very glam, is she?

8.43 p.m.

Mum says you don't need glamour when you have humour. This is TOTAL, TOTAL crap.

WEDNESDAY 26TH AUGUST

4.21 p.m.

Spent another day thinking about Dan. He'll be surrounded by gorgeous women all the time but perhaps someone ordinary will suit him better. Perhaps after years of being a huge celeb he just wants to go to Maccy D's and share a McFlurry.

5.32 p.m.

If I could persuade him to grow a beard I think we could go just about everywhere without the paparazzi noticing. Not an old man beard — one of those sexy ones that feels furry not prickly.

5.45 p.m.

Actually a Creme Egg McFlurry could get stuck in even a sexy beard so forget that.

6.12 p.m

Texted Dimple. She says we can avoid the media by having takeaways.

THURSDAY 27TH AUGUST

5.32 p.m.

Another great thing about Danny (this is what I would call him) is he is completely rich and could probably afford a log cabin in the Cotswolds away from everyone. With a roaring fire and a servant who did everything (but disappeared to a shed when you wanted him to).

FRIDAY 28TH AUGUST

(I don't know the time — it's been like a dream today...)

Oh, Dan... I can't tell you how much I am totally in love with you. I love the way you treated me — when you touched me I came alive and I know that for ever I am changed. Thank you for understanding that it's not the right time for me yet. When you held me in front of the fire and said, "I can wait," it meant the world to me. I want it to be perfect and it very nearly is the perfect time for us — I promise. I will soon be ready to give myself to you. I am a wild horse — please treat me tenderly and I can be tamed. All my love, Hxx

---

SATURDAY 29TH AUGUST

7.32 p.m.

Came home tonight from seeing Dimple to find Mum and Rob sitting on the sofa looking furious.

Mum has OBVIOUSLY read my diary because she said: "WHO IS DAN?!"

I thought, RIGHT, I am going to teach her a lesson, so I said, "Dan is none of your business!"

She SCREAMED back, "Hattie, I will find out who it is and I will be seeing his parents. HOW FAR HAS IT GONE? Where does he come from? Have you been to the doctor?"

When I said no, she went loony mental and shouted, "Hattie, boys at this age are dreadful, and just after one thing."

Then I just walked out and she started to cry. I hate hearing her upset but NO WAY should she be reading my diary!

8.32 p.m.

Mum thinks I am doing serious stuff. She actually thinks I HAVE DONE MAJOR FULL-ON THINGS!!! I am a sex goddess and all I have done is wet snogging and bum-fondling.

9.32 p.m.

Mum has just been up — she'd been crying for ages.

She said she really wants me to talk to her about what is going on in my life, especially about things as important as SEX.

She reckons it's very important that I look after myself, as there are some bad people out there. And I am a "lovely, beautiful girl with so much potential."

Yes, I feel terrible.

Oh, IT'S NOT FAIR — I've done nothing wrong. It's HER that read my PRIVATE stuff. She can suffer for a bit longer.

SUNDAY 30TH AUGUST

7.32 a.m.

Mum just came in with a coffee and said, "Please talk to me, Hattie."

I just told her I am not ready to yet. I am staying in bed all day.

5.54 p.m.

My brother just said to my mum, "Don't be ridiculous – it's all made up! Look at the poster on her wall, Mum – it's the boy who plays Harry Potter. She's just got a vivid imagination!"

EVIL. I turned into a mental and said, "YES, IT IS MADE UP – so what?! AND HE'S NOT HARRY POTTER. HE IS A REAL MAN NOW!" And Mum said, "Oh, Hattie – why did you make us think that you were...?"

"Because, MUM – everybody in this family still treats me like I am 6. Can't you see I am actually a woman now?!" This sent my brother into hysterics so I just ran upstairs.

THEY ALL GANG UP ON ME. SICK OF IT.

MONDAY 31ST AUGUST

7.12 a.m.

A note has just been pushed under my door in my brother's handwriting.

DEAR HATTIE,
SORRY I HAVE GOT TO DUMP YOU. I HAVE TO FIGHT VOLDEMORT AND HIS EVIL ARMY. PLUS I'VE MET SOMEONE AT HOGWARTS.
LOVE,
DAN

I HATE HIM. My brother is officially more terrible than the Dark Lord.

8.32 a.m.

Another note. From Mum.

Hattie – it was wrong of me to read your diary. You are a young woman now and entitled to your privacy. I promise I will never do it again. When you are a parent you will realize just how much you want to protect your children because you love them so much. I know you are not a baby any more but you will always be my baby.

NEVER GOING TO HAPPEN MUM.

9.09 a.m.

Just went downstairs and gave Mum a hug and told her I loved her. She hugged me and said, "I should have trusted you." Yes, Mum, you should have.

I think Dr Phil would think I was probably the most emotionally mature 14-year-old he had ever met, and his audience would clap and whoop for me.

2.13 p.m.

Texted Dimple and Weirdo Jen – I have called an emergency meeting of the NFPG tomorrow.

TUESDAY 1ST SEPTEMBER

4.53 p.m.

The Not Fair Protest Group today agreed on the following:

* Privacy laws that protect celebrities should be extended to teenagers.
* Reading someone else's diary should be illegal.
* If you are found reading someone's diary you should be given truth serum and be forced to reveal things you are embarrassed about on national TV. (It can fill the slot when Jeremy Kyle is on his holidays.)

Dimple told Jen and me today that she rarely thinks about boys and sex but she thinks loads about chocolate. I didn't want to say anything, but I don't think this is actually normal. Then again, Dimple has never wet snogged. She is bound to think Dairy Milk is better.

5.12 p.m.

Actually I think I would prefer a Bounty bar to snogging Jürgen again. Bet Gerda would too – LOL!

Going round to see Gran tomorrow before I go back to school.

WEDNESDAY 2ND SEPTEMBER

4.13 p.m.

OMG – I have just seen something so dreadful I may need to have counselling. When I rang the bell Gran told me to come in and she was stood there in front of her full-length mirror in just her BRA AND PANTS!!!

- Gran has stretch marks everywhere. In fact her stretch marks have their own stretch marks.
- The backs of her legs are so hairy she looks like a gorilla. She says she can't reach them in the bath any more.
- Her breasts look like they have collapsed. Gran caught me looking at her and said, "Don't look so shocked, Hattie – this is what age and childbirth do to a woman." When I pointed out that Helen Mirren is old and STILL looks amazing, Gran said, "Life isn't fair, Hattie. That woman has clearly made a deal with the devil and with gravity."

Apparently Gran was standing in front of the mirror because she has bought a new book on dressing to flatter your body shape. She was trying to work out which body shape she is. She thinks she's an hourglass. The book says she's an apple.

I can tell her now – she's a pumpkin.

I borrowed Gran's book. I am a brick, I think.

Anyway I intend to start the new school year as a new woman.

 THURSDAY 3RD SEPTEMBER

BACK TO SCHOOL.

7.39 a.m.

My school uniform has everything that the book says my body shape shouldn't wear. Pleats, shapeless shirts and ties. Might raise it with the NFPG that school uniform should be dependent on your body shape.

7.56 a.m.

Dimps says uniforms based on body shape wouldn't work as no one wants to admit they are an apple.

4.32 p.m.

School was a total nightmare. The only good thing was that Danielle Lance told us she has stopped shaving her armpits — because apparently in Germany (where she went on holiday) it's the normal thing to do. Perhaps that's why Jürgen liked me — I was smooth!

4.49 p.m.

I know Jürgen was Austrian but it's probably all hairy in that part of Europe.

FRIDAY 4TH SEPTEMBER

3.57 p.m.

Mum heard me moaning about my school uniform this morning. She thinks that we should count ourselves lucky! She had to wear a hat to school! Mum thinks we need

to get involved as with a couple of accessories
make our school uniform ROCK. Mum thinks that
gay man can truly celebrate the female body. Why
would a woman want other women to look good? Think
about it, Hattie."

Mum has a very dim view of girls.

I would LOVE a gay friend though. Perhaps Goose might be gay?

5.12 p.m.
Goose wants me to know he definitely isn't gay – though
there is nothing wrong with being gay.

5.34 p.m.
Mum watches a lot of fashion and makeover shows but
doesn't seem to act on any of their advice. Why is this?

7.01 p.m.
I love Mum and Gran but I don't want to end up looking
like them. Must find a way to look better.

Saturday 5th September

8.05 p.m.
I should be doing my Science homework but I'm writing to
Helen Mirren instead with a question. Jen is going to let
me copy her homework – because she wants to know the
answer too. I'm going to send it to helenmirren@gmail.com
and helenmirren@hotmail.com because she's bound to use
one of them.

From: Hattie Moore <helphattienow@gmail.com>
Date: September 5, 19:44:14 PM GMT
To: <helenmirren@hotmail.com>, <helenmirren@gmail.com>
Subject: OMG! You're old but you look AMAZE!

Dear Helen Mirren,

Thank you for reading this email.

As I have turned 14, I am naturally thinking of what happens as I get older. If you don't mind me saying, you are nearly 70 but still look great. Would you mind telling me:

1.   What foods you eat.

2.   What moisturizers you use.

3.   How much water you drink.

4.   What plastic surgery or Botox you have had.

I promise that this information is solely for my personal use and I will not sell it to *Look* or *Heat* magazine.

I look forward to your response.

Hattie Moore

PS You are our favourite dame. Gran says unlike most people who get one, you actually quite deserve it.

I feel bad but I might tell *Heat* if she comes back with something a bit juicy.

SUNDAY 6TH SEPTEMBER

9.12 p.m.

Goose came round after going to the boot sale with Rob. He auditioned for the school musical on Friday. I don't

---

think he'll get a massive part — I've heard him singing in his bedroom.

Monday 7th September

4.32 p.m.

OMG — TOTAL SHOCK! According to Dimple, Goose HAS landed the big role in the school play — he is Joseph. ACTUAL Joseph. The man with the amazing coat. Surely this can't be right?!

5.43 p.m.

It IS TRUE!!! Just caught Goose in the back yard doing exercises. He is trying to "muscle up" as some scenes require him to be bare-chested. Perhaps because I have known him for years I am missing something, but I can't see Goose as a big star.

6.12 p.m.

Dimple says Goose is buff — and Dimple doesn't fancy anyone!

Tuesday 8th September

4.01 p.m.

Everyone at school is talking about Goose.

Weirdo Jen says that Goose has a "deepness" that is really rare for a teenage boy (???). Apparently people who saw him audition said it was better than anyone who has ever been on *The X Factor*.

If Goose gets rich and famous it will be brilliant.

7.54 p.m.

I am trying to write a story on terrorism for English homework. It's very difficult to write about anything when all I can hear is Goose singing "Any Dream Will Do" at full blast.

WEDNESDAY 9TH SEPTEMBER

9.36 p.m.

I think today I may have written the most brilliant story in the history of English.

I have pretended to be a suicide bomber and instead of the craptacular "And then I was dead", I ended it with a news report about how many people I injure.

THURSDAY 10TH SEPTEMBER

3.45 p.m.

OMG – what if my dad is a suicide bomber or a terrorist? Perhaps the government have banned my mum from telling me who my dad is?!

4.01 p.m.

Jen says it all sounds very unlikely but if my dad is a suicide bomber he is probably dead anyway.

6.54 p.m.

Goose just came round. He says I am a mental and it's much more likely my dad is just a bit of a git than working for a major world terrorist group.

Then he let me feel his biceps. They are VERY FIRM these days.

FRIDAY 11TH SEPTEMBER

4.11 p.m.

Got my terrorism story back! I got a C+! Dr Richards called it "unrealistic"?!!

He said there is no way that a suicide bomber would have a Maccy D Filet-o-Fish as a last meal and he wouldn't spend 10 minutes agonizing over whether he should wear Gucci or Topman.

Dr Richards lives in a village with his wife and a thick dog – what would he know?

SATURDAY 12TH SEPTEMBER

12.12 p.m.

Gran was round really early this morning because she wants Rob to teach her how to drive. She wants a car and a disabled badge. This would mean she could basically park in Asda's front foyer.

Rob looked very worried but he has a strict all-age policy, and doesn't think it's too late for anybody to learn.

However, Gran is an official mental — and since she has had her cataracts done she thinks she can do anything. She keeps saying, "How hard can it be? Chavs have cars!" (I taught Gran the word "chavs" — now she uses it in every sentence.)

Rob is taking Gran out later this afternoon.

5.13 p.m.

OMG — Rob says Gran was quite good! Gran looked happy — Rob looked a bit pale. Apparently Gran nearly stalled on a level crossing but apart from that it went OK.

Isn't nearly getting killed by a very big train actually not very OK at all?

SUNDAY 13TH SEPTEMBER

7.22 p.m.

DAY OF TOTAL DRAMA.

After her last lesson Gran was feeling really confident so she decided to back out of the drive herself and wait for Rob on the road. Unfortunately Rob had left the car in first gear and Gran lurched forward straight into the shed. There was one hell of a crash and Rob rushed out and went MENTAL. He started yelling at Gran that his livelihood was on the line, and the car was his bread and butter, and what the hell did she think she was doing — was she SENILE? Then Mum started shouting at Rob, "Sod the car, what about MUM?!!"

Next thing we know, Goose rushes round and says he knows first aid and on no account should Gran move as she could have severe spinal injuries. He was brilliantly in control, even when Gran tried to get out of the car to shout at Rob for leaving it in first gear – "like a trap".

Then Gran started saying all sorts of mentalness, like: "Goose, you are lovely – you are like a grandson to me", and "Think about marrying close to home when you're older. Close to home. Really close".

Luckily the ambulance came then and they put Gran on a special board and took her to hospital. She just has a bit of bruising and whiplash.

Goose was just so brilliant today – in control like a really cool teacher. Even Gran did what she was told, and she is usually uncontrollable.

9.43 p.m.

Just want to say I do NOT fancy Goose. I just admire him in a crisis.

MONDAY 14TH SEPTEMBER

7.45 p.m.

I have asked Rob to give me a driving lesson.

He has totally refused on the basis that a) I am only 14, and b) he will never teach another family member ever again. He says his dual controls have only just recovered from Gran.

Why are ancient people allowed to drive, and under-17s not? We have better eyesight, better brains and we really WANT to drive to see our friends.

We *NEED* to drive.

9.20 p.m.

Goose popped in. I told him how great I thought he was. He said it was just his first aid training and then let me feel his calves. They are like rock! He is going to be a very muscly Joseph.

TUESDAY 15TH SEPTEMBER

6.12 p.m.

Did an amazing thing at school today. Clare said her sister and her friends had this thing called "The Anonymous Honesty Note". Basically you get a piece of A4 paper, everyone writes down a comment about you, folds the paper hiding the comment, then passes it on to the next person until you have a whole range of very honest comments about you.

We did it.

Here are mine:

- Funny in PE – though I think you are sensitive on the quiet.
- Moans about her brother all of the time.
- Has her foundation one shade too dark. You are not "sand beige". You are "ivory bisque".

- Has a fit brother.
- Has a photo of herself as a crazed podge-monster trying to eat an actual fork (obviously this is Dimple).

I have never been funny in PE deliberately. That's a worry. Do I look stupid when I run?

I am not over-sensitive AT ALL.

My brother is not attractive.

I had my foundation picked by one of the women behind the counter at Debenhams – and if anyone knows about make-up it should be them!

7.35 p.m.
Just practised running up and down in front of my mirror. It's only about 5 steps but I think I look totally fine. Nothing bounces. Unfortunately.

8.03 p.m.
Mum says everyone knows that women on make-up counters are orange.

WEDNESDAY 16TH SEPTEMBER

4.32 p.m.
I asked Dimple today if my foundation was too dark. She pulled a really weird face and said, "Yes ... a bit."

I said, "Dimple – why didn't you tell me?!! I have been looking ORANGE for months and probably now everyone is

---

laughing at me and I will NEVER get a decent boyfriend and WILL PROBABLY DIE YOUNG IN A FLAT ON MY OWN AND NO ONE WILL FIND ME FOR 6 MONTHS!!!"

Dimple reckons that she didn't want to upset me, and that sometimes I can overreact!

I hardly ever ****ing overreact!

THURSDAY 17TH SEPTEMBER

6.12 p.m.

Asked Goose if he had ever heard boys talking about me being orange. He said no – I was still just "Hattie see-through tit top". This is a good thing.

My foundation can't be that bad.

7.01 p.m.

Just put my make-up on. It IS that bad. Why didn't I see it?! What else can't I see that's actually RIGHT IN FRONT OF ME?!!

I am getting rid of all my make-up.

FRIDAY 18TH SEPTEMBER

4.57 p.m.

Goose came round and saw all my make-up in the bin. He says he needs to look tanned for Joseph so he will use my old foundation as he will look practically brown.

I've had enough of school already.

SATURDAY 19TH SEPTEMBER

8.34 p.m.

Went round Gran's. She was watching *Coronation Street* with a HUGE packet of crisps. She seemed very calm and said, "Hattie – it's important to get inner peace. I have never felt more relaxed with life. Every day is like a gift."

She puts her new-found inner peace down to the special healthy, happy muffins that her friend Denise has been baking. Apparently they have a special mix of herbs and seeds in them that will help her arthritis.

I so admire Gran. She is still thinking about diet and her figure even when most of her friends have just given up. One of her friends actually has a tub of Häagen-Dazs Baileys ice cream with a whisky for breakfast as she's going to die soon anyway.

SUNDAY 20TH SEPTEMBER

8.43 p.m.

Went round Gran's again just as her friend Denise was bringing round some muffins. I smelt them and, OMG, THEY WERE FULL OF DRUGS.

I said, "Gran, smell them – I think there might be dope in them!" (I know because my brother smokes it sometimes.) Gran kept saying, "Hattie, don't be silly – I lived through the '60s – I do know what drugs smell like. We invented drugs!"

She didn't believe me so I shoved a muffin under her nose and yelled, "ERRR, GRAN – WELL, SMELL THAT THEN!" Gran said, "OH MY LORD – IT IS MARIJUANA. I'm an illegal! I'm full of illegal. If I was at the Olympics now I'd be stripped of every medal!"

She then ran to the kitchen and threw all 4 muffins to the birds.

If my mum knew, she would explode with mentalness.

11.02 p.m.

"My gran is on skunk" sounds like the best *Jeremy Kyle Show* EVER.

MONDAY 21ST SEPTEMBER

6.32 p.m.

Told Dimple and Jen about Gran but have sworn them to secrecy.

I am tempted to try drugs but I am not going to. Jen said sometimes you start imagining the worst things on Earth and you see terrible visions. What if my breasts looked even smaller when I was stoned? Or if my zit farm actually started to grow or something? Or MGK moved into my actual house?! It's not worth it.

TUESDAY 22ND SEPTEMBER

8.13 p.m.

Gran is worried that her usual birds have not come back this morning. She is concerned that they might be confused somewhere after eating her drug muffins. She thinks the Royal Society for the Protection of Birds would HATE her if they knew that she had fed robins and blackbirds skunk. They would launch a full investigation and she'd totally be front page of the *Daily Mail*. She says she can see the headline now: "Evil Pensioner Drugs Wildlife For Her Own Evil Kicks".

9.34 p.m.

Gran has found 4 stoned birds in the garden! They are too drugged-up to fly but they're eating everything in sight. Gran is worried because they are SO chilled out it'll be really easy for cats to kill them. She then tried to give ME a lecture on using drugs!!! "See what dope does to you, Hattie?" I said, "Gran, it's your fault that they're like that — and I'm not a chaffinch!"

WEDNESDAY 23RD SEPTEMBER

7.46 p.m.

Gran has set up a direct debit for the Royal Society for the Protection of Birds. It's out of guilt.

Thursday 24th September

4.36 p.m.

Just when you thought school actually couldn't get any more BORING we found out that our trip is to the Science Museum to see ... wait for this ... "100 Years of Plastics". I cannot believe someone has actually thought it would be a good idea to fill a room full of washing-up bowls and pens and make people look at it!

Friday 25th September

10.32 p.m.

OMG – SERIOUSLY think I may have come up with the best plan ever. They always give us an hour at the end of the day to do what we want at the museum. I reckon we can EASILY get across London on the Underground and visit Topshop on Oxford Street. It'll be a Wednesday so there will be hardly anyone around at 3 o'clock! Texting Dimps and Jen NOW.

Saturday 26th September

1.12 a.m.

Dimple and Jen are ON for the TOPSHOP TRIP (TST). And it gets even better – Jen thinks we can also make it to Camden Market and get some vintage emo stuff. She has wanted a full-length velvet cape for AGES! I think I'd go more for a HOT black leather pencil skirt. OFFICIALLY even hotter than ANYTHING MGK owns.

SUNDAY 27TH SEPTEMBER

6.34 p.m.

Spent all day planning the TST. Feel guilty because Mum came up with a coffee for me without me even asking and said, "Hattie, I am really proud of you for concentrating so hard on your homework."

8.12 p.m.

The Science Museum is in South Kensington. We can get to Oxford Street in about 20 minutes. Then round Topshop in record time and back – no one will even notice we are gone!

Just realized there is no way we can do Camden Market too. I will have to break it to Jen.

9.01 p.m.

Jen is gutted as she thinks a cape would strengthen her Wiccan abilities – but she understands that Topshop MUST come first.

MONDAY 28TH SEPTEMBER

4.57 p.m.

A load of other girls have heard what we are planning to do – now they all want to come. Here is the problem – if the whole class ends up going shopping we will be in the worst trouble ever. We have had to officially ban Dibbo Hannah from being involved at ALL. We went on a school trip last year and she got her arm stuck in a postbox.

TUESDAY 29TH SEPTEMBER

7.02 p.m.

MGK threatened to tell Matfield about the TST until she realized that it is NOT COOL to tell teachers about anything. She has now promised not to tell anyone unless she is tortured.

7.55 p.m.

Who would torture MGK?!

8.25 p.m.

Dimple says torture for MGK is not wearing lip gloss. LOL. FACT.

9.13 p.m.

They have given us a quiz about plastics to fill in as we go round the exhibition tomorrow. We are paying Dibbo Hannah with a zebra bangle from Topshop to fill ours in.

9.26 p.m.

TOPSHOP HERE WE COME!!!

WEDNESDAY 30TH SEPTEMBER

8.45 p.m.

I am currently in my bedroom after the worst day of my life.

Mum just brought me up a bowl of soup. I only get soup if I'm ill or in trouble. I'm in trouble. The biggest trouble ever. I haven't been in this much trouble since I drew a poo factory in primary school.

I think I may have ruined my life — for a skirt.

10.53 p.m.

TOTAL disaster.

We left the Science Museum at 3 and the bus was due to pick us up at 4.30. Dimple had brought her rucksack so we could hide all of our Topshop bags in there. We gave ourselves 20 minutes to get to Topshop, 20 minutes to get back, and half an hour there.

First of all we got on the wrong train, headed towards Heathrow — not Cockfosters (HA!!! COCKfosters — who thought that was a good name?!). Then there was a suspect package at Green Park, which meant we couldn't change there so we had to go to some other station and then there was a naked protest by an animal rights group so we couldn't stop there! I know rabbits and guinea pigs matter but why today?!!

We didn't get to Topshop till 3.45. We only had time to buy one thing each, and Dimple ended up being searched twice because of her rucksack.

Then Weirdo Jen thought she had spotted Kate Moss going into the changing rooms so we all followed her in — and it just turned out to be another skinny woman with blonde hair.

Back on the Tube and it was EVIL — people tutting and pushing us out of the way. No one cared. Jen said we should wait for a less crowded train but every train that came was so packed you couldn't get on it. Then a man in a bobble hat carrying 6 empty plastic bags approached Dimple and asked her if she was related to Jesus. So we just got on any train we could, in 3 separate carriages.

Dimple and me managed to find each other and made it back to the Science Museum at 5 p.m. Matfield was waiting for us, and just roared, "WHERE IS JENNIFER?!" And when we said we didn't know SHE TURNED INTO A MENTAL. Did we know how much trouble we had caused? Did we know how much trouble we were in? Did we know we could have been killed? When I said we had only nipped to Topshop — not France — Bitchface Matfield SCREAMED, "GET ON THE BUS NOW!"

Just at that moment Weirdo Jen turned up — she said she was late because she was "soaking up the urban madness", and "trying to find peace in chaos". She also said it was a well-known fact that those "stuck between 2 worlds often use the Tube system", and that the "Underground is closed at night because no one wants to work on it as it's actually too scary". At that point Matfield nearly exploded.

When we got on the bus it all went TOTALLY silent. Miss Gorgeous Knickers did one of her super-smug smiles but FLORENCE (ultimate rebel) nodded her approval. She said we were beyond amazing and she would have LOVED to have come.

When we got back to the school the headteacher was waiting for us. We are not to come into school tomorrow, and she would like to see us all on Friday — to talk about "our futures".

THURSDAY 1ST OCTOBER

10.01 a.m.

Mum has been up. LISTEN TO THIS:

MUM: What the HELL did you think you were doing? You are only 14!

ME: All I did was nip to Topshop! We had seen everything else in the craptacular stinking Science Museum. I can even tell you what happens when you fart in a spacesuit!

MUM: That is not the issue — YOU COULD HAVE BEEN KILLED!

ME: But I could be killed here!

MUM: There is more chance of dying in London because it is full of mad people. It was supposed to be an educational trip and you squandered it. If you don't start taking your education seriously you won't be able to go to university.

ME: MUM, I WANT to be a fashion designer or a chef and I don't need to go to university for either of those. Gordon Ramsay

```
                    didn't. Jamie Oliver didn't.
                    Chanel didn't!!!
      MUM:          They were incredibly talented!
      ME:           OH THANKS, MUM. Are you saying
                    that I am not?!!
      MUM:          Yes, I am. You've got a lot to
                    learn.
      ME:           WELL, THANKS, MUM. THANKS A LOT.
```

And then I started crying and she said, "Don't turn on the waterworks, Hattie!" so I shouted, "I want to go and live with Gran!"

But I can't. I'm not allowed to live in sheltered accommodation.

FRIDAY 2ND OCTOBER

6.12 p.m.

Mrs Cob had us all in today. Dimple looked like she had been crying a lot as she's never really been in trouble before.

Mrs Cob said she was very disappointed with all of us, as she saw us as intelligent young ladies who were destined for really quite good things, but we put the superficial world of retail before satisfying an enquiring mind.

This from the woman who clearly last went shopping in the last century!

Anyway we are suspended till next Wednesday. And in that time we have to do a whole project on the formation of plastics to make up for what we missed at the crapping stinking rubbish SCIENCE MUSEUM, which should be closed permanently as it is the most BORING PLACE ON EARTH.

7.46 p.m.
Just remembered that the Science Museum had a pair of Roman tweezers – which means that even 2,000 years ago bushy eyebrows were a problem!

8.12 p.m.
And there was a reusable condom – URGH!!!

Actually perhaps it's an all right place.

I've messed up big time, haven't I?

SATURDAY 3RD OCTOBER

2.12 p.m.
Nylon, which is a plastic, was first used for stockings and tights.

OK, perhaps plastic is useful.

4.32 p.m.
Gran has heard what has happened – she wants to see me tomorrow.

SUNDAY 4TH OCTOBER

12.01 p.m.
Gran just went MENTAL at me. Is there anyone that isn't cross with me?

1.14 p.m.

Answer? No. Dimple's parents have rung my mum to say that I am leading their daughter into bad behaviour — and my mum agreed!

2.01 p.m.

Dimple just texted to apologize for her parents.

They are making her bath her gran every day. That's a terrible punishment. Even her ears are hairy.

7.54 p.m.

My brother just came in and said, "Hats — all this will be forgotten in a week ... until I remind them FOR EVER!!!"

I'd like to see my brother in a museum. Dead and stuffed and behind glass.

MONDAY 5TH OCTOBER

5.23 p.m.

My life just gets better... Goose came round and gave me a lecture, and said I should stop being such a pain in the arse.

When I went to say, "But I don't know my dad", Goose interrupted and said, "Hattie, that's no excuse — and it's tedious. Loads of people love you — including me. London is dangerous. Even Kate Moss wears a stab-proof Prada bra."

I think the Kate Moss bit is crap but he might be right on the rest of it.

TUESDAY 6TH OCTOBER

4.32 p.m.

Back to school tomorrow. Dreading it. Wonder if we will be seen as cool or stupid?

WEDNESDAY 7TH OCTOBER

6.12 p.m.

The answer is: stupid.

MGK has told everyone that we are really naïve as we don't understand the "true wild nature of the capital". Apparently when she goes to London she leaves a whole day for Topshop. Everyone does. "Except chavs from the Midlands who don't understand fashion."

Handed in my plastic project and the worst thing is Matfield, the evil cow, didn't even read it. She just ripped it up in front of our eyes saying, "If you waste my time, I am going to waste yours." I could have written anything or just repeated the word "pants" for 12 pages!!! Do teachers actually do what they are paid to do?!

THURSDAY 8TH OCTOBER

7.53 a.m.

Topshop disaster was over a week ago yet I am having to tell Mum EVERY TIME I do ANYTHING. I cannot even go to the toilet without a full description of what's going on. She even watches me brush my teeth.

8.34 p.m.

Miss Gorgeous Knickers has bought herself a small dog. She is carrying it around everywhere and has called it Princess. It's like this skinny thing with big eyes and a pink bow on.

Well, they say that dogs look like their owners.

AND SHE HAD THE NERVE TO CALL ME A CHAV!

FRIDAY 9TH OCTOBER

5.34 p.m.

LOL!

Like a complete DOUGHNUT, MGK brought Princess into school! She got free during assembly and went mental. Mrs Bitchface Matfield was screaming, "Who brought that dog in here? Bringing pets into school is strictly against school rules!"

Princess ran around for ages until someone managed to catch her by offering her a HobNob from the staffroom. MGK was furious: "Don't feed my darling human snacks – she'll get fat!" TOTALLY RIDICULOUS!

I bet if Princess did get fat, MGK would get rid quick.

We were all pissing – till Matfield said "TOPSHOP IDIOTS, STOP LAUGHING."

WHEN can we ALL MOVE ON?!

SATURDAY 10TH OCTOBER

4.23 p.m.

Just spoke to Dimple, who follows MGK on Twitter (Dimple follows everyone – even the prime minister.) Apparently MGK is unhappy with Princess as she ate the bow on her head, and refuses to wear fashion accessories – including her fake diamanté Gucci collar (REALLY classy).

That'll be because she's a dog – not a Barbie doll.

7.34 p.m.

Dimple just told me that MGK tweeted about "stupid Topshop chavs who are cruel to her dog". I've told Dimple we are suing. We cannot be seen as people who are chavs.

7.39 p.m.

Or people who are cruel to animals.

8.14 p.m.

Mum says no way can we afford to sue. And perhaps we are Topshop chavs as we put clothes before school. Which she thinks is really chav. No, Mum, it's NORMAL.

SUNDAY 11TH OCTOBER

2.12 p.m.

Princess has chewed the sofa and peed all over the carpet. The vet says that Princess is showing classic stress symptoms and may have small dog syndrome.

MGK is apparently regretting her decision to get a dog. Not as much as her mum's carpet is! LOL!

5.32 p.m.

I think I love Princess. She chewed one of MGK's stilettos and crapped in her wardrobe. Weirdo Jen says animals often have a very keen sense of a person's true heart. I think Princess is psychic and has picked up that MGK is pure evil.

Monday 12th October

12.34 p.m.

It's official! MGK is getting rid of Princess. Her mum cannot take it any more and she doesn't have the right Dyson to pick up dog hair.

MGK is fine with it because she has failed to bond with Princess and thinks she may be a mental anyway.

5.23 p.m.

Told Gran about Princess. She likes a dog with attitude and would be quite happy to take her on. She wants me to ask MGK how much she is selling her for. Gran says she wants MGK to realize that we are "a family with a bit of disposable income". That means tomorrow I will have to have a conversation about a dog, with a dog! LOL!!!

TUESDAY 13TH OCTOBER

4.16 p.m.

MGK LOVED the fact that my gran wants Princess and couldn't wait to ask, "But is she sure she can afford it?!"

MGK wanted £200 as she is Kennel Club registered. The thought of my gran giving that cow money so she can buy yet more gorgeous outfits makes me sick.

WEDNESDAY 14TH OCTOBER

7.34 p.m.

This is SUPERB! MGK's parents say she has to GIVE Gran Princess for FREE as well as all the bowls and everything, as it's only fair if she is taking the responsibility.

My gran is a TOTAL HERO. TEAM GRAN AND PRINCESS EPIC WIN!

8.16 p.m.

MGK's parents actually seem to be quite nice. Perhaps she's adopted!

THURSDAY 15TH OCTOBER

1.34 p.m.

Gran just texted. Princess has arrived! MGK's parents dropped her off about half an hour ago.

2.10 p.m.

Princess has been rolling in her own poo in Gran's back garden.

3.23 p.m.

Princess ripped up one of Gran's scarves and has eaten half a box of Crunchy Nut Cornflakes.

3.55 p.m.

Princess has puked up a quarter of a box of Crunchy Nut Cornflakes.

Princess is the ultimate rebel. She's her own woman — even though she's actually a dog.

FRIDAY 16TH OCTOBER

6.49 p.m.

Gran has taken Princess to bingo. Gran put her in a special harness and wore dark glasses pretending to be blind. It's all because people with visual impairments get an extra-large bingo card, a free dabber, and 10% off chicken and chips in the early-bird bingo sessions. Gran and Princess are like partners in crime.

I think they are a bad influence on each other — if they were at school they would be split up.

9.34 p.m.

Jen thinks Princess and Gran knew each other in a past life. Her theory is that they were soldiers who died in a war. When I asked Jen why Princess had been reincarnated as a dog, Jen said it's probably because it's the last thing the soldier saw before he died.

10.32 p.m.
OMG – please don't let the last thing I see be a worker ant.

10.35 p.m.
Or a massive pair of Gran's knickers.

SATURDAY 17TH OCTOBER

5.13 p.m.
I had to take Princess for a walk today. She refused point-blank to leave Gran – I had to PULL her all the way to the mini-mart, and when I tied her up outside she made such a fuss it was unbelievable. She started whining and moaning at the top of her voice, and I came back out to find there was a whole crowd round her saying, "Ohhh – are they cruel to you?" When I tried to explain to them that Princess was the most spoilt dog in the history of the universe and Gran cooked her a sirloin steak every other day and even let her choose her own TV programmes, they just tutted and said I shouldn't leave her outside in the rain. Then as soon as I untied her she ran home and wouldn't stop running till she was at Gran's front door. Gran couldn't wait to get her dry while I was just left there to get pneumonia.

8.12 p.m.

Gran has asked me to dog-sit Princess tomorrow while she has an emergency appointment at the chiropodist. When I said, "But it's Sunday," Gran said, "Corns as bad as mine don't observe the Sabbath, Hattie."

SUNDAY 18TH OCTOBER

7.12 p.m.

I think today there may have been a complete miracle, but I have got a MAJOR dilemma on my hands.

Princess went MENTAL the moment Gran left the house. While she was crying I googled <u>baby cries when parent leaves the room</u> 🔍 and basically Princess has something called "separation anxiety". It said "try to comfort and rock the baby" so I put Princess in my arms. She was fine for 30 seconds – THEN SHE BIT ME and ran upstairs straight under Gran's bed. I tried to get her out with a Mars bar but she was having none of it, so I had to get under the bed with her.

That's when I saw it: LOADS of stuff that belonged to Mum. ALL in her handwriting. Her name scribbled all over everything. Old CDs, school certificates (she was good at DRAMA!) and a box labelled:

> Memories

OMG – inside the box were 3 books dated 1994, 1995 and 1996. I HAVE FOUND MUM'S ACTUAL DIARIES. I was NEARLY SICK.

Princess tried to eat them but I barked at her and she ran off. And then — AND THIS IS TYPICAL — I was just about to read them when Gran opened the front door. I cacked it, ran downstairs and pretended I'd been to the toilet. Gran was too busy patting Princess to care.

1996. That's the year I was born.

That diary MUST have my real dad in it.

Thank you, Princess. You shall now be known as Princess the Wonder Dog.

I have to work out a way to spend time in Gran's house. There MUST be a way.

It's half-term. I've got a week to find out the truth.

9.03 p.m.
I've called an emergency meeting of the NFPG. Jen and Dimple will have some ideas. They know how important this is to me.

10.45 p.m.
I know I sound like a mental barking at Princess — but it was an emergency.

10.52 p.m.
Why are diaries belonging to Mum at Gran's house? It MUST be because there's stuff in them she doesn't want me to see. She used to hide my Christmas presents around Gran's house in EXACTLY the same way.

Half-term.

MONDAY 19TH OCTOBER

2.34 p.m.

Jen and Dimple have just been round. They thought I wanted to discuss whether it was fair or not that I read my mum's diaries! OF COURSE IT'S FAIR. SHE READ MINE!

Dimple says 2 wrongs don't make a right. Jen warned me I could be encouraging bad karma. I think this is my mum's karma for invading MY privacy! Anyway it's not about revenge — it's about finding out about my dad.

When they saw me getting pissy they started talking about ways to read the diaries. Jen suggested pretending to faint by Gran's bed and while I am "unconscious", flicking through. That would never work. Dimple, however, is a total genius as she said, "Offer to clean your gran's house. You will get to read them and she will think you are magnificent!"

That's EXACTLY what I am going to do tomorrow.

9.34 p.m.

Told Goose about the plan. He said he understood that I wanted to read the diaries but I might not like what I read.

What does THAT mean?!!

TUESDAY 20TH OCTOBER

9.28 a.m.

Gran just got massively offended at me offering to clean her house.

She snapped: "I am quite capable of cleaning my own place, Hattie. Are you suggesting I am dirty?" When I said no, she said, "I'm not ready to go into a home YET, young lady!"

Texted Dimple. She said she'd forgotten my gran was a bit eccentric.

12.01 p.m.

Perhaps I can just go round Gran's every day and pretend to go to the toilet lots.

That's gross, but what choice have I got?

1.23 p.m.

Just googled going to the toilet lots 🔍. Might pretend I am diabetic. Diabetics go to the loo every 5 minutes.

2.45 p.m.

Jen suggested that I just take the books. Gran will probably NEVER check – it's under the bed. All I need to do is sneak in there and get them.

6.04 p.m.

Just rang Gran and asked her if I could come and see her tomorrow. She said, "Sorry, Hattie – Princess and I are going to a special line dance for pets and their owners."

7.01 p.m.

Mum has heard that I offered to clean Gran's house. She's now offering to let me clean our house.

My brother thinks this is hilarious. It's not.

WEDNESDAY 21ST OCTOBER

5.32 p.m.

Mum came in today and asked me why I like spending so much time with Gran. She wondered if it was because I didn't feel like I could talk to my own mum. I couldn't say, "No, Mum, it's because I want to read your diaries", so I just pretended that it was because Gran had nicer biscuits at her house.

Mum didn't believe it but she couldn't argue as it is actual fact that Gran has M&S chocolate digestives and we have Asda rich tea at most.

THURSDAY 22ND OCTOBER

8.23 a.m.

YES!!!

Gran has to go to a funeral this afternoon of one of her bingo friends.

She had bought Princess a black waterproof dog coat and everything but apparently the crematorium doesn't allow any pets at all. So I have to dog-sit...

WHICH MEANS I GET TO TAKE THE DIARIES!!!

6.21 p.m.

I HAVE THEM!!!

I sneaked them out in my school bag. Gran didn't even care — she was too busy giving Princess 12 mini sausage rolls and the remains of a gala prawn ring. My gran always brings some of the buffet home. She went to a wedding once and put half a hog roast in her clutch bag.

I am going on about Gran because I am so nervous about what I'm about to read.

7.02 p.m.

I'll start with 1994. I need to know everything.

8.23 p.m.

OMG — my mum's life was so boring in 1994.

The diary is only half filled in and it's full of craptacular facts like "Nathan said 'cat' for the first time today" or "Nathan ate his first sausage today!" WHO CARES? I cannot believe my brother was annoying me years before I was born!

If it's not about Nathan it's about how much she loves Take That! It's pathetic.

There doesn't seem to be anything about men or love or anything. IT'S DULLSTER BEYOND BELIEF.

And she was 21 at the time — OLD!!! And she calls me immature.

9.04 p.m.

Dimple and Jen have both texted tonight asking about the diaries. I have told them the truth:

They are MORE BORING THAN RS.

I'm moving on to 1995 tomorrow.

FRIDAY 23RD OCTOBER

2.35 p.m.

I've had to get Goose round. 1995 is unbelievable. I take it all back. Listen to this:

27/4/95

I know it's wrong but all I can think of is C. I know he's moved on and I accept that. No, I don't. He's the love of my life. I have to pretend every day that I'm fine with everything but I can't — I love him. He's great with Nathan — a brilliant dad. We must be able to make it work — we were young when it all happened, but ... I have to see him every day with her. Yes, she's beautiful but she's a bit ... up herself. I pretend to be fine. But I'm not. I'm not. I'm dying inside.

Goose agrees "C" must be Carlo. I'm a bit gutted because it seems like he was nice to Nathan when HE was a baby. So what was MY problem? Goose says I need to read more before I think of things like that.

The trouble is I keep getting disturbed – Mum keeps coming in my room, Nathan keeps coming in being STUPID, and Rob keeps coming in and starting conversations that go nowhere. It's because they think I seem a bit sad.

It's not – it's because I AM TRYING TO CONCENTRATE! LEAVE ME ALONE.

SATURDAY 24TH OCTOBER

8.12 p.m.

My mum's life in 1995 was like something you see on TV.

21/5/95

C came round to see Nathan. He talked about her and how excited he is about the baby. I asked him if he was happy and he just said, "I miss you so, so much" and we kissed there and then. I said, "Stay the night", and he said, "I can't... I can't... She needs me!" I shouted, "I've GOT your baby!" And then "Back for Good" came on the radio and C started to cry and just left.

So confused. I know he wants me. He MUST do.

AND!!!

7/6/95

C stayed last night. It was amazing. How can I do this? I work with her!

I see her all the time. I know it's dreadful but I accepted it and so should she. He said, "In a way she was just borrowing me – wasn't she?" I feel awful. She's having his baby. She's vulnerable. But love is love – you can't deny it!

If I said anything like that Mum would go mental!!

The FACTS SO FAR: my mum is having an affair with a colleague's partner who used to be her partner and Mum and this other woman have to see each other every day at work. And her friend is pregnant.

Seriously it's like *Coronation Street*!!!

10.39 p.m.

OMG – suddenly realized that somewhere out there I have a half-sister or brother!

Please NOT another Nathan. PLEASE.

SUNDAY 25TH OCTOBER

4.12 p.m.

How can I go back to school tomorrow and concentrate? I am in the middle of finding out everything about my life!

Dimple thinks I should throw myself into my school work to forget about the diaries, but EVERY DAY there's a new revelation. Today it was:

14/6/95

Mum came round. She warned me about him. She says I know what he's like and I should keep well away. It will come to no good — like last time. I told her she stayed with MY dad despite the fact he went to prison for stealing letters when he was a postman. She was angry at that but she can't deny he's a great dad to Nathan. And Nathan needs a father. You can tell already he has attitude!

My GRANDAD WENT TO PRISON. The way Gran talks about him you would think he'd been a saint!

(Back to school.) **MONDAY 26TH OCTOBER**

4.09 p.m.

Who cares about ANYTHING they can teach me at school — want to get home to read!

8.23 p.m.

Mum kept talking to me tonight. Then Dimple wanted some advice on lipstick (!), then Jen texted me to say she had had a worrying sense that my aura was unsettled.

ARGGGHH!!!!!

Everyone, just leave me alone.

11.02 p.m.

Mum still sleeping with C. Nathan won't sleep at night and Robbie Williams has left Take That. Mum cried and is worried that she feels over-sensitive about it all.

No mention of ME yet.

11.10 p.m.

That was all 1995, by the way. Though Nathan is still annoying now.

TUESDAY 27TH OCTOBER

4.56 p.m.

FINALLY!!!

2/7/1995

I must be. It feels just like it did with Nathan. I am crying at everything – Yellow Pages adverts, poor Robbie leaving Take That. I daren't go to the doctor. I just know though. And I know this will make him come back to me. I'm carrying his baby now. It's a mess but I'm not sorry. He'll come back.

I hope it's a girl. I've always wanted a girl.

Mum wanted me. That's actually lovely.

WEDNESDAY 28TH OCTOBER

7.32 p.m.

19/7/1995

Told C. He went mad at me. Shouted, "You did this on purpose!" I didn't – but I'm not sorry. I wanted it. I want it. He said, "If you think this will make me come back to you, you are wrong! I love HER. She's having my child!" When I said, "So am I!" he said, "Well, that didn't make me stay with you before, did it – so why should it this time?!" Started to cry. How can he be such a bastard? I've been stupid. But I'm not sorry. I'm going to look after this little person.

Poor Mum.

8.10 p.m.

Just went downstairs and gave Mum a hug. She said, "What was that for?" I said, "Does there have to be a reason?"

But there is a reason. My dad is a pig and you love me.

THURSDAY 29TH OCTOBER

7.34 a.m.

Depressed. What if I have total bastard genes in me?

4.43 p.m.

Dimple and Jen had a word with me at lunchtime. They don't think I should read any more in the diaries as it's really upsetting me. But it's not as easy as that. I NEED THE TRUTH and finally I am getting it.

6.34 p.m.

Actually not going to read any more tonight. Might cry.

FRIDAY 30TH OCTOBER

8.34 p.m.

Goose came round and I broke down. He said he had tried to warn me that I might not like what I read but I wouldn't listen. I just thought it would be horrible stuff about my mum being a cow – which I knew already. Now it turns out that my dad is one of those people that Jeremy Kyle and Dr Phil REALLY, REALLY yell at.

Goose just looked at me and said, "Your dad has got craptacular taste, Hats, because you are really quite ... OK."

Sometimes with Goose it's weird – it's like he is not saying what he wants to say.

11.21 p.m.

I am going to leave it for a few days. Can't handle any more.

Saturday 31st October

6.13 p.m.

Gran has gone trick-or-treating with Princess
tonight. Gran's dressed up like a witch
and Princess is dressed up in a bat
costume. She wasn't happy wearing
wings — till Gran blackmailed her with
a deluxe pork pie.

7.34 p.m.

Gran collected 7 bags of Haribo Party Mix, 3 Kit Kats,
18 fun-size bars and £5.34 in cash! Someone even gave
Princess a lamb chop!

At least it's taken my mind off ... stuff.

8.36 p.m.

Dimple just called. She doesn't know how to tell me this
but apparently tonight MGK tweeted, "Just seen my old
dog trick-or-treating with the old dog of one of the
Topshop chavs."

I AM NOT A TOPSHOP CHAV!

8.44 p.m.

AND I WILL KILL HER IF SHE HAS A GO AT MY
GRAN.

I'm not telling Mum. She'll go up the school again and it
wouldn't do any good. MGK can torture me out of school
in a MILLION ways.

SUNDAY 1ST NOVEMBER

9.34 p.m.

Had to read more. HAD to.

18/9/95

It all hit the fan today. He told her. She
came round. Quiet. More scary than being
angry. "We need to talk." "What does he
want?" "I don't know – but we have to
manage this now. There are 3 children
in this. We need to act like grown-ups." I
agreed. I can see why he likes her. She's
pretty. A snob, but she tried to be adult. "I
hate you for what you've done. But you must
have hated me for what I did. So we'll have
to get over it."

Who IS this other woman? She's amazing. If someone had
nicked my boyfriend I would have killed her!!!

MONDAY 2ND NOVEMBER

8.01 a.m.

Goose was practising *Joseph* at 6.45 this morning.

How many other people in the world have to wake up to
"Give Me My Coloured Coat"?

Turned the radio up very loudly to drown him out.

7.36 p.m.

Feel very lonely at the moment. I love Dimps and Jen but even when I'm with them I feel like I'm not a part of anything. Dimple suggested a meeting of the NFPG today but I'm just not interested.

9.14 p.m.

Tell you what isn't fair. My mum NEVER uses full names in her diary — just initials. It's like she knew that in the future I would be looking.

This is just the sort of thing I wish Dr Who could go back in time to change.

TUESDAY 3RD NOVEMBER

10.39 p.m.

19/10/95

People are saying that it must be a girl by the shape of my bump! I hope it's a girl. I'd like a better relationship with her than what I have with my own mother. Would love to go shopping with her and talk to her about her problems. I would want to be more a friend than a mother.

What happened to that, Mum?!

WEDNESDAY 4TH NOVEMBER

7.12 p.m.

Gran just called my mob to tell me she is having a bonfire party tomorrow night. She wants me and Mum to bring food. I asked Gran if she was worried Princess would go mental scared at the fireworks. Gran said no – she put a sparkler in her dog food the other day as a treat and she loved it.

THURSDAY 5TH NOVEMBER

8.01 p.m.

Just got back from Gran's party. The food she organized was crisps so we've all come back STARVING.

9.20 p.m.

Mum brought me my dinner and I said, "Thanks, Mum – thanks for everything you have done," and gave her a hug. Mum said, "Hattie – it's only a cheesy beans baked potato." But it's not, is it?

Gran had to abandon the firework display as Princess kept trying to attack the rockets when they were lit. Gran says she is spirited. I say she is a mental.

FRIDAY 6TH NOVEMBER

7.37 p.m.

That's the one I have seen!

1/11/95

C has gone. He's left me a note. He hasn't gone back to her. I went round to check.

We both agree we are on our own. We keep this quiet. We don't tell the kids till we have to. Mum is saying "I told you so!" but I have to move on. This baby makes me stronger. Wish I could stop eating though. I've got through 9 Chupa Chups and an entire pineapple today.

I hope she doesn't blame me for being size 14–16. I only made her crave fruit!

8.45 p.m.
Chupa Chups are technically a kind of fruit.

SATURDAY 7TH NOVEMBER

4.56 p.m.
Chatted for ages with Dimple and Jen around Jen's house.

I know all these new things but I still don't know what my dad is called, or where he is. And I want to — more than I ever have.

Dimple couldn't understand why. When I told her it was because I wanted to PUNCH HIM. Jen and Dimps just looked really sad.

7.34 p.m.

OMG!

Gran just called to ask if I was still interested in cleaning her house as she had just read in *Take a Break* about how you should "declutter for mental well-being".

When I asked what she was thinking of cleaning, she said, "The spare room for a start! In the cupboards. Under my bed. Everywhere."

ARRRRGHHHHHHHHH!!! She will notice the diary box is gone! Gran notices how many crisps you take from a bag! Have to sneak it round there. Have to find a way!

8.11 p.m.
Texted Dimple – she thinks I should try to put Gran off cleaning and the whole idea of having a declutter. Will text Gran now.

8.13 p.m.
No point. *Midsomer Murders* is on. A terrorist could attack Gran's house and she wouldn't move during anything featuring John Nettles.

SUNDAY 8TH NOVEMBER

7.12 p.m.
Just rang Gran and asked her why she was thinking of cleaning, as she should take it a bit easier at her age. She got really pissy and said, "Are you saying I am lazy? I'm not not past it yet young lady. I marched in the '60s for equal rights, Hattie. Don't you get lippy with me, Lady Jane!"

I said, "OK, Gran. Wait till next weekend and I will help you. I promise." Gran has agreed to do it then. THANK GOD.

Who is Lady Jane?

7.51 p.m.

Thank you, Wikipedia.

Lady Jane was queen for 9 days, then they killed her boyfriend, then her. At least she got to snog, be queen — and wear a brilliant dress though. LOL!

8.02 p.m.

OMG — she was only a bit older than me when they chopped her head off. Feel bad for LOL-ing now.

In fact I feel bad about everything.

MONDAY 9TH NOVEMBER

4.37 p.m.

Dimple and Jen want to hold the next meeting of the NFPG in Pizza Express. I can guess why — it's because they know I am a dough ball maniac and they think it will cheer me up. But it won't. Not even a Sloppy Giuseppe with extra onion could cheer me up.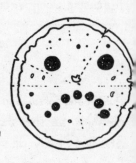

6.57 p.m.

Actually it could if some really LUSH boy served it to me. Then my dad might come in and I could punch him for dessert, instead of having the tiramisu.

TUESDAY 10TH NOVEMBER

5.35 p.m.

Haven't got much time to write here – just trying to read and write down as much as I can of Mum's diaries before I have to sneak them back.

6.47 p.m.

Goose is practising again. If he is ill on the night I could be Joseph as I know ALL the words now!!!

9.04 p.m.

31/11/95

Can't believe he just left a note. He didn't even have the balls to face us. The saddest thing is, he is a great dad to Nathan when he bothers. I'm just hoping Nathan will forget and I find someone else. But who is going to want a woman with 2 kids? It's just me, Nathan and the baby from now on.

Poor Mum. I wish I could tell her not to worry about Nathan missing his dad as he is evil and wouldn't even miss her if she left.

WEDNESDAY 11TH NOVEMBER

8.35 p.m.

LOL!!!

1/12/95

Nathan ate all the chocolate in his advent

calendar and then was sick everywhere.
He keeps asking if he can try to dress like
Mummy too.

It's TORTURE knowing this information and not being able
to use it!

THURSDAY 12TH NOVEMBER

7.39 p.m.

OMG!!!

4/12/95

The man who is teaching me to drive is
called Rob. Lovely. He keeps bringing me
banana fritters as he says pregnant women
need extra potassium so they can reverse
park properly.

Mum is hardly writing anything in her diary now – it's like
she can't be arsed.

10.12 p.m.

Just spoke to Jen – she says it's probably not so much
that my mum couldn't be arsed – it's because being 7
months pregnant while looking after a toddler means total
knackerization.

← Oh typical! Worst
day of luck to try
ANYTHING.

7.29 a.m.

OPERATION "GET DIARIES BACK BEFORE
GRAN CLEANS".

Going round to Gran's after school. Pretending that I just
fancied a cup of tea on the way home. Have got Mum's
diaries in a massive Primark carrier bag.

6.32 p.m.

The diaries are back in Gran's room!!! I don't think Gran
suspects a thing. Princess does though. She death-stared
me when I came back into the lounge.

7.14 p.m.

Dimple just texted to tell me there is a rumour going
round that I have got a new boyfriend and that I met him
after school. That's why I brought a massive Primark bag
into school with a change of clothes in it.

8.54 p.m.

According to Jen, MGK has told everyone my new
boyfriend is a fugly geek who only goes out with me
because I am a Topshop chav who sometimes wears see-
through tops.

I have enough hassle in my life without MGK starting on
me. Just why is she so EVIL TO ME?

MGK is evil to everyone. Even her clique. Apparently if
they come to school looking better than her she makes
them "ugly up".

SATURDAY 14TH NOVEMBER

8.01 a.m.

MUM WANTS TO SEE ME "FOR A CHAT" LATER. She says it's important.

She says Gran is going to be there too.

OMG.

10.26 a.m.

I've got it planned. I will say, "Well you read my diary and so I read yours, but I love you, Mum, more than I ever have." She will LOVE that.

4.35 p.m.

The chat has happened. Mum wanted me to talk to her because I have seemed so down lately and have been acting strangely. Was I making myself sick? Was it a boy? Or drugs? Or glue? (Glue? WHAT?! Apparently some of Mum's friends used to sniff glue for a laugh???)

Gran was also worried because every time I go round there I seem anxious, and as "fidgety as a ferret on Red Bull".

And get this! What has really made Mum worried is how nice I am being to her!!! I just told them, "I haven't got a boyfriend or an eating disorder. I am not on E, skunk or Pritt Stick. I just want to meet my dad."

To which my gran said, "Not that old chestnut again!" And so I came up here.

6.47 p.m.

Texted Dimple. She has never heard of sniffing Pritt Stick either.

7.01 p.m.

Just sniffed Pritt Stick. Nothing happened.

SUNDAY 15TH NOVEMBER

6.32 p.m.

Went round Gran's to help with the decluttering.

When she went under the bed I acted dumb and asked her what was under there. She just said, "Rubbish, Hattie." But she didn't throw it away. She scooped a whole load of it up (including the diaries) and put it in her wardrobe. No one goes in Gran's wardrobe. Even Princess the fearless Wonder Dog whimpers when she is anywhere near it. It's because it contains fashion horrors that even dogs understand.

MONDAY 16TH NOVEMBER

9.23 p.m.

Wish I could talk to my half-sister about this wherever she is. My half-sibling has to be a sister. I decided this today when Nathan decided to spray Cillit Bang all over my hair.

TUESDAY 17TH NOVEMBER

8.34 p.m.

Mum came up to say she understands how hard it is that I don't know my father.

She looked upset.

And then she said, "Why do you smell of Domestos?" I told her it wasn't Domestos — it was Cillit Bang, and Nathan had used it as I'd complained that my hair was greasy.

Mum didn't say anything to that.

Sister — where are you? We could swap make-up tips and everything.

9.12 p.m.

Brother — where are you? You could punch Nathan for me.

WEDNESDAY 18TH NOVEMBER

6.53 p.m.

OMG — what if my sister is an international supermodel and is MINTED?!

7.12 p.m.

OMG — what if my brother is a world kickboxing champion and someone who HATES brothers who bully?

9.33 p.m.

Goose has just been round. Apparently my mum has asked him to cheer me up! He wasn't meant to tell me this but he can't lie to me.

He thinks I should put the search for my dad "on hold", have a good Christmas and help him with his preparations for *Joseph* as he is shit-scared. I have agreed.

I can't do anything more about my dad right now anyway. And it's driving me mad. I should have realized how bad I'd got when I didn't fancy dough balls.

THURSDAY 19TH NOVEMBER

2.12 p.m.

OFFICIAL ANNOUNCEMENT:

The *Not Fair Protest Group* has decided that for one week we are "TEAM GOOSE".

Jen has bought him some special confidence-giving crystals, I am going to help him practise his lines every night and Dimple is going to rub his toes — as they are connected to your vocal chords or something.

3.12 p.m.

I know the Dimple one is weird but she wanted to help.

FRIDAY 20TH NOVEMBER

9.12 p.m.

Spent all evening with Goose. He is so nervous even though it is SO obvious he is going to be awesomely amazing. He got really tense. I had to get Dimple round to do an emergency FOOT MASSAGE.

I feel weird when Dimple rubs Goose's feet. Sort of ... NO – I AM NOT DOING THAT AGAIN. I nearly lost Dimple before because of that.

SATURDAY 21ST NOVEMBER

12.37 p.m.

Final dress rehearsal tonight. Me, Jen and Dimple are all going to cheer Goose on.

6.49 p.m.

Matfield threw TEAM GOOSE out of the dress rehearsal because we clapped after every line that Goose sang.

ERR – MRS MATFIELD – THAT'S WHAT THEY DO ON *THE X-FACTOR* and SIMON COWELL LOVES IT.

Matfield was going mental anyway because someone had painted a camel smoking a spliff on her scenery.

Goose was ... just honestly amazing.

Sunday 22nd November

2.17 p.m.

Team Goose is going to every performance of *Joseph*. Jen has made a special spell using locks of Goose's hair and threads from his multi-coloured coat. She is going to burn them just before he goes on stage. Dimple has also prepared something special for him.

10.37 p.m.

Went to see Goose earlier and he just burst into tears and blurted out, "I can't do it, Hattie." I said, "OMG, you SO can, Goose – I have been listening to you for months. You are FANTASTIC. You're just nervous. You know what Simon says – 'You HAVE to conquer your nerves'."

Goose usually hates Simon Cowell because he's ruined proper music, but he had to agree.

Monday 23rd November

9.54 p.m.

OMG! GOOSE WAS UNBELIEVABLE! You could not take your eyes off him! He got 2 standing ovations. Even Matfield was smiling!

I think it was my Dr Phil-style talk. Jen thinks it was her spell. Dimple thinks it was her "super hard" foot rub.

Mum and Gran came with us too. Mum says Goose reminds her of a young Phillip Schofield. That's a worry – Mum has fancied Phillip Schofield for about 20 years.

Tuesday 24th November

4.32 p.m.

The whole school is talking about Goose. Some people are trying to be friends with him just because he is almost guaranteed to be rich and famous. Even a dinner lady gave him free chips today. And not just Dimple wants to give him a rub. I will be glad when it's all over.

Wednesday 25th November

11.34 p.m.

The final school play performance turned into a disaster.

When it came to the bit when a load of people have to hold up letters spelling out **Jacob and Sons**, Wayne Casgill and Nick McCartney got their boards the wrong way round and it spelt

Jacob and Snos

instead.

Then one of Bitchface Matfield's prison walls fell down on top of Pharaoh's head. Goose was still brilliant though, and at the end Dr Richards came on to say he had never worked with such a talented group of pupils, and that Goose was an exceptional talent.

Then Goose did a speech where he thanked all the backstage cast and his friends and ESPECIALLY HATTIE.

ESPECIALLY HATTIE.

Thursday 26th November

9.35 p.m.

I feel really weird about Goose. I can't actually remember what he looks like half the time and I just feel I want to TALK TO HIM and CONNECT.

Our actual bedrooms are attached – we could chisel through.

Friday 27th November

8.35 p.m.

I can't get Goose out of my head at the moment – we grew up together. We used to play *Toy Story* together. He was *Buzz*. I was Jessie. And now he is basically one step away from the West End. Or *The X-Factor*.

Goose. Goose. Goose.

I feel too weird about everything at the moment.

Saturday 28th November

7.12 p.m.

Why did I read Mum's diaries?! I NEVER should have done it. I am messed up in the head now. Perhaps I should confess to Gran and ask her what to do.

7.54 p.m.

No, that's a MENTAL idea. Gran would TOTALLY tell Mum. My punishment could be Mum asking Gran to make me a dress. Mum would be THAT angry that she would like to torture me with fashion.

I need to sleep.

SUNDAY 29TH NOVEMBER

4.12 p.m.

RUMOUR HORROR!!!

Miss Gorgeous Knickers is after Goose. NO NO NO NO. She says next year the school is doing *Grease* and she is already down to play Sandy and Goose is down to play Danny.

NO NO NO NO!!! They snog at the end and everything. I have to stop it. I have to go round there and talk to him.

10.24 p.m.

Just been to see Goose. He was a bit gutted I hadn't been to see him earlier. I told him that I thought he needed rest. Then I tried to get everything from Goose I could.

```
ME:     I think you could be
        professional and that you should
        save your voice for the next TV
        thing they do with Andrew Lloyd
        Webber.
GOOSE:  Well apparently next year the
        school is doing Grease.
ME:     Yes. Don't do it. Seriously I've
        heard that if you use your voice
        too much you grow big lumps on
```

your vocal chords and can never
sing again.

GOOSE: Hattie — that's not going to
happen to me now. I love being
in shows.

ME: Yes, but I think you're
forgetting your old real friends
like me and you've changed.

GOOSE: I have NOT changed, Hattie. Who
did I thank at the end of the
show?

ME: Me.

GOOSE: Totally shut up then. I didn't
mention any other girls did I?

ME: No. Talking of girls, now that
you're Mr Celebrity at school
have any girls ... you know?

GOOSE: No! Well — a few might have
tried but I'm ... I'm tired
after being Joseph.

LOL! Yes, MGK. Goose is too tired to see you!!!

MONDAY 30TH NOVEMBER

6.12 p.m.

There is now a rumour going round that Goose is gay.
Goose says this is because he is good at theatre, which
other boys think makes him gay. In reality they are
actually mentally 2 years old.

I asked Goose. He said, "No, I am not gay — I like girls.
Well, some girls."

And then he smiled at me.

And then it all went a bit weird.

OMG!!!

TUESDAY 1ST DECEMBER

4.55 p.m.

Miss Gorgeous Knickers is going out with Goose.

I feel sick.

No, Mum, I can't eat tea. One of my best friends is going out with the world's most horrible woman. Yes, I know we've all got our problems, but actually what problems have you got compared to mine? NONE. Has Rob run off with someone totally hot and sexy that you HATE?! NO.

WEDNESDAY 2ND DECEMBER

8.12 p.m.

I'm not stalking but MGK has just left Goose's house after spending 2 hours 27 minutes and 16 seconds there. I just happened to catch her arriving and leaving as I was getting up from my desk. She was wearing a black top and short skirt and I could hear them talking through the wall. I whacked on the wall and told them to shut up as I was trying to learn about the Muslim pilgrimage of the Hajj. Where women should be veiled.

I wish I could veil Miss Gorgeous Knickers FOR EVER.

THURSDAY 3RD DECEMBER

7.13 p.m.

Apparently Goose's mum Donna isn't keen on MGK as she is far too "forward" for her son. I have always liked Goose's mum and she has always liked me. MGK stands no chance against me and Goose's mum. We are like ... a very powerful thing that's feeling very powerful indeed.

FRIDAY 4TH DECEMBER

6.12 p.m.

YES!!!

I think I can hear through the wall that Goose is trying to finish with MGK as he wants to concentrate on his GCSEs. LOL!!!

Everyone knows this is the biggest lie ever. No one wants to concentrate on their GCSEs except for total nerds and geeks.

7.12 p.m.

MGK just came out of Goose's house. She looked really upset so I smiled and waved (I was in my room at the window and safe!). THEN she yelled something really weird: "You won't be smiling for long. I can only keep my mouth shut for so long and THEN you'll be crying, chavvy!"

I AM NOT CHAVVY!

And what does she know that I don't?

7.43 p.m.

Spoke to Dimple and Jen. They swear on their lives they have heard no rumours about me except for the fact (and Dimple said she was really sorry for telling me this) I once pretended that Daniel Radcliffe was my actual boyfriend and stalked him like a mental outside his house.

I hate my brother.

8.01 p.m.

Jen just remembered that there was a rumour going around a few months ago that my brace was fake and I was wearing it to get attention.

Who makes this stuff up?

8.12 p.m.

MGK obviously.

I think EVERYBODY is talking about me now.

8.54 p.m.

Just rang Goose — his mum answered. He is doing his Chemistry homework and does not want to be disturbed.

Goose is mahoosively lovely but mahoosively geeky.

SATURDAY 5TH DECEMBER

4.32 p.m.

Goose came round. He is doing a huge car boot tomorrow with all the things he couldn't sell on eBay — including some fake Prada bags marked PRAGA. He asked me if I wanted one – and I just burst into tears. He gave me a massive cuddle and said it would be all right – MGK was only winding me up. I had a snot full of nose so I couldn't say anything.

4.58 p.m.

"Snot full of nose"! Nearly true – as there was hardly any nose left under all the snot.

I'll go round to talk to Gran tomorrow. She'll know what to do about MGK.

SUNDAY 6TH DECEMBER

9.23 p.m.

I told Gran I needed her advice and she just started saying stuff like "the course of true love never runs smooth", and "all the best relationships start from just being great friends".

She also said, "Hattie, do we need to have a special chat right now about sex?"

I shouted at her, "NO, GRAN, NO!!! I have had that chat at school. I know all about everything—" Gran just interrupted me with: "Just promise me one thing – never sell all the stock in your shop the first day you are open."

I don't even want to THINK what this means!

Anyway I said, "Gran, it's nothing to do with boys. MGK says she can only keep her mouth shut for so long and that she would wipe the smile off my face. I'm really worried she's going to make up craptacular rumours about me that people will actually believe."

There was a massive pause then Gran just pursed her lips and said, "Don't worry about it, Hattie. She's just confused. It's her age."

What help is that?!

MONDAY 7TH DECEMBER

6.23 a.m.

Bizarre!

Gran just called Mum. I thought she was ill because it's so early.

I could hear Mum saying stuff to her like: "Don't be silly – why should she say anything now?" and "I don't care if you've been awake all night – it's not going to happen". Then she really got pissy and said, "Look – I'll talk to her mother. I'll get her to warn her off. Yes, I know Hattie is a pretty, funny, clever girl. She is MY daughter, you know."

4.34 p.m.

Told Dimple that behind my back my mum actually thinks I am pretty, funny and clever. Why doesn't she ever say that to my ACTUAL face? Dimple reminded me that she has – OCCASIONALLY. Dimple was more interested in what my gran was going on about anyway. Who knows?!

I am sick of only getting half the story and not being officially told what the hell is going on.

7.23 p.m.

Weirdest conversation with my mum in history tonight. This PROVES I cannot win:

MUM: Hattie, have you heard anything … odd recently that you want to talk to me about?

ME: Er … Danielle Lance says that if you put an egg in your hair when you dye it the dye stays in for a year.

MUM: I don't mean that. I mean, has anyone upset you?

ME: Well, MGK called Gran a dog and me a chav about a month ago and then the other night she also said that she was going to wipe the smile off my face.

MUM: Oh?

ME: Yes. She says she can only keep her mouth shut for so long. Just forget about it. Please don't call school. She can get to me in loads of ways you don't even know about. That's what being bullied is like these days.

(All of a sudden her forehead developed massive wrinkles — hope I don't get them.)

MUM: It will be all right.

ME: No, it won't, Mum, as she is
         actually evil and hates me.

Then there was a massive pause, and Mum just said, "Hattie, tonight we'll have a special dinner. Your favourite."

9.34 p.m.

Mum has been on the phone ALL night. I don't know who to. And dinner was not special. It was Rob's spicy pasta. Which is just random stuff from the cupboard. With chilli.

I've just been chatting with Jen on Facebook. She thinks my mum is just trying to treat me differently as I have shown "increasing emotional maturity".

10.11 p.m.

I can hear Nathan crying. Bet he has been dumped AGAIN.

TUESDAY 8TH DECEMBER

11.53 a.m.

OMG!!!

OMACTUALG!!!

I ... don't know what to write. Seriously. I... It's ... OMG – it's like ... WHERE DO I START?

OMG!!!

12.34 p.m.

I can't actually write today. Trust me.

4.35 p.m.

Dimple and Jen want to know why I wasn't at school. What can I say? Just having to ignore it.

WEDNESDAY 9TH DECEMBER

11.39 a.m.

Got up yesterday morning to find my mum, Rob, Gran and Nathan all waiting for me in the front room. My mum said, "Hattie, sit down. You are not going to school today. We need to talk, sweetheart."

And when she calls me "sweetheart" I KNOW I'm in trouble.

I sat down, and then – I still think I might be dreaming – she said, "Hattie, there are some things about your life we haven't told you because there has never really been a right time to tell you. But now we have to tell you. And I hope you'll understand why we haven't told you before, and ... that ... you will..."

She was really struggling, so I said, "Mum, I know. I'm sorry – I read your diaries. I know about my dad, and I know about my half-brother or sister. And I know that Nathan wanted to dress like a girl."

And then it all went MENTAL.

Mum shouted, "WHAT?" Nathan screamed, "I NEVER wanted to wear dresses!" and Gran said, "I knew you'd been sneaking round my house!"

Then Rob yelled, "CAN WE ALL REMEMBER WHAT'S REALLY IMPORTANT HERE?"

Then my mum said, "Hattie – you have got a half-sister ... And it's Ruby Slack."

I could see her mouth moving, but it wasn't actually making sense. It was like the time I came off my BMX when I was 8. It all went in slow motion. And I said, "Ruby Slack?"

"Yes, darling," Mum said. "Ruby Slack is your half-sister. She's known for a while. That's what she was threatening to tell you. That's why we told you first."

Ruby Slack.

Ruby Slack.

AKA

MGK

And all I could think of to say was: "Well if I need a kidney transplant that's a good thing because she could give me one of hers."

This made Gran cry, and she started shouting, "The poor girl is in shock. Give her a brandy." But Mum just came over and hugged me and kept saying sorry.

So MGK, the most evil disgusting torturer of my actual soul for years and years is my actual half-sister.

It hasn't sunk in yet.

4.34 p.m.

Perhaps that's why she's always been so evil to me.

Perhaps she was jealous. Or just hated me because she didn't want to be related to a chav.

Not that I am actually a chav.

Why am I so calm?

4.44 p.m.

Just asked my mum why Nathan knew before me. She said, "We told Nath first because we thought he could be a support for you and help you through all this. He is older."

Could my life get any more mental? Nathan tortures me nearly as much as MGK! Haven't they noticed?!

5.55 p.m.

Text from Dimple:

> We are so worried about you, Hats. Please tell us what the matter is.

7.02 p.m.

Goose just came in.

He said, "Hattie – Mum just told me."

I just looked at him. "But what do I do now?"

Goose looked at me and said, "Well at least you have a sister you can gang up against Nathan with."

OMG – that and the kidney thing are good but WHY DIDN'T THEY TELL ME?! WHY DID SHE KNOW BEFORE ME?!!

I NEED ANSWERS.

Everyone is acting so odd with me. Mum keeps asking me how I am. I tell her fine but the truth is, I don't know.

7.48 p.m.

OMG – Goose's mum knew before me. Who else knows? I am NOT calm.

I am also officially NOT going back to school till Monday. Even Mum agrees I need time to get over the shock.

THURSDAY 10TH DECEMBER

5.23 p.m.

Met Dimple and Jen after they had finished school and told them everything.

Jen had to take half a bottle of Bach Rescue Remedy to cope with the shock. Dimple just hugged me for about 5 minutes.

They have sworn not to tell a soul.

FRIDAY 11TH DECEMBER

4.55 p.m.

Jen just texted. MGK has told Danny Fenton (she fancies him), who told Rachel McGuff (he fancies her), who told Katie Hayes, who told EVERYONE.

MGK has been officially told off for spreading rumours.

She has to do an essay on something called "The Charge of the Light Brigade", so she learns how dangerous gossip can be.

LOL!

Just keep her away from me.

SATURDAY 12TH DECEMBER

11.09 a.m.

The thought of seeing MGK makes me feel like PUKING like you would NOT believe. It's like finding out your half-sister is Hitler. But worse because she's alive without a moustache (she has a Brazilian every month in fact) and has the best wardrobe in the area.

4.56 p.m.

I asked my mum tonight about relationships. She explained they could be complicated, and she was very confused about my dad.

Apparently she was going out with him first and had Nathan. Then MGK's mum went out with him after they had split up — but then she got back with him.

I asked, "What was so special about him?" Mum said, "He had charm, Hattie, but he couldn't stay put. He could never settle. When he got something he wanted, he wanted something else."

OMG – I think I AM like my dad.

SUNDAY 13TH DECEMBER

7.23 p.m.

I need to face up to things. I need to face my fears. I need to face MGK. I've called an emergency family meeting tomorrow.

Bet she turns up looking stunning.

How long has she known?

8.12 p.m.

OMG – what if we can actually be friends? We are about the same size. Surely it's impossible to really hate your actual real half-sister and not lend her your clothes, bags, shoes and collection of Pandora charms!

MONDAY 14TH DECEMBER

4.01 p.m.

The stares today were unbelievable. I could see everyone was whispering about me. And the best thing – MGK wasn't even at school today! Apparently she has a "virus". Hope she still manages to turn up tonight. I'm dreading it but I need to face it.

OMG, I'm mature.

4.34 p.m.

Just took Goose round his birthday card. He said, "Look, Hattie, if there's anything I can do PLEASE just say. Even if it's just a hug."

It went weird again — so I had to go.

5.23 p.m.

"FAMILY" MEETING.

THE FIRST THING MGK said was: "You're not borrowing anything."

She's known since she was 11. Her mum didn't bother telling her till we both got to high school and saw each other every day. MGK never told anyone because she "didn't even want to admit to herself that it was true". Plus she "loved having it over me".

Her mum said, "Ruby!" when she told me that. MGK just smirked. COW.

My mum didn't tell me when I was 11 BECAUSE SHE DIDN'T THINK I COULD COPE WITH IT!!!

AND they all wanted everyone to just forget about it.

When I shouted that that was TOTALLY LAME, Mum said, "Then the older you got, Hattie, the harder it seemed to tell you. You've never got on with Ruby and I knew you would ask questions about your dad that I couldn't answer. Or didn't want to answer. We didn't want a scandal. We didn't want people to know."

So I shouted, "BUT EVERYONE DOES KNOW NOW, MUM!!!" And then Mum said, "But you're older now, Hattie. And you're clever and witty and you can cope."

I know she is just being nice to me so I'm not totally mental with her.

Then Gran said, "I wanted people to just forget about it. I couldn't show my face at bingo for a fortnight after it all came out."

So just to confirm – they didn't want to tell us because of my gran's social life.

ANYWAY...

THE FACTS:

- Our dad is not called Carlo. He is called Keith.

Keith. Keith. The only name more un-glam than Keith is Bernard. There have never been ANY famous Keiths EVER.

Carlo was a nickname because the only food he ate was spaghetti bolognese. According to my mum he would "make a huge load of it on a Sunday, then have it every night till Saturday, when he had a kebab".

- He is not a hairdresser. He is a plumber.

He is from STOKE-ON-TRENT. I went through there once when Rob got TOTALLY lost on the way to Alton Towers. IT IS HORRIBLE.

- He emigrated to Tasmania.

GRAN HAS HIS LAST-KNOWN ADDRESS and is GOING TO TRY TO CONTACT HIM. Apparently he wrote to her about 3 years after he left to ask how Mum was "getting on". She didn't reply and she doesn't hold out much hope as he is – according to her – "a useless waste of space that needs a foot up his arse".

MGK just sat there looking gorgeous. She isn't bothered about finding her "biological" father because her real dad is "the man who has been around since she was 2".

The man who just happens to be a very nearly millionaire.

She also isn't bothered about being friends with me as I'm "not really anything like her and a Topshop ch—"

Gran cut her off there and said, "Oi, lady, blood is thicker than water. And I'll tell you something, Hattie may not have your style but she knows how to look after a dog. Unlike YOU."

At this point Princess the Wonder Dog growled and MGK stormed out and nearly fell over her stupid lap-dancer heels!

I LOVE GRAN.

6.18 p.m.

Just looked Tasmania up. It's in Africa. No WAY am I going there – no Facebook, no mob, no TV – NO LIFE!!!

6.34 p.m.

Texted Dimple. She says I am looking at Tanzania. Tasmania is an island off Australia. I still doubt Facebook works there either though.

TUESDAY 15TH DECEMBER

6.32 p.m.

Just written this. Sending it off tomorrow.

From: Hattie Moore <helphattienow@gmail.com>
Date: February 15, 18:19:29 PM GMT
To: <jeremykyle@itv.com>
Subject: Jeremy – this would be your best show EVER! It could get you a Bafta SERIOUSLY

Dear Jeremy Kyle,

I know you do not normally allow under-16s on your show but I wonder if you would make an exception for my family.

My mum has refused to tell me who my real father is for years. Then last week she told me that my father is a plumber called Keith from Stoke-on-Trent. He is also the father of the girl who has been my total enemy since starting high school!

On top of all this my gran has dabbled in drugs, and my brother abuses me by forcing me to perform nursery rhymes in return for money that I need to actually stay alive.

I think they all need to be told just how badly their behaviour is affecting me.

If you can find my dad we could do a DNA special results show too.

Love,

Hattie Moore

7.12 p.m.

OMG!!!

Didn't ask Mum what my dad's ACTUAL surname is.

7.34 p.m.

RAMSBOTTOM!!!

RAMSBOTTOM!!!

KEITH RAMSBOTTOM!!!

If MGK EVER hears about this, socially I am dead.

7.55 p.m.

Hang on. THAT'S MGK's dad TOO. Her power OVER ME HAS ENDED!!!

8.12 p.m.

It hasn't ended. It's a bit reduced.

WEDNESDAY 16TH DECEMBER

4.34 p.m.

Matfield said my painting in Art today showed "great promise". Apparently if your parents ring up the school and say you've got family problems. Matfield is MADE to be nice to you.

6.12 p.m.

Mr Rathod has refused to ring up the school to pretend to be getting divorced just so Matfield is nice to Dimple. Dimple is sick of Matfield telling her that she has as much artistic ability as a monkey.

THURSDAY 17TH DECEMBER

8.12 a.m.

Woke up feeling furious today.

I think I HAVE been in shock. OMG – I BASICALLY HAVE AN EVIL TWIN AND NO ONE TOLD ME!!!

AND OMG – my dad is called Keith – and no one told me!!!

5.32 p.m.

I'm in MAHOOSIVE trouble. I WENT MENTAL at Matfield today.

She was picking on Dimple again for not being able to draw hands properly, and I just shouted, "You know what Mrs Matfield? If you are so pissing good at drawing hands, WIND IT IN AND DO ONE!!!"

Everyone went quiet and Matfield screamed, "Go and see Mrs Cob – NOW."

Mrs Cob was angry but said, "Hattie, I know you've had some problems at home but that's no excuse. Go home today, and think about how you have acted."

Mum went MENTAL. Usual craptacular stuff like: "You have to control your temper", "I know things have been hard but you need to mind your tongue". I just walked off.

She had an affair with a man called Keith. I don't have to listen to anything she says!

6.45 p.m.
Goose heard the row. He says we need to try to "understand".

7.12 p.m.
Gran has asked me round tomorrow. She wants to talk to me after school.

FRIDAY 18TH DECEMBER

BREAK UP!!!

10.41 a.m.
I am NOW known as "Hattie see-through tit top MATFIELD-SLAYER". Jen says someone is even thinking of starting a Facebook page in my honour called "Hattie Moore is a TOTAL legend".

5.35 p.m.
Gran sat me down and told me I had to stop acting like something terrible had happened.

She said, "Have you once thought of how your mum feels? Or Nathan? Or Rob? You couldn't have got a better

---

father than Rob. Its not like you've lost a member of your family. You STILL have a fantastic mother. So start being nice and stop acting like a brat."

She's right. I have been a cow. Not sorry I shouted at Matfield though.

She also said, "I know that you've read the diaries so let me just say this. Your grandfather going to prison was a mistake. He was just keeping the letters at our house to keep them dry ... and the police got the wrong idea."

Yeah, Gran. Whatever.

SATURDAY 19TH DECEMBER

7.36 p.m.

Conversation between me and Nathan:

```
ME:        How are you, Nath?
Nathan:    Me? Fine. Why? How much do
           you want to borrow?
ME:        Nothing, you massive
           FAILURE. Just checking you
           are OK.
```

That surely proves to him that I care?

8.34 p.m.

Gran just rang my mob. She said, "Hattie, I have to admit something to you — I put pressure on your mum not to tell you. I couldn't cope with more scandal after what had happened with your grandad. People called me 'Mrs Percy the Pinching Postie' FOR YEARS."

So just to confirm – they ALSO didn't want to tell me because my gran was married to someone who basically could have been on *Crimewatch*.

SUNDAY 20TH DECEMBER

6.12 p.m.

Me and Goose went to the car boot with Rob today. Rob couldn't believe it when I said I wanted to go. It was full of craptacular tat but Rob came over at the end and said, "Thanks, Hattie. Was great to have you here today."

I think I'm actually quite good at being lovely.

7.01 p.m.

May start a blog next year. I can offer people advice. Especially people who have dads who don't care, grans with mental dogs, and Art teachers who are actually the devil.

MONDAY 21ST DECEMBER

4.32 p.m.

Came home from Christmas shopping with Dimple to find everyone in the front room again. Goose and Nathan were smiling but Gran, Mum and Rob looked VERY pissy.

Mum said, "Hattie, got some news for you. Gran has found your dad. And he's flying over. He gets here Christmas Eve."

Christmas Eve?!

He gets here Christmas EVE?!!

Gran said, "Yes – he's staying with me. He realizes he's been an idiot. But I am telling you, Hattie – don't expect a bloody miracle. I know it's Christmas but a leopard doesn't change its spots. There's more chance of another virgin birth than him being a decent father."

Mum told her off but I don't care. I finally get to meet MY ACTUAL DAD. I gave Goose a hug. I didn't hug Nathan but I smiled at him.

OMG – I AM GETTING A DAD FOR CHRISTMAS!!!

8.12 p.m.
OMG – I am SO NERVOUS I could puke.

8.23 p.m.
Rang Jen. She said she was going to put a ceremonial Yule log in her front garden, as the placing of wood encourages good family relationships.

8.42 p.m.
Texted Dimple. She said:

> Don't be nervous, Hats. Think of him as Father Christmas. Just a Father Christmas called Keith.

I don't know what I'd do without my friends...

9.13 p.m.
In fact my friends have TOTALLY saved me this year as I've had the biggest life journey EVER.

OMG that sounded mahoosively Dr Phil. BUT if you write down what I have learnt since I started this, it's *mental*.

- When the biggest cow at school picks on you, it's probably because she is your half-sister.
- Anybody could find out their real dad has a craptacular name and mends toilets. Unless you get Jeremy Kyle to do your DNA you can NEVER be totally sure.
- Some boys like girls to be bad at *Grand Theft Auto* because it makes them feel better. All boys who think like this cannot actually use their tongues properly. LOL!
- Some English boys think texting 14 times in 1 day is unreasonable – which shows they are TOTALLY immature.
- Austrian boys kiss like hot love-beasts but get really boring quickly.
- Karaoke makes normally sensible adults act like they are on *The X-Factor* final and should be banned.
- Evil teachers at school can be forced to be nice to you if your family life is craptacular. WHY DOESN'T ANYONE EVER TELL YOU THIS?! IT'S THE MOST IMPORTANT FACT OF LIFE.
- My gran is the world's most mental woman.
- Blackbirds, sparrows, blue tits and robins cannot handle drugs.
- Grans cannot handle drugs.

- London is MAHOOSIVE and you can't get anywhere in 5 minutes. The Underground map is also a bunch of squiggly lines that make NO SENSE.
- Your best friend can basically be Miss World and you CAN control your jealousy so it doesn't ruin the greatest friendship ever.
- I am a fully sensual woman who can slightly rock braces.
- When you are friends with a boy sometimes it can get confusing. And it goes weird. Actually I don't know what I've learnt from this. I'm still confused.

The point is if I've learnt all this THIS YEAR what's NEXT YEAR going to be like when I have my ACTUAL DAD in my life too?

Have to go — Goose is knocking on the wall. He says he needs to speak to me urgently and "It can't wait — it needs to be face to face". OMG why are things always so dramatic with men?! They need to be like me, Dimple and Jen ... ACTUALLY UNCOMPLICATED...

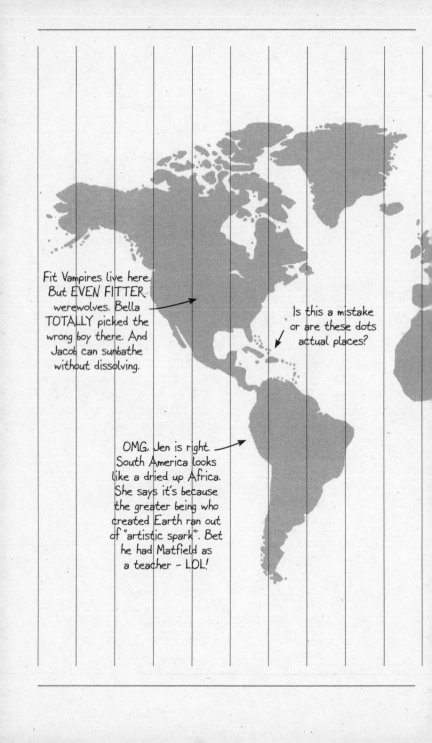

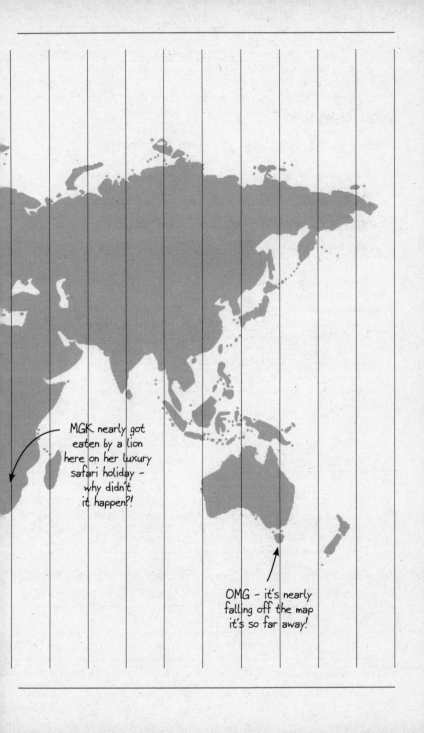

Notes about what?!

Gran says it's for things you have to remember.

REMEMBER: never to let Gran and Princess share
a packet of Werther's Original Toffees EVER AGAIN!

NOTES

NOTES

Acknowledgements

Kevin Johnson
Thank you for building my writing shed and letting me fill it with photos of the 'Carry On' Team.

My Mum
For having her hair done at least 4 times a week. Even at 70. (Thanks Sandra Jackson BTW – you're super.)

Emma Drury
My best friend – thank you for sharing everything including the HELL and INJUSTICE of GCSE art.

Lucy Kearney
The brilliant Gnu for the greatest chats and health advice – 'Dates Rae Dates!'

Sarah 'Saz De P' Powell
For all the giggles wherever we are in the world. I'll never make you go to Mona again.

Daphne and Peter Johnson
For packing furniture so brilliantly it survives even the roughest baggage handler.

Richard and Sylvia Moore
(Adopts Richard's Northern voice) 'Thanks for being RIGHT lovely with your hospitality and kindness.'

Roo Green
(Performs Roobot) for brilliantly reminding me that we are in the most competitive era of mankind EVER.

My brother, Kevin Earl
'TROUT!"

Acknowledgements

Andy Cattanach
For introducing me to the KLF chill out album.

Rob Wagstaff
For being a living legend and for sending me the Nightlife clock.

Donna Sookee
'The Don'. For the greatest mornings of gossip and for the phrase 'You're bloody killing me Rae.'

The wonderful Paul Robey
Yootha Joyce. Coro. Mrs. Bridges. Betty's hotpot. It's ALL the law.

Michelle and John at L.V.P.O.
Thank you for all your legal/spiritual/postal/magazine advice!

Lee Price
The marvellous not so fat-face – though please get a laptop or an iPhone or SOMETHING!

Love and thanks also to Lloydie James Lloyd, Lesa Compton, PK & CK Koukoularides, Erica Hodge and to all my friends from Stamford High School.

The brilliant Eve White
Thank you for always asking the questions I'm too wimpy to ask AKA money ones.

All at Walker Books
Denise Johnstone-Burt, Ellen Holgate and Daisy Jellicoe. Daisy I'm nicking your name. It's too good not to use. This is your legal notice.